The Nantucket Tuck You Inn
Book One

Becoming Santa

To Trisha –
Your Christmas
Story
Jacqueline Gillam Fairchild

JACQUELINE GILLAM FAIRCHILD

The Nantucket Tuck You Inn Series
Becoming Santa, Book One
By Jacqueline Gillam Fairchild

For editorial requests or to purchase multiple copies at wholesale, contact The Editor at SubmissionsLRP@gmail.com.

Door Image for cover www.depositphotos.com/sandralise
Nantucket Photo for Cover: Jacqueline Gillam Fairchild

Library Cataloging Data:
1. Christmas 2. Nantucket 3. Romance 4. North Pole 5. Bakeries 6. Cookies
7. Bed and Breakfast 8. Grandmas 9. Candy Land

ISBN: 978-1-7359337-1-9
Kindle eBook ASIN: B08LTRXBJS
V.11182020
Published by Little Roni Publishers LLC, Clanton, AL
www.LittleRoniPublishers.com
In association with Hartline Literary Agency
http://hartlineagency.com/

Published in the United States of America

For Ira

Acknowledgements

For Nancy Watkins, Jim Hart
and Chad Gillam.

Thank you to MacKenzie Taylor and Kathleen Visione who
have helped me endlessly.

With a special thank you for her endless work
and friendship, Ellen Sallas.

Endorsements

"Jacqueline is one of the most creative and interesting persons I have ever met."

J. Peterman,
iconic catalog
entrepreneur,
TV character
and author

Also by Jacqueline Gillam Fairchild

Make Me Over

The Scrap Book Trilogy:
- Creating Memories
- Grand Memories
- Charmed Memories

Greater Expectations:
- Trish's Story
- Maggie's Story
- Pandora's Story
- Jillian's Story

Estate of Mind

In praise of Estate of Mind:

"I love your book! I love your book so much that I have to argue with myself about how many chapters I can read in one sitting because I don't want to finish it! What an inspiration. After the first few chapters, I cleaned my entire porch (some years I haven't used it at all) and have lunch there on weekends while I read. I love the characters, your descriptions are fabulous. I can't say enough good things and just wanted you to know. Thank you for writing this absolutely delightful book. When I finish, I guess I'll just have to read it again!"

Bonnie Mason
Community Business Development Manager
Barnes & Noble, Inc

From the Author, about Becoming Santa:

Becoming Santa is the story of a little boy who believed impossible things and of a man forced to face his grief.

It is the story of a young woman's mysterious appearance to the windswept island of Nantucket, and how the magical place of Santa's Village is as real as any other town (only harder to get to).

It's about cookies, reindeer, and a colorful children's board game that might have been inspired by a real place.

Becoming Santa introduces the formidable loner Miss Tabatha Tucker, from the Tuck You Inn, a place where (some say) you can check in, but no one ever checks out.

What if you were destined to become the next Santa Claus, yet you not only fought the idea, you couldn't grasp it, even after you fall in love with the person proposing the idea?

When you come to your senses, what if you find yourself on a train to the North Pole and looking out the window, the pines turn to candy canes, and the mountains to gumdrops?

Read on and you, too, will believe in love (and Santa)!

Intro

JINX STRODE UP THE COBBLESTONE PATH TO THE British shoppe she owned with her husband Jefferson.[i] She pulled her parka close against the crisp fall air as Jefferson tripped the lock. Jinx flipped the sign to OPEN to begin another day. After heaving her canvas tote to the counter, it was time to click on lights. Jefferson released their two Pekingese pups to find their shoppe beds and headed to the CD player. Jim Hart's latest CD wafted over gourmet groceries, British chocolate bars, and hard-to-find clothing items setting the proper tone.

Jinx straightened a pair of red glitter shoes and raised her eyes to check the dogs, their squat bodies rounding as they each circled, seeking the best position against their bolsters. In a faraway voice she said, "Let's go to Nantucket."

"Sure," Jefferson replied, booting the PC. "We'll do it next summer. Sounds excellent."

Jinx turned now to run a feather duster over a jewelry display. "No, I was thinking…well, this fall."

Jefferson stopped his work and turned to see her face. "This fall? This is our busiest time of the year." He waited for the punchline. Instead, Jinx offered a pout.

"We need a little escape."

"The island shuts down for the winter," he said and returned to arranging the sales counter.

"Not completely." Jinx said with defiance, moving now to a basket of brightly-colored striped sweaters, folding and refolding, her eyes unfocused.

"Hon, the beach roses won't be in bloom."

"The air will be crisp."

"There won't be any tourists."

Jinx stared into middle space picturing the gray shingled cottages, the cobblestone streets, imagining her tastebuds immersed into a steaming plate of scallops.

"Exactly," she said as if the topic had closed. "Exactly."

one

THE CLOUDS SWIRLED FASTER AND FASTER AND the wind rushed through her hair, its roar deafening the moment. She shrieked, calling for help, and still the world spun. Belle hugged her velvet bag close to her chest as her surroundings flipped upside down. Then she was ejected, falling downward with violent velocity.

"Don't let me die. Don't let me die. I have too much to do. Please don't let me die," she prayed in what became a mantra until her world went black.

"Oh, dear, did you see that?"

"I'm right here."

"I … I think he crashed."

"That he did."

"Do you think he survived?"

Her husband took her hand in his. "No, my dear. I don't think he did."

A tear welled; she couldn't help it. He was, after all, like a son.

"It is terrible, but be happy it was only a practice run," he offered still holding her fingers.

"I can't be happy." She wept in earnest, allowing the fat tears to fall down her plump creased cheeks. She pushed back a strand of silver hair and wiped her eyes with her free hand.

"Please, don't cry, dear. It's not your fault."

"You're darn right!" she snuffled back. "If it's anyone's fault, it's yours. If you …"

"Ifs will do no good, dear."

She persisted in a stern tone. "If you'd laid off the cookies and lost that extra weight, your knees would never have gone out and you wouldn't have needed knee replacements."

"It wasn't the cookies, my dear." Her husband hid a butter cutout behind his back and their faithful Samoyed nipped it from his hand to then swallow in one bite. "We're old, both of us, and parts of us are wearing out."

"Speak for yourself." She pulled in a breath and her lower back twinged. "Whatever happened to them saying your knee replacements would make you good as new?"

"A good as new in some ways, but recall they also said there were many things I could never do again." His arm encircled her wide middle.

She sighed. "Do you suppose he was drinking?"

"When *wasn't* he drinking?"

"It's my fault. I thought when we found him as an orphan at that monastery that he would grow into a good man."

"He was a good man."

"Who drank too much," she added in a sad timbre.

"The monastery made brandy. He grew up on it, my dear, couldn't be helped."

"He had all the *other* qualities we were looking for," she said wringing her plump hands.

"He was kind. He loved children," he agreed. "He was good husband material."

"Husband…? Oh, no…"

They both froze, sobered, and stared at each other. Together they whispered, "What about Belle?"

Belle squeezed her eyes tight, both arms gripping her precious tote tight against her person. The sensation of air whooshing past was gone. Belle peeked out one eye; she wasn't spinning through space. It was her *head spinning,* that's all.

"Look! She's waking up," a small boy said, leaning over her, his freckled face inches from Belle's.

Another boy his size stood back a piece. "Is she dead?"

"Not if she's opening her eyes, Billy," Boy One replied.

Ambulance sirens drowned out any next words and flashing lights pulsed in Belle's vision. Boy Two wandered toward the source of the strobing, but Boy One stayed close and hunkered low, still looking into Belle's face.

"Step back!" the volunteer paramedic shouted at the gathering crowd and they made a path. "Walter?" one of the first responders said coming closer. "What are you doing here?"

"I found her, Dad. Me. I found her right here."

The gurney was lowered. Gently, the man lifted her body to the foam mattress and raised the contraption to roll to the ambulance. Her long skirts dragged the ground, and he was careful not to step on them. "Ma'am? Can you hear me?"

Belle opened her capacious cinnamon eyes and stared into the indigo sky, or were they his eyes? "You, you *saved me*," she whispered.

Harv drank in her ivory face, pink heart-shaped lips, and cascading honey curls, entirely struck by her beauty. In the next moment, the young woman's eyes fluttered, and she was out.

They rushed her to the Cottage Hospital, lights on, pushing through traffic. Harv considered the theatrical Victorian outfit she wore, the long red velvet cape, a plaid taffeta full-length skirt, a fur-trimmed red sweater. Where was she going? The theater was closed for the season. And what happened? A hit and run? Walter had not reported any other vehicles. Plus, it was off-season on Nantucket, not much traffic. It was as though she had been thrown from something, fallen into their laps. Whatever happened, Harv thought, it was very odd.

The doctor said she is unconscious. Surely someone knows something that could help explain who this is and what happened…

Harv took one last peek at her through the glass door of the observation room and turned for the exit. Time to head home. Against the hospital's exterior north-facing wall, Harv grabbed his bike from the rack. With his mind on the young woman's shimmering blonde hair, pushing back the fact of her mysterious appearance, he headed home to his gray shingled beachfront cottage.

It was the perfect house for a single dad and *compact* described it in full. He had always meant to add on, make it roomier, but when his wife was struck down by a tourist, those plans died with her. Walter had been just a baby when it happened and did not remember his mother. Now Harv's family was just the two men, camped out together, getting by.

Harv circumvented his low white picket fence and dropped the bike on his tiny patch of lawn. His garage door stood open. This was more his workshop than a garage, and as he thought might be, he stepped in to see his son at work. Five-year-old Walter was sanding a runner for a rocking boat they were making for the Toy Boat, Nantucket's premier (and only) toy shoppe. Walter had always been brighter than average, talking, reading, and writing sooner than the other children his age, and it seemed he had a knack for toy-making as well.

"How's it going, buddy?" Harv asked and looked over the boy's shoulder.

Walter kept at it, back and forth, back and forth, his #220 sandpaper giving the oak the finest sheen. "How is she?" he asked in his high voice, eyes to his work.

"Still out."

"Who is she?" he asked the same way.

"Don't know."

"Can we go back and see her?" He still didn't look at his dad, but instead leaned close to the runner and flicked an errant shaving with a fingernail.

"After we eat."

Finally, his son turned, Walter's huge eyes hopeful. "We could eat on the way."

Harv made a *humph.* Why not? He wanted to see her, too. To his son he said, "Good idea."

Walter tucked the sandpaper in his special-sized toolbox. Harv's main occupation was teaching shop at the high school, so his son surely knew how to take care of tools.

In minutes, Harv and Walter were biking away from their cottage pedaling down the cobblestone, the salt air tangy and brisk. As they turned up Orange Street, the distinct island smell disappeared to make way for the delightful aroma of bread in the ovens. At The Bake Shoppe, Magee, the flour-covered owner, stood out front and saw them approach. She called a greeting as they left their bikes to head inside. The bakery was tiny, but the old wooden cases were loaded to the brim.

"Any of Jay's donuts left?" Harv asked touching his grumbling middle.

"Long gone," Magee said with a single shake of the head. The compact little lady not only managed the bakery but also worked alongside her husband who did a great deal of the baking himself. "Got some meat pies."

"Got any Chocolate Chunkers?" Walter peered into a case, his hands and nose pressed to the glass.

"Any chance you'll sit and eat?" Magee asked. "You must'nt always eat on the fly." She handed Walter his meal first, wrapped in a sheet of wax-paper.

He dove right in and said after a big swallow, "We're going

back to see the lady!"

"At the hospital," Harv supplied maneuvering his longish black hair behind his ears to take a bite of his own portion.

"I can cut your hair, you know," Magee offered as an aside.

Her husband bellowed from out of sight, "Don't fall for it!" and then poked his face around the threshold of the showroom, flour dusting his cheeks. "I used to have hair to my middle!"

Harv gave a grin at Jay's bald head and Magee waved the air.

"Never you mind," she said. "Aren't you the one that found her?" she asked Harv, all the while bagging their order of Chocolate Chunkers.

"No, I did," Walter said puffing out his small chest. "And I'm gonna keep her."

"What?" Harv and Magee both looked over.

Walter assumed an innocent face, wide eyes, head to the side. He grinned. "If nobody comes for her, I think we should keep her." He was so serious that Harv marveled.

"She's not a stray puppy," Magee said with raised eyebrows.

This caused Walter to giggle and he turned for the door, double-nibbling his meat pie from one hand and a cookie from the other. After calling goodbye, Walter and Harv headed out, the wind-stripped screen door banging behind them. They pedaled down the street, and because they were eating at the same time, they weaved onto the lawn of the island's oldest bed-and-breakfast, the grandly constructed Tuck You Inn.

"Harvey Nichols!" a woman's shriek sounded through the ocean air, "watch where you're riding that bike! You and that boy of yours just hit my hydrangeas!"

"Sorry, Miss Tucker!" they responded in unison.

The old woman shook a pointer finger to their faces. "Sorry's not good enough! You boys slow down."

"We're going to the hospital, Miss Tucker! To see the lady!" Walter called over his shoulder.

"The one that fell out of the sky?" Miss Tabatha Tucker asked, her silver-gray eyes flashing

Harv hit his breaks annoyed at her preposterous question. "She did no such thing, Miss Tucker. Come on." Harv tipped his chin Walter's way, as if the woman should know better than to fill a boy's mind with such nonsense.

"Oh, really?" she said putting balled fists to her ample waist. "Where do you say she came from?" She looked then to Walter who usually had a reply for anything an adult might ask.

"No one knows," the boy stated, having stopped beside his dad. He dug out a Chocolate Chunker from his basket. Harv noticed he was careful to stay off Miss Tabatha's yard. "And she's still asleep."

"She is, is she?" The old woman focused back on Harv. "When she wakes up, if she needs a place to stay, tell her I've got room."

Walter made an obvious noise, his eyes going to the inn's façade. Harv knew what he was thinking—all the kids thought the place was haunted, or cursed, or any number of oddball descriptions of what was in reality, simply an old inn. Shingled roof missing a tooth here and there, white trim in need of a coat of paint, a wraparound porch that could use a little extra shoring before another winter passes, but it was still just an inn.

"Dad, we gotta go," Walter whispered, sucking his palate with drama as if his mouth suddenly went desert. "Nobody ever comes out of the Tuck You Inn…" he said even lower and Harv hoped Miss Tabatha did not hear. To make sure, Harv made a noisy goodbye and promised to inform the young woman of Tabatha Tucker's offer.

That of course depends on if she's awake, he thought pedaling along now with Walter. *And if she's staying in Nantucket while she recuperates.* Harv felt no guilt as he sincerely hoped she would.

two

"LOOK, DEAR! THEY TOOK HER TO THE HOSPITAL!" she announced openly fretting.

"How'd you find her?"

"My sister called."

"Ah." Her husband nodded once. "Do they know who she is yet?"

"Aren't you concerned with *how* she is?" she asked, again wringing her hands.

"I am sure she is fine, my dear," he said but when his wife narrowed her eyes, he added, "How is she?"

"I think she's waking up."

"Excellent," he said and they watched on.

Belle wiggled her toes; her first sensation was of awaking from a sleep that lasted decades.

"She's coming around," a woman said nearby. Dozens of islanders had gathered in her hospital room so when Belle opened her eyes, the crowd gave her a start.

"Oh!" she exclaimed and quieted, realizing she was in a hospital room and the people closest to her were obviously medical attendants. *Something happened to me…*

"Welcome back!" a high voice called and the little boy from before came close and took hold of her hand to give it a pat. "My name is Walter. What's your name?"

What a darling little boy! Belle thought as she noted his blue eyes and bridge of his nose covered in freckles. He had black hair in need of a trim, and maybe a wash. *Do I have a son?* she asked inside. Was this darling boy hers? Had she neglected to tidy him up? Her gaze went to his tee-shirt smudged with paint and what might have been chocolate.

"Walter…" A hand went to the boy's shoulder. "Give the lady some room."

Belle looked up. His eyes were a deeper more brooding version of the little boy's, his black hair also scraggly and in need of a trim. *Why, he's the one who saved me…*

"Hello," she said testing her voice. At the sound of her first word, a sigh went round the room.

"Everyone out 'cept Harv, move on," the doctor barked clearing the room. Belle noticed that Walter stayed by his father's side. "Welcome back, young lady. You gave us quite a scare."

This was a kindly older gentleman, a medical professional, and he gave Belle a generous smile. *Do I know him?*

"I'm Dr. Wolke."

The name meant nothing. She moved to rise, her taffeta skirt crinkling. Wondering how long she had been out, her eyes went to her velvet cape on a nearby coat rack.

"So, young lady, can you tell me who you are and what happened?"

Belle looked from the doctor, to the brooding man, to the sweet little boy. To buy time, she held Walter's eye. "You were there, right?" she asked, the memory of whatever happened refusing to return.

"Yes, ma'am. I found you," the lad said with a tinge of

pride.

"Found me? I don't understand." Belle tested her neck all ways and looked at her arms. She turned her face to the doctor. "What happened?"

"That's what we'd like to know," Dr. Wolke replied.

Belle turned to Harv and a small silver bell on a silver chain around her neck tinkled. "I… I… fell… I think." As she put her feet to the floor, she realized she wasn't dizzy. "I think I'm okay. I guess I should be going." Going where? She wasn't sure. Maybe when she got outside she'd know. Belle reached for her cape. "My backpack…"

The nurse retrieved it and handed it over. Yes, her velvet backpack. She grasped it and the tiny bell around her neck rang again. She clasped it and closed her eyes. *Bell.*

"My name is Belle." There, she knew that. "And…" Try as she might, she couldn't piece anything together. "And I need to leave."

The nurse gave Dr. Wolke a concerned look. "She's not hurt and she can't stay here just because she lost her memory." The nurse squinted at the doctor. "Where will she go while she recovers from this amnesia?"

"Call Miss Tabatha Tucker at the Tuck You Inn," Dr. Wolke replied. The nurse raised her brow and he added, "It will be a quiet place." He looked to each face. "Miss Belle can rest and get her memory back on her own time."

"And if she doesn't have any money?" the nurse proposed.

Dr. Wolke sighed. "If that's the case, let Miss Tabatha run me a tab. I'll take care of it until she is back to normal."

The nurse agreed with a tentative hmm. "I went in there once a few years back, a guest needed help from a fall." She licked her lips. "I'm sure the silly stories about the place being haunted are rot and rubbish."

"Nurse Kim has an active imagination," Dr. Wolke provided, patting Belle's forearm. "The Tuck You Inn and its twin, the deserted mansion next door, have a long history of urban myths attached to them. I know Tabatha Tucker personally," he said making sure all in attendance heeded his next phrase. "She's good people."

"We passed Miss Tabatha and she said we should ask the lady to come stay at the Tuck You Inn," Walter piped up, his small voice sure and filled with serious inflection. "Me and dad can take her over there. Make sure she's safe."

"You forget, we rode our bikes, Walter," Harv said and the doctor dug around in his coat.

"Borrow the Jeep. It's out back like last time, same place, beside the dumpster," he said and Harv nodded, the exchange revealing they shared vehicles often. Belle sensed the small-town community connection displayed by all involved and it was nice.

She had no certainty of where she was from, but at the spoken name "Miss Tabatha" she had a sense of something positive. Maybe wherever she was from, there was a person with that name. Or a nice innkeeper with an eccentric reputation…

Belle shooed her rambling thoughts and to her rescuers, said, "I won't be a burden. I promise. Thank you for everything."

"Let's go," Walter said and put out a tiny hand to Belle.

"Hold on, Walter," Harv said and his manner gave Belle the impression he was working hard not to look in her direction. "Doc, didn't she have any ID? Has anyone checked her backpack?"

"No ID, no driver's license, no wallet," Nurse Kim volunteered and set down a medical chart with nothing to add.

Belle opened the flap of her velvet bag and pulled out a bundle of papers carefully tied in red ribbon. "I was afraid they were gone," she said low, her eyes filling with grateful tears. They were important, but she couldn't grasp why.

"Is that your ID?" Harv asked with his hand coming up.

Belle handed them over and Harv carefully untied the bow. He looked a long moment at the one on top, his brow knitting, and then he flipped slowly, one after the other. He glanced at the doctor and the nurse and back again

"It's recipes…" he said.

"For what?" Walter asked leaning over to see.

"Well…" Harv mumbled, a grin touching the edge of his mouth. "They're recipes for Christmas cookies. Sugar Bells, Decorated Santas, Gingerbread Reindeer," he read aloud, peeking to Walter's face when he giggled. "Candy Cane Shortbread, Chocolate Kris Kringles, Coconut Snowmen, White Chocolate Snowballs, Mrs. Santa's Toffee Squares, Christmas Nut Horns, Pecan Chimneys…" Harv finally met Belle's eye and he grinned by reflex. "Dozens of recipe cards but no wallet?"

Belle resumed possession and she re-tied the ribbon.

"Why Cookie recipes?" Harv asked, incredulous.

"Not just *any* cookie recipes," Belle defended. "These are special cookie recipes."

"Oh? Tell us about that," Dr. Wolke said, listening for clues to her identity.

Belle's gaze went soft as she searched her memory. "Hmm… I don't know…" she said and the doctor allowed it to drop. For the life of her, she couldn't recall anything more on the subject. Safely re-bundled, she dropped her recipes into her bag and reached for her cape off the hook. Once she had donned it across her shoulders, she clutched her backpack to her chest and followed them to the exit.

"Doctor's orders are for you to get plenty of rest and let it come. I bet you'll be remembering yourself any minute now," the kindly physician said and bid her farewell.

Walking between Harv and Walter, they steered her to the rear hospital exit and to the borrowed Jeep. Harv insisted she take her place in the passenger front and Walter climbed up into the rear and buckled the seatbelt. Once underway, Belle gazed at the scenery.

"This place is beautiful!" she exclaimed to anyone listening. "Everywhere I look, I see something more wonderful than before."

Behind her, Walter made a new giggle and she looked to his sweet face. He had scrunched his eyes and wrinkled his nose. Belle got it – to him, it was just "home," things he saw every day. She gave him a grin and faced front again. Now her vision was filled with roses that grew right over the buildings.

"My goodness!" she exclaimed and reached a hand to the window as if she could touch them.

"I think you've never seen beach roses before—that's a clue," Harv said in a kind tone, his eyes to the road.

Belle made a nod but did not take her eyes from the beauty outside.

"They're finishing up. You should see them in the height of the summer," Harv added.

"They remind me of when I was a little girl," she said and allowed her voice to dissipate. They drove past the Congregational Church just as the bells tolled and Belle went white, her skin prickling.

"Where was that?" Walter asked from the backseat leaning as far as the belt would allow.

"Doc said not to pry too much, Walt," Harv gently admonished. "It will come back on its own if we're patient."

"She said the roses reminded her of when she was little," Walter said his face to Belle's profile.

Belle swiveled to look at the church out the back window. "I think it was at a church. Yes, yes, I'm sure it was."

"You grew up at a church?" Walter snuck out.

Belle faced front again with a definitive nod. "I believe I did, for a while anyway. Maybe I'm starting to remember some things."

"People don't live in church," Walter said and Harv cleared his throat. Belle grinned and took in the hotel as they pulled into the drive.

The Tuck You Inn appeared to be a historic establishment with an enormous wraparound porch populated with wicker rocking chairs. A woman stood at the front steps to meet them and Harv told Belle that was the owner, Miss Tabatha Tucker.

Tabatha stood in wait, her eyes on Belle exiting the car. The sea air tossed wisps of silver hair across the innkeeper's weathered and round face. To her left and right, magnificent hydrangeas formed a brilliant puffy blue hedge. Multiple window boxes on oversized sills spilled over with crimson geraniums. Belle thought the woman seemed familiar and her place seemed filled with magic. As Harv and Walter remained at the car, Belle instead rushed toward Miss Tucker, smiling. Miss Tabatha opened her arms in response.

"I'm Belle," she said as the hug ended. "Thank you for letting me stay with you. I'll pay. I mean, when I remember." A fat tear snuck out as Belle realized she had no idea when that would be.

"Nonsense, honey child. There'll be no talk of pay. I have all these rooms, tourist season is over, and I rattle around by myself. You are to be my guest, you are."

Belle gushed a thank you but was aware that Harv and Walter hadn't come up the steps. She overheard Harv say, "guest?" and then they snickered. Belle grinned thinking she had befriended the town grandma and for whatever reason, her rescuers found her odd.

Walter broke from his dad and ran to Belle, grasping her legs. "Be careful," he said as a whisper. "Nobody ever comes out," he said again when she bent low to hug him.

"Don't be silly." She looked at the other adults in turn. "I feel as though I know Miss Tucker already."

"Call me Tabatha, honey child."

Belle touched Walter's cheek with a delicate finger. "Come in with me and see for yourself. I'm perfectly safe." She took his hand, linked her other arm through Miss Tabatha's, and started up the walk. She looked back at a stunned Harv. "Are you coming?"

Harv closed his mouth and inched forward.

"Miss Tabatha, aren't these men being silly?" Belle said, her voice singsong.

"Very silly, my dear. I'll make us some of my Tuck You Inn Magic Cocoa," Miss Tabatha replied with a twinkle in her eyes.

"That would be lovely," Belle sighed already feeling better. "With peppermint sticks to stir in the marshmallows?"

"Is there any other way to stir it?" Miss Tabatha responded and led the way.

three

"DO YOU THINK HE'S THE ONE, MY DEAR?" SHE asked, twisting the end of her apron.

He was reading an ancient and gigantic book. Each page he turned produced a shower of dust that sprinkled like glitter. "With a name like Harv? *No.*"

"Well, it's Harvey." She worried her bottom lip and stirred a pot of hot chocolate on her resplendent cast iron stove.

"Harvey was a rabbit."

"Harvey Nichols."

"Worse, that's the name of a department store in London."

She sighed. Was he always so unreasonable or was it the knee surgery bringing that out? She couldn't decide. Finally, she decided it didn't matter.

"He has a son," her husband said open ended.

"Walter." This time, her sigh was tender.

"Yes…" His finger touched the writing on the facing page "Walter Nichols..." Then he snapped the big book shut, waking the dogs. "We have bigger problems. Belle needs to remember."

She agreed with a *tsk,* spilling cocoa as she poured it into the oversized mugs.

"After all," he mumbled, now truly cranky, "We're on a deadline."

Walter couldn't believe he was actually going *inside* the Tuck You Inn. He held his breath sure it would smell weird, be full of black cats and strange noises, but it smelled of warm gingerbread and clean linens. He inhaled and sighed at the same time; it was nice. He looked around. They were passing through an open foyer into the main living area. It wasn't scary at all, but was very Nantucket—crisp white walls, shiny white wood, blue-and-white striped plump sofas, and a grand view of the ocean. Grinning, Walter ran to a huge bow window and reached a hand up as if able to touch the water.

"Ah, my lad, I see you've found my favorite spot," Miss Tabatha offered with a smile.

Belle walked up behind him and he sensed her before she even put a hand to his shoulder. She smelled of peppermints, and at that moment, she reached into her backpack and produced two candy canes. One she unwrapped and popped in her mouth like a lollipop, the other she handed to Walter. Walter gave it a skeptic onceover. Candy canes could be bitter, not really a favorite treat.

As if she read his mind, Belle said, "Go ahead. I think you'll like it. It's a special recipe."

Sure enough, with one lick, Walter found it tasted like a pouf of whipped cream with the slightest hint of mint.

"I thought you only carried recipes in that backpack?" his dad said then eyeing Belle's bag.

Belle paused and thought. Then she grinned with a tiny shrug. "Must have been stuck in the corners."

Corners? Walter thought. *She has corners in her velvet bag!* He didn't mind; he liked Belle and her magical bag. She offered a candy cane to Walter's dad who looked skeptical.

"Try it," Walter challenged, really enjoying his. His father peeled the cellophane and popped the cane into his mouth. As he expected, his dad's face broke out in an approving smile.

"Like a cloudy sky, don't you think?" Belle asked her face to the billowing cloud formations out the picture window.

Walter grinned. That's what it tasted like, somehow, it made him think of the best days. His dad was saying the same thing to Belle and Walter forgot he was afraid of the Tuck You Inn and its proprietor.

He allowed his eyes to drift. The place was cozy, yet formal, like he would need to be careful walking through. Lacquered bookshelves held nautilus, and starfish, and sand-dollars. Oil paintings of seascapes covered the walls. In one corner stood an iron clock on an ornate base, a pendulum shaped like an anchor swung the seconds. The numbers on the open face were in fact jewels from the sea, with high noon being a monstrous pearl. The hands of the clock were those of an octopus pointing to the time. For all its seriousness, Walter found the clock funny and he allowed a grin.

"Ah, my clock!" Miss Tabatha said then seeing where he looked. "It belonged to my great, great, great." Miss Tabatha never said great what. "It's a perpetual motion clock—it never stops."

"There's no such thing," Walter's dad said, and he turned to see Miss Tabatha's response. His dad knew everything important, so what would she say? Would she dare disagree?

Miss Tabatha sat down a tray of hot chocolate he hadn't noticed her getting, never mind making, and said, "Well, my lad, I guess there is, because there it is."

"I've heard of these," Belle said and walked closer to examine its details.

"You have?" Walter and his dad asked at the same time.

"Yes, they just go and go and go. It has something to do with the balance of the works, but I think they're rather magical."

"Magical?" Walter whispered.

Belle's laugh was again, like a tiny bell. "Well, not *magical-*

magical. More like mermaids, and, you know, other things you can't see unless you truly look."

Walter didn't have any idea what she meant but he stole a quick look at the ocean for mermaids. Belle might not remember who she was, but she had a lot of ideas that sounded strange and wonderful at the same time. Walter didn't see any mermaids and he softened his gaze to see if that would help. Behind him, his dad said the word as if he didn't believe in such a thing.

"I'm serious," Belle said and returned to look at the water beside Walter. "Surely, with all this water you have mermaids."

"What do they look like?" Walter asked squinting to see. A flash of silver in the water grabbed his attention, but it was gone again.

"Have some cocoa," Tabatha said. Walter turned inhaling the rich chocolate goodness. When he approached the tray, Belle lifted a mug for him and plopped marshmallows into it.

"Three is perfect, right?" She slipped a candy cane in and handed the mug to Walter who took it with both hands as Miss Tabatha's mugs were three times the size of his at home. He wrestled the cane a little with his lips and Belle giggled a sweet sound.

"Use it to spear the marshmallows," she suggested and poked one gooey pillow with the cane from her own cup, and then popped it in her mouth. "Mmmm, they're best just before they melt away."

Walter mimicked her action, nodding in agreement. His dad huffed and hadn't take a mug for himself.

"All this talk about mermaids and, well, it just isn't right."

Belle turned her face to him. "Now surely, a grown man…"

"Yes," Walter's dad agreed, "a grown man." He had narrowed his eyes, which Walter interpreted—his dad didn't believe in mermaids. Walter turned to see what Belle would reply.

"…Has had lots of years to see between the layers."

When Belle smiled at his dad, Walter watched his father's face soften completely. That made sense—Walter felt the same way when Belle look at him. She made him feel… happy. Just pure joy.

"That's enough visiting," Miss Tabatha said then and bustled between the men and Belle. "Off you go. I'll show Belle to her room. I'm sure she would like some rest. You two men can come again another time. Bye now…"

Without another word, Miss Tabatha whisked Walter and his dad out the door. A mermaid weathervane swung creakily on the porch as the massive front door slammed behind them. Walter didn't say anything about it, but he would be looking for mermaids in the sea every day now. Belle believed, and that seemed enough reason to keep his eyes peeled.

Each day, Miss Tabatha took Belle into town and introduced her around as they shopped for basics. Nothing jogged her memory, but a pattern emerged. They would begin the day with Belle making waffles, fluffy and delicious with just a touch of vanilla. Then they would run their errands in town where everyone they met became enamored with Belle as soon as she greeted them. Lastly, they would settle back at the inn with Belle baking cookies in the Aga.[ii]

"Honey child, that shortbread simply melts in my mouth. If I'm not careful, I'm going to be big as a house," Miss Tabatha said in a giggle on her second plateful.

"Nonsense, and what matters a few pounds?" Belle said grinning as she packed a wax bag of shortbread for Walter and his friend Billy. They had taken to stopping by in the afternoons to visit. The funny thing she learned was that before now, Walter and Billy were afraid of the Tuck You Inn, their minds filled with all sorts of scary stories related to the place and its owner. But now, both boys disregarded the former as nonsense and told Belle it was their favorite place to come. When she mentioned this to Tabatha, the old woman smiled with flashing eyes.

"Like all of us, the lads are simply under your spell."

Belle appreciated her generous spirit and kindness. She still felt the woman was familiar, but not as if she *knew* her. When she concentrated down on it too long, she'd get a headache. *Let it come,* the doctor's words returned, and Belle did her best to allow for the process.

The boys had arrived, evident by the sound of excited chatter at the front door. They left their bikes against the fence, careful not to touch the lawn or the hydrangeas, and they clanged the porch's ship's-bell.

Miss Tabatha heaved herself to the door to swing it wide. "Hello, my lads! Belle has a new recipe! Shortbread with chunks of candy cane."

Both boys inhaled; the house smelling entirely of cookies and hot chocolate. Belle came out of the kitchen to greet them, dusting her hands on her apron. Miss Tabatha had set up a gigantic jigsaw puzzle on the coffee table and was busy turning the pieces face up.

"Is your dad still at school?" Belle asked aware Walter spent a good deal of time at Billy's house since his dad taught school. She had not seen Harv since the day he brought her to the inn, and she had hoped he would visit with Walter by now. Tabatha informed her that the man wore many hats, not only as a volunteer paramedic, but he taught shop at the high school and built toys in his garage for the town's toy store. When Belle heard he made toys, this thrilled her to the core and she determined to ask him about that next time they met.

"What are you guys working on in the workshop?" Miss Tabatha asked as she continued preparing the puzzle for assembly.

"Rocking boats for the little kids for Christmas," Walter replied his pudgy hands flipping puzzle pieces as quickly as Tabatha.

"Christmas?" Belle stopped so short with her platter of cookies that a few slid off the side.

Billy raced for them mumbling, *"God made dirt and dirt won't hurt,"* which is the sacred two-second rule even Belle recalled, and he popped one in his mouth.

Walter also reached for a dropped cookie. "Dad says it's never too early to start!"

"No, it's never too early," Belle repeated in half-time.

"We picked up a new puzzle in town today," Miss Tabatha began, holding the lid so they could see the complex picture.

"All right! You didn't get a baby one!" both boys said with glee.

Belle set the platter of cookie survivors next to a stack of small plates which the boys loaded up without delay.

Tabatha gestured to the picture on the box, a scene of Santa flying over the rooftops in his sleigh. "You like it? Belle picked it out."

"A Christmas one!" the boys squealed with delight.

"A Christmas one," Belle said repeating, her gaze soft as if in thought.

"Santa comes to town on a Coast Guard boat December 1st," Walter said smugly. "That's a fact-jack."

"He does?" Belle squinted and then looked off.

Walter hesitated and Billy caught his eye as if they shared a secret. "On Nantucket he does. But before that, there's the Festival of Wreaths," Walter said, his five-year-old tongue pronouncing the word as *reefs*.

"Festival of Wreaths?" Belle again repeated looking off.

"Uh-huh, and then the Festival of Trees," he added in a teaching tone that he probably got from his dad. "That's at the *end* of November. The trees are even more beautiful than the wreaths!" he added, his voice amping with excitement. "Everyone works on them, the whole town. Then the pageant, which is always the same and sorta boring," he said with a titter that Billy matched. "But on December 1st, Santa comes and the magical talking tree is set up."

"Magical talking tree?" Belle repeated with curious eyes.

"Yeah, at the bank by the food tents. But the food tents are better at the parking lot," Walter said looking as if he could taste the seasonal treats in his mind right now.

Belle thought maybe Miss Tabatha noticed because her face grew soft looking at the boys and she said, "Walter, why don't you come back tonight for supper? And bring your dad. I know he could use a home-cooked meal."

"We can't. I'm meeting him at the Toy Boat and then we'll go to Magee's."

"The Bake Shoppe," Miss Tabatha mouthed to Belle. But Belle was still trying to picture Santa coming in on a boat.

"Santa comes December 1st? What about Christmas Eve?" Both boys froze, shortbread halfway to their mouths.

"The Santa-Boat Santa…" Walter lowered his voice. *"…is my dad. He stands in for the real Santa."*

Billy nodded along with Walter's words as if his revelation was the most important semi-secret in the world.

"Growed-ups know it's my dad, but don't say nothing to the little kids..." Walter tipped his chin with seriousness, but Belle was still pondering the ideas of a stand-in.

"A fake Santa," she said in thought.

"Not fake," Walter said, and his face scrunched as he explained himself. "He's a stand-in."

"What does Santa say? To the stand-in, I mean?" she asked suddenly pensive and twirling a long strand of blonde hair.

Billy and Walter looked at her like she was nuts. "Um, no one actually ever *sees* Santa, I mean, he's very, very busy."

"Oh." Belle said, but something didn't sit right and it had to do with her memory. Why couldn't she remember where she came from? The mystery was not solving itself fast enough and only when she caught Tabatha's tender eye-meet did she allow her calm to return.

For the rest of the afternoon, they worked on the puzzle and nibbled cookies, all talk of Santa put aside. When Billy announced they had to go, Belle handed the prepared waxed bags of shortbread for the boys and reluctantly sent them off.

From the doorway, Belle's gaze wandered down the cobblestone street, as far as she could see, the rows of trees balding for the winter and the sky white, threatening freezing snow or rain. When Miss Tabatha invited Harv, her heart had thumped. On the flipside, when Walter declined, her stomach sank. What was that about? Had she attached her emotions to a man she'd only met once? *Is it because he rescued me from whatever happened? Or because he's handsome enough to make me blush?*

"His wife died, very tragic, when the boy was still in arms," Miss Tabatha said with a *tsk,* coming to stand behind Belle facing out. "All these years, he stays to himself, him and that boy against the world."

"He doesn't date?" Belle asked without thinking and watching a painted bunting tip its head on the picket fence rail. "I mean, it seems he'd have plenty of women chasing him…"

"Oh, honey lamb, I believe they do," Tabatha chuckled, her upper body bouncing. "But he pays them no mind. He works and sleeps and works and sleeps according to the local buzz. I'll keep inviting him here since Walter likes it so. It's time Harvey Nichols rejoined humanity."

Belle turned her face to catch the innkeeper's expression, but Tabatha turned with a smirk and disappeared into the house. Belle smiled, tiny and to the side, no longer watching the road that led to the inn, but recalling the toymaker's beautiful eyes.

"Dad, are you ready for dinner?" Walter called through the store having ridden his bike to the Toy Boat. He tried not to let the door slam as he raced into the back room. He found his dad working on a miniature kitchen cupboard with hand-stenciled daisies.

"Just a sec," his father said dabbing a sparkling pinpoint of gold fleck inside each flower and then capping his tube of glitter. He stood and miniscule sparkles floated to the floor causing Walter to think of Belle and her magical tales. Once his dad tidied his tools, they mounted their bikes for the ride to the bakery.

Behind the counter, Magee put out a fresh batch of oatmeal cookies, lining them carefully in the case. "Hi, guys. I have some spinach quiche left."

They both grimaced.

"And a few meat pies."

That sounded better. A meat pie was exactly what it sounded like, a fluffy pastry folded over ground beef, boiled potatoes, and baby carrots. *Yum.*

"Want some cookies for later?" his dad asked but Walter shook his head.

"Got some in the bike," he mumbled between mouthfuls.

"From the Trading Post?" Magee raised an eyebrow.

Walter shook his head.

"Not from the Stop and Shop?" Magee asked as if she didn't want him eating commercially packaged cookies.

He shook his head again since his mouth was full and he held up one finger like Dad did to excuse himself. Then he ran to his bike to return with the peppermint shortbread. He handed the wax bag to Magee. "Try one."

Magee plucked one out and gave it tentative nibble. After all, she and her husband were master bakers. But her scowl turned to a sigh. "Heaven," was all she said.

"I know," Walter agreed grabbing one for himself.

"The peppermint is subtle—hardly there," Magee said trying to explain it.

"I normally don't like peppermint," Walter confessed, "until I tasted Belle's."

"Belle?"

"Uh-huh, the lady I found."

"She's still here?" Magee looked over at Harv with a question mark.

"She's at the Tuck You Inn," Walter informed with pride.

"With Miss Tabatha Tucker?" Magee's eyes popped. "My stars, even I've never been in there."

"Billy and I go every day."

"What?" Harv and Magee asked in unison.

"Yeah, it's fun." Walter was oblivious to their shock because, after all, it was the highlight of his and Billy's day.

Magee furrowed her brow.

"We're doing a jigsaw right now. Miss Tabatha makes us hot cocoa and Belle makes cookies."

Magee's brow remained furrowed. "She makes cookies?"

"A new kind every day," Walter said with shortbread in his smile.

Magee tried to catch Harv's eye, but he was busy digging out another shortbread. "What does she do with them?"

"We eat them."

"And you say they're different every day?" Magee pressed.

"Uh-huh." Again, Walter was oblivious. Isn't that what moms did all day? Bake cookies for the boys they loved?

"What kind of cookies?" Magee asked, unsure if this was true.

"You know, ones shaped like Christmas trees with M&Ms for ornaments, and ones she calls Snowballs with coconut all over. And springer something, the ones with pictures on them."

"Springerle?" Magee scowled. "Are you sure? Those are tricky and take a very long time to make."

"Yeah! Those! I didn't think I'd like them but they're great when you dunk them in cocoa. She said next time she makes them, Billy and I can help."

"Does she need a job?" Magee asked half-joking.

"Maybe." Walter wasn't sure what she did when she wasn't baking.

"Ask her to stop by. Goodness knows, we'll need help with Christmas coming," Magee asserted. "Does she remember anything yet?"

Walter shook his head and continued nibbling. And as far as he was concerned, there was no rush.

Rolling out a buttery dough for cutout stars, Belle asked Tabatha in a faraway voice, "Why can't I remember who I am? I mean, I remember how to bake…"

"Oh, honey child…" Miss Tabatha sipped her morning cocoa. "I don't think it can be rushed. It's in there." She tapped her own head. "And it will come out when it's ready."

"Are you sure?" Belle rolled in her bottom lip as she stamped out the stars.

"Yes." Miss Tabatha looked at her from faded silver eyes. "Yes, I am."

A knock at the door startled them both. Belle slipped the first tray of stars in the oven as Miss Tabatha toddled to the foyer to get the door.

"Magee?" Tabatha stared in disbelief. The locals never called on her. *Ever.* And she was never really sure why.

"Tabatha," the local baker said with a somewhat forced smile. "How are you?"

How am I? I've lived in Nantucket forever and not a soul has ever asked me that question. But what she answered was, "Why, my dear, I'm fine! Just fine. Thank you."

Magee got a whiff of Belle baking something buttery and rich inside. The visitor closed her eyes, as if able to taste it in the air. Miss Tabatha inhaled, too, thinking the first batch of stars must be coming out. She softened.

"Smells heavenly, doesn't it? Would you like to come in?"

"Come in?" Magee repeated with a pensive glance over Tabatha's shoulder.

"Sure. Smells like Belle's first batch is out of the oven." Miss Tabatha's smile spread.

"If it wouldn't be too much trouble," Magee mumbled and clasped her hands to her breastbone. "Little Walter swears by Belle's baking."

"The little dear! It is no trouble whatsoever. Come on in. I'll put the kettle on. Unless you'd be wanting cocoa?"

At the utterance of the word, Magee grinned with a nod.

"Cocoa, it is!" Tabatha announced and led her new guest to the grand foyer framed by magnificent seascapes. "Make yourself ta-home."

Tabatha noted how her guest marveled at everything and she let her to it. What had she been expecting, anyway? A cauldron? The thought made Tabatha grin and she turned for the kitchen. She invited Magee to follow, and the baker did, likely excited to meet the one causing such lovely aromas.

Belle was stamping out Springerle while more star cookies baked. Tabatha did not miss how close Magee watched her every move now that she'd entered the space. Surely, Belle's stamps were the most intricate anyone in town had ever seen, and Magee's entranced expression said she thought so, too. Belle looked up from her work and considered her flour dusted hands.

"Don't stop on my account. I'm Magee," she said in way of introduction.

"Magee runs The Bake Shoppe down the street," Tabatha said with a nod, all enjoying the heady aroma of butter and crisp cookies.

"The Springerle need to set up overnight but the stars are ready," Belle said still stamping away. A timer chimed and Belle pulled a cookie sheet from the oven. She carefully slid several hot, tender stars on a Christmas plate. Miss Tabatha looked at the pattern of snowmen on the china and wondered where Belle had found it.

"Would you like cocoa with that?" Belle turned to a pot simmering on the stove. She gave it a stir with a wooden spoon.

Miss Tabatha couldn't remember having snowmen mugs but then again, it was a huge kitchen full of forgotten china.

Magee sighed with delight as she bit into the hot, buttery cookie, her eyes on Belle stirring her cocoa with a candy cane. "These melt in your mouth!" Magee shoveled in another one amazed. "You may have heard that I am a master baker, but these? Exceptional!"

"Thank you," Belle said meaning it.

"No. Sincerely, where'd you learn to bake like this?" Magee took another bite. "So thin and crisp yet retaining such buttery tenderness. I don't know how you do it!"

Belle surfaced. "I, well… I don't know...."

Magee's face fell as if remembering their new friend had lost her memory. "It doesn't matter," she said to cover any awkwardness. "What else can you make?"

Miss Tabatha let out a laugh. "What *can't* she make?"

"I remember as a child a butter cake that tasted like these cookies," Magee said between mouthfuls. "Can you make that?"

Belle didn't hesitate. "No, I only make cookies."

By the force of her answer, Magee stopped mid-bite.

They were interrupted by the front door slamming and Walter calling out, "Is it okay if I come in?" Followed by, "sorry

I let the door bang."

The boy found them in the kitchen and crawled upon a stool before snagging a cookie.

"Hi, Magee," Walter acknowledged, not even questioning what she was doing there. Then he gave his best smile to Belle, one that exploded off his face.

"Hi, Walter," Magee said and turned to him. "Belle was just telling me about the cookies she makes."

"She can make anything!" he boasted with pride and Belle turned ten shades of red. "Belle, how about some Halloween cookies? I mean it's coming up. Pumpkins and bats and…"

Magee jumped right in. "Absolutely! Black sprinkles and maybe some witches."

"No, I don't do witches," Belle said with a firm headshake.

"Then some cutout bats! And maybe some shortbread you could cut and frost like giant candy corn," Magee offered.

Belle shook her head and stirred her cocoa.

"Just no?" Walter and Magee repeated.

"No," Belle said matter-of-fact. "I only make Christmas cookies. Coconut Snowballs, cutout Gingerbread Reindeer with red hot noses, Sugar Bells, and Pecan Chimneys. I'll make those tomorrow if I can find pecans at the market." Already her mind was busy shaping the caramelized pecans into little chimneys.

Magee waved both hands in a pish-posh. "If you only make Christmas cookies, that's great. We all love Christmas cookies. Would you like a job at The Bake Shoppe? I sure could use you."

"A job?" Belle resurfaced from the Pecan Chimney side trip.

"Goodness knows somebody will snap you up if I don't!"

Magee added with a nod to Tabatha and the boy.

"Gee. I guess I could use a job. I mean then I could pay Tabatha." She thought of the kindness her hostess had bestowed on her but Miss Tabatha shrugged.

"Don't think anything of it." She gave Belle an encouraging wink. "But I think you'd enjoy baking at The Bake Shoppe."

"Even if it's only Christmas cookies?" Belle asked Magee softly and already thinking it would be great fun.

"No!" Walter shrieked, and everyone turned. "She can't work for you!" A fat tear snuck out and rolled onto his sugary cheek.

Belle gave him a gentle smile, understanding what might be the issue. "Doesn't Billy's mom have preschool at her house in the morning?"

"Y… e … s," Walter confessed.

"But your afternoons are free until your dad is done at school," Belle continued.

"Uh-huh…"

"So, if you had to, you could have a job after preschool, with me at the bakery."

"A-a-a job?" Walter repeated looking at all three adults in turn.

"Uh-huh." Belle's mind clipped along. "At the bakery. You could help with the sprinkles and rolling the dough…" She could come up with countless things Walter could manage and enjoy. Miss Tabatha and Magee stared on, open-mouthed. "You can use a computer, can't you?" It seemed as though even babies used computers, though Belle wasn't sure how she knew this.

"Absolutely! Billy's mom teaches us. She's getting us ready for the real world."

"Then if Magee wants to send out a newsletter to her customers telling them about the new cookies, you could fill in addresses."

"A newsletter would be wonderful," Magee sighed. "I've always been too busy to do it."

"I could do it!" Walter said with confidence. Then he backed down adding, "If you help me." He looked to Belle with serious eyes.

"Absolutely!" Belle used his word.

Miss Tabatha and Magee finally closed their mouths.

"So … do we have jobs?" Belle asked Magee.

Magee gave a definitive nod. "You both start tomorrow. Let's look at your recipes and I can bring in supplies this afternoon." She turned her face to Walter. "When you get home tonight, tell your father."

Belle watched the boy nod and Magee clapped her hands once before turning to the pile of recipe cards. She lifted her cell phone and opened a note to make a shopping list. In five minutes, she called toodle-doo and was gone.

Miss Tabatha handed Walter another cookie and said it was time for him to get home. He only shrugged and continued to nibble, his eyes on Belle.

"Come on," Belle said and held out her hand. "I'll go with you. I need a walk anyway."

"Excellent idea," Miss Tabatha said and Belle did not look at her face, knowing she was match-making.

But is it such a crime to want to see Harv's toy workshop? Belle didn't think so.

Once underway, Walter was careful not to touch Miss Tabatha's hydrangeas and Belle walked beside him down the cobblestone street. When they reached the bend, the ocean view opened wide and Belle was looking out to sea.

"What're you looking at?" Walter asked following her gaze. "Mermaids?"

She resurfaced. "No. Well, maybe. I was just wondering where I came from, that's all."

"Where did you come from?"

The five-year-old had the nerve the adults didn't. Maybe it was the innocent way he asked things inside his honest curiosity.

Belle looked him in the eye. "I don't know."

"You must remember something," he persisted.

Belle shook her head, blonde curls bouncing each way, sure—*very sure*—that she in fact, did not remember a thing.

Walter didn't believe her. "But you know about cookies. Maybe it's all in there bouncing around and the cookie part just bounced out."

Belle smiled with a cautious nod. "Maybe so."

"And," Walter continued in teaching mode, "you were wearing those strange clothes when I found you … like a costume."

"Oh." Belle scrunched her face. "Were they that strange?"

Walter nodded. "Yeah. Don't they seem strange to you?"

"Where I come from, that's how you dress." She stopped. Walter was right; it was all in there and a new thing had popped out.

"Where is that?" Walter asked to see if more would come.

"I don't know."

They passed a stand of beach roses still in bloom and the salt air was tangy.

"But you know they all dress that way," Walter said and his tenacity was helpful.

Belle stopped her forward motion. "There weren't very many of us." Her eyes widened. *Was that a memory?*

Walter also stopped his bike. "If you remember, are you gonna leave?" he asked almost too small to hear. Belle did not answer before he added even lower, "If so, I don't want you to remember."

Without a proper response to what he didn't really ask, she touched his shoulder. He looked at her and then the Nantucket clothing Tabatha got her in town, a sleeveless madras blouse and short denim skirt.

"Aren't you cold?" he asked. "Those look like summer clothes."

"No, I'm actually pretty warm," she replied.

"Maybe you're from somewhere cold," Walter ventured, "with fewer people."

"Maybe so," she conceded.

"When you remember," he said wobbly but louder, and she knew what was coming.

"If I remember …"

"If you remember, you'll go back?"

Belle stared far off and gave a slow nod.

"If you leave, Miss Tabatha will be alone and sad…"

Belle turned to see his meaning.

"Didn't you notice that? Everybody's scared of her."

Belle's grin tucked into her cheek. "No, they're not. She's the sweetest, kindest person…"

"Yes, they are."

"Well, I'm not." She lifted her chin. "And you aren't."

"No." Walter looked out over the water. "Not anymore."

Walter started pedaling again, nice and slow and Belle resumed beside him.

On the next corner, he said, "You'd leave Miss Tabatha?" Then it slipped out. "You'd leave me?"

Belle couldn't reply before Walter raced away as fast as his stubby legs could take him. Belle stood in place, the air whipping her honey hair across her face. He was a darling and she hadn't meant to make him upset. But she had a serious issue to face—where was she from and how did she get here? Her desire to see the toymaker dissolved with the pressing need to remember *something*...

Dusk beat out the late afternoon and still Belle stood, watching the waves lap against the shore, the gentle rhythm lulling her racing mind.

"Where am I from? Did I wander here from somewhere else? It's an island so if I did, wouldn't I remember getting on the ferry and coming here?"

A small prop plane circled up above, the noise breaking her endless circle of thoughts; a circle that repeated, looping back to her first question. A car pulled to a stop, its headlights causing her to blink.

"Belle?" It was Harv in his ancient woody. He leaned out the window, "I was running into the Fast Break. Wanna lift?"

"No, thank you." Self-conscious, Belle started forward.

"Come on." Harv had pulled to the curb and was out of the car. "I'll drop you back at Miss Tabatha's."

His voice was so compelling Belle lightened up. "Okay."

"Fast Break is on the way. I told Walter I'd get some Doritos." They pulled into the convenience store. "Come on in. Let's get a coffee. Caffeine fixes anything and everything."

The florescent lights cast a greenish glow and further in, the coffee pot sat on a wobbly stand. Harv poured two cups as if he were at home. Belle took a sniff and squinted her eyes but still politely sipped. Harv found Walter's junk food and they headed to the checkout. Polite smiles to the car and he opened her door to settle in beside him.

He drove slowly without speaking until finally, he blurted, "So, you really don't know where you're from? How you got here, who you are?"

"Uh, no." Belle looked up from her Styrofoam coffee cup. "I just sort of landed."

"You fell from something, like off the back of a truck?"

"No, I don't think so. Surely I'd remember that." She pictured bumping off the end of a pick-up and rolling on the brown autumn grass.

The car neared the Tuck You Inn. "Look," Harv pointed and just in time, Belle looked at the sky over the water. "A shooting star. They're lucky, you know."

Belle mimed reaching for it. "Are you sure?"

"No doubt." Harv smiled. "Shooting stars are rare and lucky.

"No, I mean are you sure it was a shooting star?" Belle asked in all seriousness, her mind whirling.

"What else could it be?"

"I'm not sure." She sounded wistful. Then she turned and changed tempo. "This is a very odd place."

Harv raised an eyebrow.

"Is it true Santa comes in a boat?" Belle asked thinking it might have been a joke.

"Yep, a Coast Guard boat." Harv grinned as if talking to a child.

"Walter said you're one of Santa's stand-ins."

"I am."

"How'd you get that job?" she asked in all seriousness.

"I guess because no one else wanted the job."

Belle thought there must be more to that but just then, Miss Tabatha rattled open the front door with a loud noise.

"Harv! Walter called! Said you were coming right back. He's worried."

Harv made his goodbyes and Belle watched him go, her mind adding him back into the mix; his smile, his walk, the way he scratched the crown of his head when he puzzled. Belle wanted to decipher her own mystery, but Harv was very interesting, too.

four

"CAN'T WE DO ANYTHING TO HELP HER REMEMBER? it's getting late," she said, setting down a tray of fudge brownies glazed in apricot jam. As she cut them into squares, she placed a sugar bow on each, creating diminutive chocolate packages.

"I don't think it would be right to mess with her memory, my dear," her husband replied tasting the brownies with a humming nod. "Even if we wanted to, I don't know what we could do."

Belle bounced to the bakery, her recipes secure in her backpack. When she reached the door, nerves overtook her and she hesitated.

"This is crazy. I'm starting a job and I don't even know who I am!"

Before she could turn and flee, Magee waved her in. Once inside, the aroma of baking bread enveloped her, and the time-worn wooden display cases loaded with goodies distracted Belle from all other thoughts and insecurities. Her smile grew as she realized she was precisely where she wanted to be.

"Come on," Magee encouraged, "Grab an apron, wash up, and settle in. I think we'll start with your Christmas Nut Horns since that dough needs to chill. Then maybe your Coconut Snowballs."

Belle's eyes watered with the joy of it. The work area had tables and mixers and a *wall* of refrigerators. She fingered a bin of flour and moved to a bin of rolling pins. A plethora of supplies and plenty of space to work… "Oh, Magee! I won't let you down."

"Of course, you won't," she responded with a grin. "This is my husband, Jay. He'll be making rolls, bread, and meat pies most of the day. When I'm not busy at the counter, I'll be decorating Halloween cakes."

Belle considered the chocolate loaf cakes with candied pumpkins stuck in the frosting. The scent of warm chocolate caused her trepidation to melt away. Releasing a deep breath, she began softening butter and mixing ingredients. Before long, she found herself humming. A short time later, Magee checked in to make sure everything was okay.

"Is that Jingle Bells?" Magee asked with an eyebrow raised.

"Hmm," Belle said with a smile. "I guess it is." She continued her work, humming. Now and then, she added a few words about one-horse open sleighs.

When the Christmas Nut Horns were cooling, the scent of cinnamon filled the kitchen. Belle was rolling soft cream-filled frosted cupcake balls in coconut when she heard Walter on the sales floor.

"I'm here to work!" he hollered.

Magee was boxing a banana cake for a customer as Belle dusted off her hands and rushed out of the workroom. Walter looked excited with a tinge of nerves; Belle could relate since that was how she'd felt only a few hours ago. His eyes met hers and he grinned, relieved, and released a pint-sized breath.

"Did you tell your father you would be here?" Magee called over without leaving her work.

Belle looked to the boy for his answer and he hollered to Magee, "Not yet, gonna tonight."

Magee must of thought that was good enough for she went

back to work. Belle reached out her fingers and he took her hand.

"Okay, young man. Let's wash up and you can come into the kitchen."

"In-in the back?" Walter asked in obvious amazement. "I never been back there!"

"Where else would elves help make cookies?" Belle asked with a mischievous grin. "Besides, I need some advice. I began rolling the Snowballs in coconut and I'm not sure if I'm putting it on too thick."

"I can help with that!" Walter said with enthusiasm and Belle got him started with the soap.

Not too long after, Belle brought Magee trays of Christmas Nut Horns and Coconut Snowballs which began to sell as soon they were placed in the showcase.

"You're such a good little helper!" Magee said to Walter who peeked from the back room. "And so quiet! I forgot you were here!"

Belle patted his head as she rejoined him in the work area where they worked until five o'clock. Then it was time to leave. Walter tucked his wax sack of Snowballs into his bicycle basket, waved goodbye, and pedaled away. Day One had been a huge success.

By Friday, word had gotten out that there were some new items at the bakery. Belle had shown Walter her ideas on emailing Magee's customers, and together they scanned digital snapshots of the newest cookies and developed a fine newsletter.

"Do you think it should say your cookies are *magical?"* Walter asked Belle as he rolled out shortbread dough for cutouts.

"You tell me," Belle replied, rolling right next to him, showing him how to properly thin the dough. "You best know how they taste." She considered her cookie cutters, choosing which to use. In the end, she selected a Christmas tree. Walter hadn't replied and she nudged him with her elbow. "How would you describe them?"

"Yummy?" Walter pondered. "Melt-in-your-mouth delicious!"

"I like the sound of that," Belle praised. "We'll go to the computer while these are cooling." She had a very strict rule that they never left baking cookies unattended—too easy to burn them, thus ruining the magic her number-one fan loved so well.

In the tiny office, Walter positioned himself in the desk chair sitting on his knees, hands to the keyboard. Belle didn't recall her past, but she recognized nonetheless that the boy was brilliant beyond his years.

"You are so smart," she told him as he carefully typed in the server web address. He beamed her a grin with cookies in his teeth and returned his face to the monitor.

"Did you get the email list from Magee?" Walter asked when he was ready, the first mailing being his responsibility.

"I did," she replied and set the pages to his right. Over the next few minutes, he pecked names and emails into the form and Belle watched over his shoulder, amazed at his accuracy. When the cookies were done, they returned to the kitchen, saying they'd work the list in between batches until all data was entered.

Back to baking, Walter asked after a wistful pause, "Are we only ever going to make Christmas cookies?"

"Yes," Belle answered, transferring thin dough trees to her silpats.[iii]

"Some of them don't look like Christmas," Walter offered referring to the Christmas Nut Horns and the Snowballs, which could be called anything with those shapes.

"They *are* Christmas cookies, traditional and classic, made at Christmas for Christmas." Belle frowned in thought and swiveled her face to his. "Do they need to look more Christmas-y?"

"Maybe the Thumb Prints," Walter informed with confidence. "They don't have red or green sprinkles or anything that make them Christmas-y."

Belle chewed the inside of her cheek in thought. "We could make them look like little wreaths."

Walter shrugged with a tiny head shake. "All cookies don't have to be Christmas cookies."

"Of course, they do! Where I come from, that's all we made and all we ever ate—" Belle stopped short. Was she having a breakthrough? Beside her Walter paled, likely worrying again that if she remembered herself, she would leave.

"What?" he asked in a soft voice.

Breaking her frozen posture, Belle shot him a grin and slid the cookie sheet in the oven. She hit the timer and tenderly touched the crown of his head. "A little bounced through like before. Maybe it will drift in like that until it all comes back."

"Maybe it won't." Walter's mouth drew down and Belle knew why.

"Walter, honey, I *need* to remember. I want to remember. I feel there's something urgent I'm supposed to be doing."

"But then you'll leave me," Walter whined, cleaning his work area, and therefore not meeting her eye.

Belle gave an understanding nod; she'd become fond of him, maybe overly so, and she was afraid he might be right. She didn't want to hurt him or any of her new friends.

"Except you're staying at Miss Tabatha's and no one ever leaves there."

Belle *tsked* recalling Walter assertion that *no one ever left* the Tuck You Inn. "Now, now. I'm very fond of Miss Tabatha and

I think you are, too." Beth watched his face for an apology, and he softened. "She's like an aunt I always wished I had." Belle liked the sound of her words but nothing else came.

"I don't have any aunts," Walter said wistful. "I don't have relatives. Only Dad."

"Neither do I." The melancholy spread to Belle and they grew quiet in their own thoughts.

Walter first broke the silence. "How about a mom or a dad?"

"Um—no, no I don't," Belle replied soft.

"You're sure?" Walter's eyes were sad.

"I feel it." Then she looked off. "Could I have *guardians?"* She said it so easily that it *felt* right.

"I don't know." Walter turned and raced from the work area to the front of the bakery. "Magee! What are guardians?"

"Well, they're like parents," Magee answered, closing the cash register. "They take care of you. Why?"

"Belle thinks she has some," he replied and raced back to the kitchen. Magee followed after him.

Perplexed, Belle scrubbed the counter, flitting around, cleaning one section and then jumping to another, deep in thought. Magee called her name and she looked up.

"Are you remembering?" Magee asked, her voice gentler than ever. "I read on the internet that with amnesia, we shouldn't force it or ask too often. But it might be okay since Walter said you might remember having guardians."

Belle set her dishtowel to the countertop. "Maybe," she said thinking over the past few minutes. "We were talking about Miss Tabatha being like an aunt and..." Belle again nibbled her bottom lip looking aside.

"You have guardians instead of parents?" Magee pushed with care. "Are you an orphan?"

"Orphan?" Belle tried the word aloud and then sighed. "Aren't I too old to be an orphan? I'm twenty-seven."

"You are?" Both Walter and Magee's eyes popped hearing the new recollection.

"Hah, maybe I am. That came easy enough."

"Another one bounced out," Walter said with a giggle.

"Maybe you were an orphan, you know, when you were little," Magee said in the same careful voice.

"Maybe," Belle said, trying it on inside. It sounded close enough if not exactly right.

"You were an orphan and you had guardians," Magee added.

Belle smiled and nodded; it was feeling pretty *right*.

"So, someone loved you…" Magee said leaving it open and Belle understood her meaning. This could help her remember and she went along.

Belle relaxed her eyes and then her face clouded. "There was an accident."

"Well, of course there was an accident!" Walter piped in. "I know cuz I found you!"

Belle continued undaunted by his exuberant interjection. "He was driving and crashed and … and I think died. Oh!" Belle inhaled and focused on the kitchen counter. Her head fuzzed and she must have paled because Magee sent Walter for a glass of water.

"Water?" he asked in a near whine.

"And some sugar," Magee added, her eyes on Belle's face.

"Sugar? Which kind?" he asked, scanning the trays of cooling cookies.

"Anything! To clear her head. Hurry now!" Magee said.

Belle did not move and allowed Walter to bring her a measuring cup filled with tap water.

"This okay? Don't got glasses in the kitchen," he said and then presented her with a broken Christmas Tree cutout.

Belle nodded, sipped, and then nibbled the cookie.

Magee reached out a hand. "You're remembering. Let's go

with it. Think what happened."

"We were speeding," Belle began and set down the cup. "No, we were *rushing*. It was dark. We crashed." Belle had been concentrating too hard and she needed to relax and let it come. She told herself to breathe and she placed both palms to the smooth counter. She saw the speeding and the darkness, and then she felt the crash all over again. Her body shook as if she had been hit.

"Belle?" Walter whispered and touched her hand. "I knew it was a crash," he said and he began to weep, his frail frame shaking. Magee found a paper towel and tucked it in his fisted hand and Belle took him into a hug.

"Don't cry," she said over his head. "As you can see, I'm fine. I made it. Chris didn't, I don't think, but I did." She forced a shaky smile for Walter's sake.

"Chris?" Walter rasped, his face wet with tears.

"My husband." Belle's expression dropped aware she must be as white as the flour on the pastry board. "Oh!" A shake was coming on and traveled over her like a bad tick.

"You had a husband?" Walter whispered.

Magee handed Walter the measuring cup of water. "Drink, Walter, there you go. Good boy."

Now it was Belle weeping. At first, only a single tear squeaked from one eye, but then, more and more fell until she sobbed, as if she had been holding it in for an awfully long time.

Walter and Magee both hugged her, rocking her for comfort. Eventually, the tears slowed as she used them up.

"I guess that explains how I got here." Belle made a pitiful attempt at a laugh and her mind reeled back.

"If you crashed, where's your car?" Walter asked curious. "And all the pieces and crash stuff?"

Belle looked off, squeezing her brain. "I don't know. I don't think I was in a car."

"And your husband's body?" Magee added sounding kind despite her words.

"I think it was blown up," Belle said and started to cry all over again.

Walter rode his bike home, his mind spinning. All he could come up with that made sense was that she was brought here for him. How? He had no idea. Why? Because he needed a mother. It was simple and it made sense. *I needed a mom and now she is here!*

Walter forgot about meeting his dad at the Toy Boat. Instead he crawled into his bed, jeans, ratty tee shirt with frosting smears, and sneakers, and willed himself to sleep.

His dreams were frantic. A rocket was soaring through the sky. He could see Belle through a porthole-type window. His dad was the pilot. Suddenly, they hit a meteor and exploded. The rocket disintegrated into a million shiny pieces flying off in every direction. His dad was nowhere to be seen, but Belle was flying through the black sky. Falling, falling, falling, until she landed on the grass on Main Street by his feet.

Harv rushed into Walter's room, past the tiny basketball hoop, his feet hitting a few stray stuffed animals. When his son hadn't shown up at the Toy Boat, he went home only to find him sound asleep. Without waking him, Harv sat on the edge of the small bed, brushing a strand of unruly hair off Walter's forehead.

Am I doing enough for him?

Harv frowned. He couldn't be. He was making it, but he was really only getting by. Juggling a full-time teaching career, a part-time job making toys, volunteering as a paramedic, managing a house, raising a boy…

And babying a frozen heart.

Harv wiped his face, one swipe. A heart still in shock over his wife's accident. Grief had hardened him, shut him off, and this he countered by staying busy.

But then, listening to the quiet rhythm of Walter's breathing, he wished…

Harv looked out the window at the first star of dusk. He wished it *wasn't so.* He had no more to ask than that and he had no idea what normal would be. Over the years, he and Walter had formed a very small team, had made their own normal. Harv eyed the bakery sack on the quilt where Walter must have left it. With a sad grin, he planted a kiss on his son's forehead, retrieved the bag, and tiptoed out.

In the small dinette, Harv settled in the chair without turning on the light and sampled a cutout Christmas tree cookie from the bag. His mind tickled the memory of who loved Christmas cookies the most when he heard his son wail at the top of his lungs. Harv leapt to his feet and bolted down the hall.

"Walter! Wake up!" he said and scooped the boy into his arms. "You're dreaming. It's just a dream!"

"Dad, Dad!" Walter grabbed his father's neck with both arms, his hair matted with sweat. "Dad, you're okay!"

"Of course, I'm okay." Harv rocked him as he had when he was no more than a baby.

"You're not dead!" Walter said, his eyes glazed, his voice panic stricken.

"Of course, not. See? I'm right here," Harv reassured. Walter kissed his head and held him close. "You're okay. *Shhh.*"

"You blew up into a million pieces!" Walter said, his eyes not yet focused in Harv's. "I saw the crash!"

"I'm okay. Come on, look. I'm fine." Harv stroked his back as he spoke over the boy's hair.

Walter shook his head, still trembling. Then after what seemed an eternity, his respirations slowed, and he relaxed from his rigid posture.

"If it wasn't you, who was it?" Walter whispered.

Harv had no answer and he continued to rock his son in his arms. When finally ready to tuck him back into bed, Harv noticed his clothing. "Come on, change into your pjs and I'll get some milk and cookies."

He lowered Walter to the floor and his son gave a careful nod. Harv left him to change clothes and entered the kitchen. He poured a tumbler of cold milk and grabbed what was left of the cookies. When he returned, Walter was sliding under the covers wearing his Gingerbread Man pajamas and leaving his discarded jeans and tee shirt in a pile at the foot of the bed. Harv sat on the edge and together, they ate the end of the cookies.

"Feel better?" he asked when the treats were gone.

"Yeah," Walter said and nipped the point of his last tree cookie, the part with the yellow M&M for the star. "It wasn't you in my dream." His voice was thoughtful and sure.

"Good." Harv brushed cookie crumbs from the quilt to the floor.

Finished eating, Walter snuggled deeper into the covers. Calmed and fed, his eyes were heavy, ready for sleep. "It wasn't you. It was Belle's husband." Then Walter fell asleep.

Harv stared at his now sleeping son. "Belle's husband?" he repeated. His son must have heard that from Belle. And he saw her when? With his busy schedule, he didn't have long chats with his son every day like he did when it wasn't the holiday season. Somewhere, some time, Walter was able to talk to Belle.

She must be starting to remember…

Did Belle have a husband? The thought brought a chill down his back. There was no denying he was attracted to her, though he refused to act on it. He tried not to seek her out, though he sometimes couldn't help it. It was that darn smile of hers; it *did something* to him, softened him. He understood why Walter was so fond of her. Despite his own precautions, Harv was fond of her, too. Maybe too much.

A husband?

Harv didn't want her to have a husband, dead or alive. With that odd thought, he wandered to the kitchen, poured himself a double scotch, and went to bed.

Harv should not have had the drink before sleep. It was a guarantee his mind wouldn't rest. In his dreams, Belle walked alone, along the beach with a basket looped on her arm. She was toeing a stone, bending over a piece of driftwood, looking for the million pieces her husband had been blown into. But of course she wasn't finding body parts. There was a sand dollar in her basket, a tiny shell, and a shiny piece of green beach glass. Still she was looking.

Harv was over a dune watching her. She had on her red velvet costume, the one she'd worn when they'd found her. The breeze off the shore caught her long golden hair and it flowed behind her, wisps catching on her face. He knew what she was looking for and thought maybe he should offer to help. But he couldn't. He could only stand and watch, mesmerized by her beauty, haunted by her grief. Where was the carefree, childlike girl he had rescued? The one without a memory, fascinated by everything on the island as if she had never seen a beach or a New England town.

Dream Belle continued to pick up bits of beach minutiae, now wading into the tide, the hem of her delicate plaid skirt becoming soaked. She reached for something, the fur cuff of her sweater dipping into the water. Then she stepped in further, reaching, and was gone. The sea had claimed her. Harv could not even see her honey hair. As her red velvet cloak drifted to shore, he raced down the dune.

"Belle!" he screamed. "Belle!" Then he dove in the water searching and screaming…

"Dad, Dad!"

Harv was shaken to his senses by the sound of his son's voice and the wiggling of his near arm. His body was twisted in the sheet and with effort he kicked the blankets to the floor.

"Dad, wake up!"

Walter crawled onto the bed and looked down on his dad, patting his chest. "Dad! It's just a dream!"

"Okay, okay" Harv whispered, scattering the cobwebs to clear his thoughts. He was semi-back; part of him was still on that beach, screaming and searching for Belle.

"Dad, you were dreaming."

"I know, I know." Harv hugged his son as his mind cleared. But he could still feel the cold ocean water. He shook his head again, clearing it away. He kept an arm around his boy, the closeness anchoring him to reality.

"You had a nightmare." Walter sounded shaken. "Just like me."

Harv nodded and a word slipped out before he could stop it. "Belle…"

Walter pulled back and looked at him. "Belle?"

"I was dreaming about her." Harv ran his free hand through his disheveled hair, shaking the memory, yet at the same time holding tight to it, as if not sure which way to go.

"Is she okay?" Walter asked, his lip quivering.

"I don't know," Harv admitted. He really didn't.

"I think she's starting to remember," Walter said low.

"Did you see her today?" Harv asked and his son nodded. "Where?"

"At the Bake Shoppe. She said she remembered a husband named Chris."

Harv gave him a skeptical look. "What else?"

"The crash. Only I don't think it was a car crash." Walter scrunched his face trying to explain.

"Do you think it was at sea?" Harv let slip, not meaning to play a guessing game on the topic.

"No." Walter grew pensive. "Her clothes weren't wet when I found her."

Harv remembered. *Ah, he's right.* Her dramatic costume would have been soaked. Her clothes were so heavy that if they were wet, they would have dragged her under.

"I think she fell from the sky," Walter offered.

Harv considered his son's sincerity. He meant it; he wasn't fabricating a complicated story.

"Has everyone given up wondering where she came from?" he asked, his voice cautious.

Harv sighed. Walter had hit upon it; the town had returned to normal. No one thought twice about the mysterious woman, where she came from, or where she was going. Each man and woman had moved onto the next interesting thing in their respective lives.

"Well, maybe so, but she didn't fall out of the sky," Harv mumbled, feeling as if he should say something. He hadn't forgotten, and neither had his son.

"I think she did!" Walter said with his familiar stubborn puss. "Besides, she thinks she did, too!"

Harv looked at his determined son and shook his head. What could he say? He had no answers and it was too late to grill the boy on how he ended up at the bakery when he was supposed to meet at the Toy Boat.

Harv settled on, "All right, we both need to turn in. Tomorrow we'll see if we can't learn some more."

With that appeasement, Walter curled up next to his father and fell asleep. Harv's mind pitched and swayed like a ship at sea. *...Maybe she did fall out of the sky like Walter said.*

Until finally sleep claimed him, too.

five

BELLE CONSIDERED THE MOON, A WHITE EYELASH IN the velvet black sky. The water lapped the shore and tiny sprinkles tickled her skin as it rode past on the breeze. How long she had stood on the beach she wasn't sure, but Miss Tabatha left a soft light on in the window. Belle smiled at the illumination, happy to have someone care so about her wellbeing. It would be painful to leave such a great new friend; if she left, that is. Miss Tabatha seemed familiar, yet how could that be?

I was an orphan…

But where?

Nowhere like this place. The beach was new, as were the beach roses that grew wild in every spare corner, lacing rooftops and arbors with their charm. She had never seen hydrangeas, the poufy blue flowers that lined Miss Tabatha's walkway as well as decorated the entire island with such delicate beauty. Belle considered the tang of salt in the air—it was not only the people here that were strangers, but the place itself was very, very new.

I remember I had guardians…

She hummed. These were guardians who cared for her, who rescued her. When they entered her life, she didn't know. Who they were was on the edges, and she couldn't yet pull it in. Where they were also returned a big blank. All she knew was it wasn't a place like Nantucket.

If that is so, what am I doing so far away from wherever I came from?

Belle turned her mind to the other great revelation. Her husband. Who was he? Where had she met him? What did he look like? Belle squeezed her brain for an image of a man she felt was attractive, someone she would pick out of a crowd. Again and again, the only face that arose was Harv's.

But that wasn't right. Harv lived right here, in Nantucket.

Chris…

What was his last name? How long had she been married? Taking in a lungful of the night sea air, she thought, *it couldn't have been very long. Was I in love? If I'd been in love, wouldn't I be heartbroken now that he died in the crash? Did I not love him?*

Belle stilled her mind.

He had been more a *friend*.

They had wanted her to marry him. They said it would be perfect. They knew what was best. After all, they had rescued her from the orphanage. They assured her that she would love him with time and she had believed them. The recollections came faster now, and Belle nodded with caution.

It had been snowing. An outside wedding?

Yes, she had an outside wedding by an ice sculpture. Or was it an ice palace? Of course! It had been a palace made of ice and the snowflakes drifted down, huge as paper doilies. She had carried poinsettias, her favorite flower, and she had worn red, her favorite color. Why, she'd worn the red cape, the tartan silk skirt, the fur-trimmed sweater they'd found her in! Belle's eyes grew huge.

Those were my wedding clothes!

A tear squeaked free and she put her hands to face and she dropped to both knees.

"My wedding day! I should be able to remember my wedding day. As a little girl at the orphanage I dreamt of a wedding to a man I could love with my whole heart. Help me…

Help me remember."

A shooting star soared across the inky sky. Belle reached up as if she could capture it. She remembered reaching her hand up and someone taking it and leading her under a crystal arch where ivory poinsettias cascaded with gigantic snowflakes and flickering ivory candles. All around were her closest friends—a pair of snowshoe rabbits, three white fluffy Samoyeds, her guardian's dogs.

"Oh! My guardians have three Sammys! Snowy, Sparky, and Sunny," Belle whispered to herself, lowering her hands from her cheeks. She remembered their personalities that fit their names. And the baby polar bear was there, only weeks old! He stood beside her puppy.

I have a puppy!

Belle grinned wider at the memory of her malamute puppy, Sprinkles, who wore a white velvet bow around her neck. Her mind continued to clear, and she saw reindeer, all with silver bells, standing in a huddle, heads bobbing with kind and loving eyes. Belle's heart swelled with affection as she imagined them.

Are all my friends animals?

As the happy tears fell, she realized, yes, these were her friends. She could see the reindeer's breath frosty in the night and the robin's egg blue of Sprinkles' eyes twinkling.

Where is my husband? Belle wondered. *Take a deep breath, Belle, breath. In. Out. In. Out. Clear your mind. It's all right there.*

The same hand reached for her and they stepped together into the... what was it? A car? A coach? She couldn't see, couldn't remember.

"Try, Belle! Try!" she said under her breath sending gentle plumes into the night. But the next thing to come was an explosion of light, like fireworks, only she was in the middle of the array.

And then she was falling.

Falling and screaming.

Not asleep, Harv caught the phone on one ring having seen Miss Tabatha's name on the Caller ID.

"It's Belle!" the woman shouted to him and then said to the side, "Honey child!"

Harv heard Belle scream through the phone before the call dropped. Harv leapt from bed, threw on his coat, and flew like the wind for the Inn. For Belle.

As he ran up the walk, something inside steered him to the beach and he raced around the building. Miss Tabatha and Belle stood under the stars; Belle was weeping and Miss Tabatha cooed words of comfort. Harv charged to their position and without a thought, scooped the young woman into his embrace.

"Belle … Belle …" he said low, his face ashen. When she did not calm, he put his hands so gentle to either side of her face. "Belle," he whispered. "Are you okay?"

Her beautiful eyes focused and he watched her work furiously to control her emotions. Snuffling back tears and hiccups she managed, "I remember crashing."

Harv held her tight, not understanding, but intuiting her fear of whatever happened. "Where were you?" he whispered.

Belle tipped her head and pointed upward.

"The sky? You were in the sky?"

She nodded yes as the tears began again.

"You were in a plane?" he asked still trying to sew up the details.

Belle grimaced. "I don't know. I don't think so…"

"Who else was there? Can you see?" Harv asked and still held her close. Maybe if she talked, her memories would continue to solidify. "How many people are there?"

"Just one," she said and then pushed her face into the lapel of his coat. "Only him. Only my husband…"

Harv held her tenderly and sent Walter a mental well-done. He'd been right. Belle had a husband. Hadn't Walter dreamt of Belle hurling through the sky only to crash, she and her husband? Harv considered; Walter thought it had been *him* hurling through the sky with Belle and crashed and died. What made him put that together?

Miss Tabatha came out of the shadows, having heard everything. "Should I go to Walter?"

"Walter!" Harv turned his face toward town with a jerk. "I left so fast…"

"I'll bring him here," Miss Tabatha said, and she was gone.

Harv and Belle stood under the stars, the autumn air settling them both with its comforting charm. Finally, Harv asked, "You have a husband?"

"*Had.* I had only just gotten married the day we left and then crashed."

"Left where?" Harv had to hear it; he had to ask.

"Home." She turned her tear-flooded eyes his way. "But I'm not sure where that is."

"What do you remember?" he asked with care.

"I … I started to remember the wedding. Everyone I loved was there." Belle still clutched him in their embrace, and he hoped she'd never let go.

"Who was there?" he asked in the same tone.

Belle looked pensive but started said with a slow nod. "My guardians were there, but I couldn't quite see them. I only heard their comforting voices. But I saw Sprinkles, my malamute puppy, and the Sammys, and the thumpers—two snowshoe rabbits, and the reindeer and …"

"Animals?"

Belle nodded. "It was outside. Did I mention the new polar bear cub?"

"Polar bear cub," Harv repeated, his mind racing to understand. Her face literally shone as she recounted her life and Harv watched, amazed. "And…" he tried again, "Your husband?"

Belle's smile faded and she swallowed. "I can't picture him."

"Yet, you're sure it was a wedding?"

"Yes, it was a wedding, with a crystal arch and all the animals as my guests. It was a wedding. It was *my* wedding." She sounded certain. "A girl wouldn't forget her own wedding."

"But you would forget your husband?" Harv hadn't meant to say it that way and Belle's expression fell.

Her eyes widened, and then flared. "Who do you think you are? How dare you judge me!"

He was shocked, and the fury was contagious. "Don't yell at me! I'm only trying to help!"

The fight was cut short as Walter ran across the beach screaming, "Stop yelling!" He raced to his dad, arms flapping.

"Whoa!" Harv caught him under the arms and lifted him off the ground. Walter's legs continued to kick.

"You upset Belle! You upset Belle!" he screamed.

Belle watched wide-eyed, so did Miss Tabatha.

"Not so fast there, Walt. She started it!" Harv said aware he sounded younger than Walter just then.

Belle defended herself. "How could you challenge me for remembering my wedding and not my husband?"

Walter went still in his father's arms. "You remembered your wedding?" he asked and scrabbled down until his feet met the ground.

Belle opened her arms and Walter jumped into the hug. "Yes. Yes." She brushed a stray lock of hair off his forehead. Then she looked at Harv. "I'm sorry I yelled at you. I can't understand why I can't remember him. I want to."

Miss Tabatha gave a weary sigh. "Everyone…" Harv, Belle and Walter all turned and fell quiet. "It's very late. Let's go in, have some cocoa and maybe, just maybe, tomorrow this will all make more sense."

She held out her hands like the grandma everyone wanted, and at that moment needed. They followed her in, Walter back in Harv's arms and Harv's hand in Belle's. Across the lawn and to the porch, Harv marveled how easily he pictured Belle there, beside him, completing their family. Unwilling to rush the moment, he cleared his mind and hoped for time.

six

"MY DEAR, I THINK SHE'S REMEMBERING," SHE SAID fussing with a flower arrangement of hemlock, snowberries, and white roses. To finish, she added pompom ivory poinsettias and stopped, pleased.

"She better, it's the end of October. We're running out of time," he grumbled, patting one of the Samoyeds silky heads. "Has she found her tote bag?"

Belle awoke exhausted, the process of remembering prematurely draining her energy. Or maybe it was the interaction with Harv. Either way, she did not feel rested as she followed the aroma of French toast wafting from downstairs.

"Ah, you're up," Miss Tabatha said from the stove. Deftly, she slid the toast from the cast-iron skillet onto a plate. She caught Belle's wondering glance. "They're gone. Harv to work and Walter to preschool at Billy's mom's."

Belle sighed with a nod of thanks.

Miss Tabatha patted the back of a chair. "Eat up. You had quite a night."

Belle agreed and once seated, poured an inordinate amount of syrup onto her breakfast. She ran the tines of her fork back and forth and back and forth in the sugary fluid.

"Will remembering be this hard all the time?" she asked, her gaze to the forming and reforming lines.

"Oh, honey child," Miss Tabatha sighed bringing a strong cup of coffee, "I don't know. But you have to keep trying."

Belle exhaled; her hostess was right. How it would be easier to drift along as she was now, but a nagging sensation urged her to keep trying as if she had a very important deadline she couldn't ignore. Belle pondered this as she ate. Before long, her head felt clear and her strength renewed. One thought circled her mind without ceasing:

I need a husband! And I need him before Christmas Eve!

Shortly thereafter, Belle had bid farewell to Miss Tabatha and walked through the delicious crisp fall air to The Bake Shoppe, her mind chumming all the way.

Why do I keep thinking I need a husband?

What in the world could it mean? And what did it have to do with remembering her past, the crash, her identity? Belle was happy here, she had a fun job baking cookies, doing what she loved best. She was thinking on all this when Walter came in, ready to work.

"What can I do?" he asked, making a big show of washing and drying his hands.

"I'm making gingerbread reindeer, so why don't you press red hots on their noses for me?"

"Cool," Walter said and got to work. After eleven or twelve little red noses were complete, he looked up to catch her eye. "Tonight's trick-or-treat. Can't we make Halloween cookies for once?"

"No," Belle replied and continued rolling, cutting, and arranging.

"How about pumpkin-shaped cookies out of this gingerbread dough?"

"No," she replied as before still working the dough ball.

Walter pouted but kept working. After another minute he looked for her gaze once more.

"Yes?"

"Want to come trick-or-treating with me and Billy? Billy's mom is sick and his dad has to stay home to give out the candy. We always have a grownup with us to make sure we're okay."

Belle stopped turning the dough. "You want me to come trick-or-treating?"

"Yeah, why not? It would be neat. You can wear a costume." His eyes brightened. "You could wear the stuff we found you in! It looks like a costume!"

Belle frowned in thought. Her wedding clothes for Halloween? "I've never gone out for Halloween," she said, pensive.

"Never? Even when you were little?"

"I was at the orphanage and we didn't celebrate Halloween. As a matter of fact, we didn't even speak English!" Belle froze in place, her eyes wide. "We spoke French. I was in an orphanage in the French countryside."

Walter jumped off his stool growing excited. "Maybe that's where you learned to bake!"

"Yes," Belle replied with certainty. "Yes, it was. I remember! The older girls made bread and croissants for the local bakery. We smaller girls made cookies."

Walter rushed up and threw his arms around her. "You remembered! You remembered! What else?"

Belle grinned and looked upwards. "I lived there for a long time. I was quite old before anyone came for me. I remember watching the other children get families—it was always so bittersweet. I was happy for them of course but…"

"Sad that no one wanted you," Walter supplied.

She gave a nod.

"But then someone did."

"Yes, a couple. They were very, very old."

"Like grandmas and grandpas?"

"Like Miss Tabatha." Belle's face softened. "Maybe that's why I like her so much."

"Must be!" Walter was practically dancing. "So, you left the orphanage, and then what?"

Belle closed her eyes. It was in there, she just had to will it out. "I missed the other children. I only spoke French, so that became a big part of my day. My guardians taught me proper English."

"And what else? What else did you do?"

"Um… I baked cookies. *Christmas* cookies." It was coming back. If she wasn't studying English, she was baking cookies…

"Did your guardians have other children?" Walter asked.

"No, they had animals." She squeezed her eyes. "And these odd little workers who ate the cookies."

Walter scrunched his face. "What do you mean?"

Belle tried, but it was lodged somewhere she couldn't pry loose.

"You said they were little. Were they children?" He looked at her sideways, very serious, and for a moment, Belle saw Harv in his face.

"Hmm, they were small," she offered and hummed. "They were short. I suppose, maybe your height. Some I think were not quite as tall as you."

"Children! Child labor! Dad says that's against the law!" Walter sounded agitated at the thought and repeating what an adult must have said within his hearing. Belle put out her hand and touched his shoulder. It occurred to her that some would think Walter laboring since he helped bake cookies, but she kept it to herself and gave the boy a smile. "No, they weren't children. They were very small adults."

"What about school? Did you go to school?" Walter asked next.

"School?" Belle's eyes widened. "There were no schools."

Walter didn't believe her. "Are you sure? Maybe you just didn't want to go," he said with a snicker.

"No, honest, there were no schools."

"Then I want to go there!" Walter's small chin jutted forward.

Belle tossed back her head and laughed, "When I figure out where it was, I'll bring you there!"

"You mean it?" Suddenly serious again, Walter sought her eye.

"Of course, I do. You, Miss Tabatha, Magee, and your dad are my friends. You will all be invited."

"Yay!" Walter clapped his hands with a wide smile. "So, tonight will you take us trick-or-treating?"

"I will," Belle replied with a bow, in her mind already donning her taffeta skirt and red velvet cape. Wedding clothes for Halloween. She clicked her tongue and went back to the cookies.

Right on time, Belle left her borrowed room at the Tuck You Inn dressed in her wedding clothing, her beautiful red cape dragging along the cobblestones once she reached the peaceful street. She turned her long gaze to the sea and allowed her mind to run. Something about the coolness in the air and quietness of the early evening invited her to stop and consider.

"I don't have much time left," she whispered to the air shuffling past and bringing with it the aromas of the sea town. She was on a schedule and she needed to remember why. If she didn't remember soon, time would run out. Then where would she be? Belle clenched her fists and then looked at her left hand.

If I had been just-married, why wasn't I wearing a wedding ring?

Pondering these things, she continued the walk to town. The Toy Boat was lit and open, so she wandered inside.

Immediately, her heart was filled with joy, her vision filled with not only toy boats—so apropos to this place—but also dolls with curly long hair and gorgeous big eyes. She saw tin toys of various ilk, armies of toy soldiers ready for play, Parcheesi and Monopoly, and any other board game folks might enjoy with their loved ones.

A crinkled older woman nearby eyed her up and down, likely aware she was the rescued girl with amnesia.

"Hello," Belle offered, her fingers running along the closest game of Fairy Land. She lifted another entitled Santa's Trials and turned it to read the back. "You have the new games in," she said as an observation and continued to read.

The woman made an obvious nod. "Unpacked 'em this morning." Then she paused and waited for Belle to look up. "These are brand new—not even in the magazines yet," she said with her eyes narrowing. "I'm surprised you know about them."

Belle smiled, oblivious to the dig. Then she smiled full-wattage. "You have the new robots! Aren't they the best ones yet?!" She picked up a brightly painted tin robot and wound the key, making its feet move forward. Little sparks shot off its head every third turn step. "Great touch, the flying sparkles! I knew it would be."

Her grin remaining, Belle set it down and picked up a baby doll, plopping it on her shoulder as if for a burp. It crooned out *mama* and then *papa*. She gave an approving nod.

"We had to bring these up to date; so many dads are more involved with their children then used to be."

"Huh?" the clerk mumbled, confused by Belle's comments.

Belle did not react to the woman's bepuzzlement, but instead crossed to a beautiful dollhouse with a slate roof and shuttered windows. The outer walls were layered with tiny gray shingles and roses had been painted trailing up the side along a miniature white trellis.

"Why, it's a little girl's Cape Cod house!" Belle said with glee clasping her hands beneath her chin. "It's… *it's perfect.*"

Belle leaned low to peer into the windows, the tiny furniture, the paintings on the wall, of the sea, of course and one of a lighthouse. Her mind fuzzed and she lifted her upper body to stare off into space, seeking a fleeting *something.* Then she nibbled her bottom lip and said with a resigned sigh, "I've never seen this one before, *ever.* I'm sure I'd remember. It's *so perfect.*"

"Thanks." Harv stepped off the threshold where he must have been standing, for how long, she couldn't say. Belle looked up from her concentration to take in his face, still tanned from the summer, so handsome even more so today than ever.

"You built it?" she asked and he nodded wiping both palms to his workpants.

"Sure, in my workshop. They provide a small space here, but I make most of my stuff at home."

"Wow, this is amazing," she said returning her attention to the dollhouse. She touched the stone surrounding the chimney top and shook her head once in awe. "You said *stuff.* What else do you make?"

"Toys," Harv said with a smack. "I make a lot of toys."

"Toys?" Belle asked, one finger twirling a long strand of her hair on its own accord.

"Yeah, you know..." Harv delivered his own full wattage grin as he spread his arms. "For the Toy Boat."

Belle looked around growing embarrassed at how huge her smile remained. She turned to the side pretending to study a horse and carriage parked in front of the dollhouse and put both hands to her cheeks. They were warm and she did not want to appear so silly.

What is wrong with me?

"I heard you're taking Walter and Billy trick-or-treating," Harv said changing topics. "I was just leaving. I'll walk with you and show you my workshop at the house."

With a gentle grin, Belle nodded, and Harv put out his elbow. Minutes later, they strolled through town, enjoying the clean briskness of the intermittent breeze. Maintaining her expression, inwardly, Belle's mind raced.

He makes toys? And not only that, but beautiful, amazing, one-of-a-kind toys? This means something!

With a careful exhale, she gave his arm a squeeze. "What made you decided to make toys?"

Harv allowed a shrug. "I've made toys since I was a boy. When Walter came along, it seemed natural to continue." Harv then gave her arm an equal squeeze in return. "He's always been a big helper, like the perfect elf."

Belle stopped walking and Harv turned, eyebrow raised.

"Elf?" she stammered.

"Yeah. You know—a great helper."

Belle pressed her lips together, but she was grinning wider, new memories crystalizing in a rush.

The little people I made cookies for at home were elves!

Unaware of her epiphany, Harv pulled open the garage door. Belle's eyes could grow no wider as her gaze slipped along an old-fashioned workshop housing children's bobsleds, stacks of wooden gameboards in the midst of being painted, rocking horses half-carved with friendly eyes begging to go for a ride, and much more.

"Belle!" a high voice yipped as Walter and Billy came storming into the garage opening both dressed like space men. "Where've you been?" they asked in tandem. Before she could answer they were taking her hands, dragging her away. "Bye, Dad! Don't give away all the candy." Then with Belle between them, the boys pulled her for the first street of homes, swinging their Toy Boat shopping bags.

Belle followed along, her mind still pondering the completed toys in Harv's workshop. The beauty of the craftsmanship! She was floored, and remembering the elves? How was she to play trick-or-treat when all she wanted to do was scream to the heavens, *I AM REMEMBERING!*

"TRICK-OR-TREAT!" the boys' voices rang out as they reached the first door. The next moment, they were celebrating with, "Giant Hershey bars, yeah!"

Belle allowed their glee to hold her attention and she laughed at their innocence.

"Gummy worms!" they shouted at house #2, dropping the candy into their bags, ready to move on.

Belle nodded to the other adults escorting their children, dressed as wizards, witches, and goblins, along with the occasional alien for her own spacemen to laugh with. It overcame her like a wave. "I want this..."

Belles eyes darted left and right as she realized she'd spoken out loud. No worry; she stood on the sidewalk beside a cluster of beach roses and no one was nearby.

Billy and Walter clamored back holding open their bags of booty. "Wanna Snickers bar?" Walter waggled one under her nose. "I got extra."

"Oh, no, no. Those are for you," she objected tenderly.

"No, the extras are for you! We did it on purpose!" Billy piped up, gesturing for the still-dangling treat.

Belle accepted and the trio ripped into their respective Snickers and resumed walking. Biting, chewing, and then swallowing in a thoughtful manner, Belle gave a huge nod with her upper body. "That was really delicious!"

Still walking, Walter and Billy leaned around her on either side and exchanged a look. With a suspicious giggle, Billy said, "You've never had a Snickers bar?"

Belle smiled amused by his serious tone. "No, I don't think I have. Any chance I can have another one for later?"

Walter laughed and took her hand. "We're gonna figure out where you're from and were gonna bring them lots of

Snickers!"

They had reached the business end of the street and the boys begged to stop at the Bake Shoppe.

"Look!" Walter yelled, pointing at the store porch where Magee and Jay sat on the bench dressed as proverbial bakers. In another step, Belle saw they were passing out apple cider donuts in wax bags.

"Hey, guys!" Magee hollered. "Wanna sit and rest?"

Walter and Billy rolled their eyes; they would never take a break because of the chance of missing something.

"I like your costumes," Magee's husband volunteered to the boys.

Walter puffed out his narrow chest. "We're space men from where Belle came from."

Magee and Belle said in unison, "Oh?"

"Yeah," Walter replied going into teacher mode. "Billy and I figured since she fell from the sky, she's an alien, so we dressed up like space guys to show our support." Billy nodded, his eyes serious.

Belle knelt to the boys' level. "That's sweet, but I don't think I'm an alien. I'm not from outer space." Belle licked her lips to allow time to form the right words. "I think I was traveling *through* space."

"In your rocket ship?" Billy chimed in.

"With your husband," Walter added.

Magee and her husband listened on, their eyes concerned.

"No, no, I wasn't in a rocket ship. I am confident of that fact." She sighed and her gaze softened. "I remember feeling the cool wind whoosh through my hair. That doesn't sound like a spaceship."

"We dressed as space men for nothing!" Billy complained but Belle opened her arms to give them a hug.

"Dressing as space men on my account is the sweetest thing anyone has ever done for me. You're even sweeter than

Sprinkles."

"Sprinkles?" Magee asked and all faces turned to her as if they'd forgotten her presence.

"Sprinkles is her malamute puppy," they replied at once.

During this, Magee's husband had risen and gone inside. When he returned, he held out two large paper sacks with The Bake Shoppe's logo. Belle smelled donuts as the boys cheered and grabbed the bags.

"Thank you!" she sang, looking inside.

"There's a little time left to trick-or-treat, but you better be closing it up," Magee said and gave Belle a wink.

Maybe she guessed at Belle's sore feet, they did ache, but not terribly. With a few more thank-yous and goodbyes, they were off to the next street. In a half-hour, porch lights were going off and Billy's eyes were droopier than ever as bedtime drew nigh.

"Did you have fun?" she asked the upturned faces.

Billy turned to Walter, squinted, and then laughed. "She doesn't get it, does she?"

"I told you. I don't know where she's from but not from anywhere like this."

"I had fun, thank you," she said, smiling by reflex at Walter's new yawn; his spaceman costume looking more like pajamas. In another minute, they walked up a tidy front sidewalk trimmed with orange electric lights on a string. Tiny Jack-o-lanterns had been positioned every third step.

"Here's Billy's," Walter said and his friend waved and hurried to the front door. When they started home, Walter said in a low voice, "My stomach hurts."

Belle grinned and patted his head. "Hold off eating any more candy until tomorrow. You'll be fine, trust me." She grinned wider with a new chuckle. "I know an elf that eats too many sweets—cookies, not candy bars. He has to pace himself, too." Belle tossed Walter a *what-can-you-do* look.

Walter knitted his brow. "You know an elf?"

"Sure," she answered with thought. "The little people I make cookies for. Tonight, I remembered they're elves."

"Real elves?" Walter asked dubious.

"Yes, real elves." Belle took a moment to flex her ankle, first one, then the other. The entire town seemed paved with cobblestones. Gorgeous to look at, but to walk across for two hours?

"That doesn't sound real." Walter scrunched his little face. "Maybe you didn't remember right."

"Oh, it's real." Belle glanced up; they had reached Harv's cottage and he sat on the porch waiting.

"Hi, you two. Big haul?"

"Tons, Dad! And donuts!" Walter ran up the steps to his dad. "Did you get many trick-or-treaters?"

Harv nodded with victory. "I went through eight bags of candy."

"You didn't give them all out!"

"I saved the ninth one for us. Mini Snickers."

Belle's heart melted then for a dad who would hold back a bag of candy of his son's favorites.

"Belle never had a Snickers until tonight," Walter explained as if it truly was an impossible thing.

Harv met Belle's eye and heat rushed to her cheeks. "And I loved it." She smiled in Harv's face too long and looked away. "I should be heading to the inn."

"Dad! Please take her in the car—her feet!" Walter said, pointing downward.

"No, really," Belle said, but she relished the idea of a lift.

Harv picked up the cues and the three piled into his car. On the way to the inn, Belle's heart swelled with something new concerning Harv and she wanted to discover its identity as much as her own.

Walter dumped his candy stash onto the bed, amazed at the haul. He lined up the big bars and then the mini ones before sorting the apples, granola bars, and anything that looked "healthy."

"Geez! Somebody gave me a pop tart!" he yelped and put it in the rejects stack. Since he started working at the bakery, he had acquired a taste for not only quality, but warm quality—right out of the oven. The way he always pictured a mom, one who stayed home and baked her little boy cookies, day in and day out.

Walter pondered this as he sorted the Starbursts and Reese's Peanut Butter Cups to the good pile. Someone had the nerve to give him candy canes! And it was the sticks, no crooks, probably left over from last Christmas. Prior to meeting Belle, he had thought candy canes were bitter, but hers were creamy with a hint of mint. He set the dummy canes on the edge of the bed, thinking he'd give them to Belle for a laugh, when they rolled off.

Walter lowered to fetch them, but they had rolled under the bed. Lifting the quilt, he first found his red sock, and then he felt around in the abyss only to close his fingers around his G.I. Joe which he hadn't seen in forever. He grabbed at whatever and pulled out next his stuffed white dog from when he was tiny.

"Puff!" he said squeezing the toy tight as he dropped cross-legged to the braided rug. Puff reminded him of when his father was too depressed to play or even visit, and Walter spent his time talking with Puff. It had been such a lonely time that sometimes back then, it felt like he didn't even have a dad. After a last kiss to its nose, Walter set his beloved dog aside and reached further. His fingers brushed cloth and he tugged it closer. It was Belle's tote!

"I forgot!" Walter said with a laugh. He had shoved it under his bed the day he'd found her, intending to keep it safe. Walter wasn't sure why, but he had wanted to *hide* it. Whether from people, Dad, or himself, he didn't know. But here it was and he looked it over with a happy smile.

The bag was soft red velvet with two loopy handles. He hadn't looked inside it that crazy day but instead had stashed it, sure it was important. At first, he literally forgot it was there, but then as he grew to know and love Belle, he forced himself not to think about it when it came to mind. After all, there was a chance she would find out who she was and when she found out she might leave.

She might leave *him*…

A fat tear escaped and he brushed it aside. He had to open the tote. It might hold the key to Belle's past, and he had no right to withhold it even if it meant Belle leaving.

Leaving *him*…

Walter closed his eyes and slipped a small, pudgy hand inside, to empty it one item at a time. But his eyes popped open at the only thing inside. *A book.*

Walter scrunched his face. Belle crashed clutching her tote bag with only a dumb book inside?

Taking both hands, Walter slid the book free of the velvet bag. Maybe he had been a hasty in being annoyed. The oversized tome looked like a Grandma's bible, but this huge volume wasn't tooled leather. *It was gold* and it nearly *glowed.* A huge golden book and written in raised script, in shiny red letters, were two small words: THE LIST.

"The list?" Walter puzzled, his jaw slack. Carefully, he lifted the ornate cover and gold glitter danced in the air. He watched the puff dissipate and then he looked at the first page. It had no index, no title page, only an ornate red "A" followed by a list in small, black, probably handwritten letters. Walter squinted and began to read, sounding out the syllables as he learned at preschool.

"Ab-by Smith-son. A-dam Wolke, An-dre-a Hoops..." Walter giggled, realizing these were names and someone was named, hoops. He looked at the next and the next.

Why names? It was a list of names starting with A.

Walter gingerly turned pages, eventually reaching a similarly ornate letter "B". He read again, having new fun sounding out the new words.

"Bar-ba-ra Welsch," he said, at first pronouncing it *wel-suh-cha* before trying it with the more natural choice of *Welsh.* He continued, "Bar-ney Apple-ton, Bet-ty Pe-ters... What's going on?"

The "Cs" were the same. The "Ds" followed suit. And on it went, nothing more than name after name after name.

Gently, Walter leafed through, not knowing how to feel. It was weird, but not too fun or interesting. And it was *endless.* Why did Belle have it with her?

Just then a light bulb went off and he flipped to the "Ws". Walter ran his finger down the list and then froze, his eyes round. There it was. "Walter Nichols".

My name? Why is my name in this big weird book?

Walter frowned, his gaze fixed on his name. What did THE LIST have to do with Walter Nichols?

Fearful and worried, with shaking hands he flipped past the "W's" and slammed it closed. More gold glitter fluttered out with the bang. Walter pushed the book back into the velvet bag and with his toes, he pushed it as far under his bed as his legs could go.

seven

"SHE'S REMEMBERING, MY DEAR. BE PATIENT."

"I know but it's already November."

"Well, I think we've got a handle on things here."

"We're pretty much on schedule. Still, it all hinges on…"

"Don't say it. I know. I know."

"I think the dough for the candy cane cookies is chilled enough for us to roll out." At the double-door fridges Belle removed a bowl with mounds of red and ivory dough. She glanced at Walter. "You okay?" she asked, her voice gentle.

"Me? Oh, yeah," he lied. He was sick to his stomach. The big gold book haunted him as much as his guilt for keeping it hidden.

Belle pinched off some red shortbread dough to roll into a rope. She handed a clump to Walter who first warmed it in his hands and then mimicked Belle, running his hands back and forth over the roll. They both repeated the action with dough that hadn't been tinted and then very carefully, Belle showed Walter how to twist a strand of red with one of natural.

"This is cool," Walter remarked, for a few minutes forgetting his troubles. With a sharp knife Belle cut the twisted ropes into six-inch strips and gently lifted them to the silpat cookie sheet.

"Now we'll make the cane part," Belle said and rounded one end of a strip.

"Hey! They really do look like candy canes!" Walter said grinning.

"Wait until you taste them," Belle said with a smile. She slipped the first sheet in to bake and returned to rolling and shaping.

Before too long, the first batch came out and Belle slipped a couple finished cookies on a plate to cool. Then she got a carton of milk and poured two glasses recently added to the private cupboard.

An improvement on the measuring cup, Walter thought and bit into the cookie. "Mmm! These are the best yet!"

"You think?" Belle then laughed a joyous sound Walter had come to love. "Your dad and I are going out to dinner tonight," she said the next time she met his eye.

Walter thought he caught a different sparkle in her face, and he scrunched his nose. "Dad said I was going to Billy's for pizza but he didn't say anything about you guys. He's taking you on a date?" Walter knew all about guys and gals going on dates.

Belle grinned. "I think so. I was surprised when he called."

"But happy?" Walter asked, his cookie mid-air. This sounded like a good idea. Did she want to go?

"*Very* happy," Belle replied and twitched her nose. Then she pointed to the tray. "Why don't you bring one of those candy cane cookies out front for Magee to try?"

Walter carefully plucked a cool pastry off the silpat and put it on his dish. As he headed to the sales area, the bell on the front door tinkled.

"Walter?" It was Dad, his voice raised. "What are you doing here? Why aren't you at Billy's?" His father ran a hand through his shaggy hair, frustrated. "Magee, I'm sorry about this." Then he turned back to his son. "So?"

Surprised to see him, Walter set down the dish and gave his father a defiant stare. He hadn't had to chance to tell him about his new job. And maybe he forgot on purpose, afraid his dad might not approve. He puffed his chest. "I work here, Dad. I got a job."

"Walter," his father warned in the tone he least liked, "what are you talking about?"

Magee stepped in. "He works here after preschool every day. I thought he told you."

"No. He sure didn't."

Walter frowned in increments; he was about to be in trouble.

His dad faced Magee. "And what do you mean he works here? He's only five years old."

"He's helping me bake cookies," Belle added entering now from the back kitchen, dusting off her hands on a Christmas-y apron stenciled with poinsettias.

"*You* work here?" his dad asked Belle.

"You didn't tell your father?" Magee asked Walter in the same stern tone as his dad. She looked at the grownups and Walter needed to calm everyone down.

"I'm a big help! I can sweep and I don't get in the way, and I made Magee an email list on her computer!"

Walter's voice had hyped, but his dad was looking at Belle with eyes full of questions. Walter waited to see what Belle might do to fix his father's expression.

Harv awaited an explanation. The girl who fell in their laps had no memory, but was baking cookies with his son for money? "How long has this been going on?"

"A few weeks," Belle said uncowed, "Magee hired us together, a package deal."

Harv shook his head, perplexed. "Shouldn't you be spending your time figuring out who you are and where you're from? Somebody's missing you somewhere. Have you forgotten about that?" Harv asked reluctant to admit inside that he'd been too sharp.

"No, this was what I needed. Because of Magee and Walter's help, I remembered a lot already." Belle jut out her chin and crossed her arms.

"What did you remember now?" Harv asked, still edgier than he wanted to be. "Last I heard you remembered a wedding, but not your husband." He had tempered his tone but was bordering on starting a fight with a young woman he liked quite a bit. Thankfully, Belle did not take the bait and her smile remained soft.

"I remember a bit more about where I'm from."

"She's an orphan from France where she baked cookies until her guardians came for her," Walter piped in, his voice elevated and his tone protective.

Harv's eyes widened. "Is this true?" His tone had normalized, probably because she was so calm. He watched for her reply, her face so lovely, flour powdering her nose and apron front. How long would it have taken him to notice she was working at his favorite bakery? And Walter, too? Had he been that distracted by his own little chores? Exactly *when* had he become an absentee father?

"Yes," Belle replied, her cheeks turning pink as Harv held her gaze. "Most of what I've remembered happens when Walter and I talk. He's not afraid to ask me questions and sometimes I find out that I know the answer."

"Wow. Well, that's great. Really." Humbled but also happy that his son was getting through when no one else could, Harv made a big exhale. "What else?"

"Don't be mad about him coming here. Walter's learning more here than at any daycare," Magee said before Belle could answer. "He's a huge help, not to mention a great cookie tester." She sent Walter a grin. "He's never been any trouble and he makes Belle smile." She gave Harv a tiny shrug. "It wasn't a secret; we all assumed you knew."

"Well, I wish I had, but..." Harv felt boxed in, which was never good. "Why didn't you tell me?" he asked his son.

"I was afraid you wouldn't let me," Walter said low.

Harv wasn't mad, only disappointed that he had set his son up to lie. They had always been a good team, but recently, Harv's loneliness may have made him more distant than ever.

"It's okay, Walter. I'm not mad. Next time just tell me. Deal?"

Walter gave a slow nod, his face that of a child sorry he hurt his dad. He walked close and Harv engulfed him into a hug. When he stood tall, Harv gave the women a nod.

"If Magee doesn't object and Belle could use the help…" At this he smiled at Belle because it was, in reality, glorified babysitting. Harv had never challenged what Billy and Walter did after preschool, but this choice was constructive and safe enough under Magee's mature and watchful eyes.

"I'm sorry," Walter said then and his face said he meant it.

Harv forgot that he had come to buy snacks and stepped over to the case and picked out a few items for Walter to give Billy's mother. He then gave the sack to Walter and asked him to wait by the door. Once the little guy scooted away, he stepped over to where Belle still stood in the kitchen threshold.

"Thank you," he told her low and the other people present gave them some room. "Thank you for being so great to Walter."

"He really is helping me, honest," she said, her voice feminine and filled with affection for his son.

"Okay, good," Harv said and fell silent. Up close, Belle's brown eyes were edged with a bright tawny rim and her lips were as pink as an Easter rose. He needed to go. Walter was waiting. "Besides remembering, how is everything else? You feel good? No lingering effects from the accident?"

Asking about her health? Boring! Harv chided inside, but she gave a serious nod, holding his eye.

"Not even bruised. It's a miracle," she said low.

"I agree," he said and after licking his lips and swallowing too big, he backed away and wished her goodbye until their date. Magee had returned to her customers so he slipped to where Walter waited.

"What'd she say?" he asked as if it might be about Belle's memory.

Harv pat his head and steered him for the sidewalk. On the way to Billy's house, Walter wiggled his hand.

"Belle said you're going out to dinner."

"Heh, what?"

"Are youse going on a date?"

"I guess so." Harv wondered how Walter would feel about it and was surprised when his son grinned.

"I'm glad," he said and continued walking. "She's awful nice."

"She is, is she?"

"Yeah, and funny, too, when you least expect it. Plus, she makes the best cookies in the whole wide world."

"Sounds like you like her a lot," Harv said. "Tell me something funny she said."

Harv did not expect what happened next. For the rest of the stroll to his little friend's home, Walter told his father all about Belle's orphanage, the little people, the animals, and many more unbelievable things that couldn't be real. Harv pressed his lips and listened.

By the time Walter finished sharing her "funny recollections," they were at Billy's house and Harv stored up his questions. The possibility of him having the courage to ask Belle about any of it was still in the air.

Belle peered into her closet wondering what to wear to dinner. Miss Tabatha stopped at her room and saw her considering her paltry choices and Belle blurted, "I have a dinner date with Harv."

"And you don't know what to wear?" Miss Tabatha asked in her kind voice, her weathered face shining with love.

Belle grimaced. "I don't even know what I used to *like* to wear."

"Oh, honey child," Miss Tabatha said, a comforting arm lifting to encompass Belle's shoulders. "Let's go up to the attic. We'll see what is in the old trunks. Maybe there will be something wonderful and beautiful in one of them for you to wear tonight."

Enjoying the mystery and promise in her tone, Belle nodded and followed to the stairwell. It took several flights to reach the tippy-top, but once in the final room, the attic turned out to be a world unto itself. Spectacular wayfaring oil paintings leaned against the walls, huge pieces of forgotten furniture slept under sheets like ghosts, and an iron dress-form stood in the back window as if watching for a lover to return from the sea. And, oh! The trunks were everywhere!

Some were humpbacked leather, others painted with sea scenes and crafted of ancient wood, and along one wall sat a chorus of Louis Vuitton steamers. Belle gawked in amazement but watched the innkeeper make a beeline for a particular trunk with a shell-encrusted mermaid gracing the frontage. Miss Tabatha opened the lid and a cloud of silver and turquoise glitter filtered into the air.

"Did you see that?" Belle asked eyes wide.

Miss Tabatha reached in without looking. "It's only dust, honey child. Nothing but dust."

"No, it was silver and turquoise and it glittered!" Belle looked for it now, but it had dissipated.

"It is sea dust, that's all." As she spoke, the innkeeper pulled free a film of seafoam fabric and as she shook it open, the cloth materialized into a long flowing dress. Ruffles of gauzy film ran diagonally from bodice to hem and a swirly pattern emerged where more of the silver and turquoise glitter clung like embedded jewels. The neckline dipped just low enough and the hemline trailed the ground.

Miss Tabatha's eyes glowed. "This one is perfect! No need to look further." She snapped the lid closed and took Belle's hand.

"You must try it on!" With a smile and a gentle tug, she led Belle down the staircase.

A few minutes later in her borrowed quarters, Belle slipped it on. The effect was ethereal, as if the queenly garment had been custom-made for her dimensions. It slid over her slight figure and flowed about her body like water.

"Give us a twirl!" Miss Tabatha instructed.

As Belle did a gentle turn, more colorful glitter appeared, seemingly emanating from the fabric itself.

"It is perfect!" her hostess proclaimed. "What time will your young man arrive?"

Belle glanced at the perpetual clock. "Soon," Belle returned and excused herself to fix her face and fluff her streaming hair. When that was done, she turned in time to see Miss Tabatha at her bedroom door holding a pair of heels with thin silver straps covered in seashells.

"I thought you might enjoy these..."

Belle did not question if they would fit; something told her they would be as perfect as the dress. She slipped them on, and they not only felt custom made, but they were so comfortable she thought she could wear them around the clock.

The doorbell chimed. "That would be Harv!" Miss Tabatha said. "Off you go, honey lamb, and have a lovely night." The innkeeper leaned back with a happy sigh as Belle promised she would.

eight

HARVEY LOWERED HIS HAND FROM THE DOORBELL and considered the bouquet of flowers in his grip. Constructed entirely of shells, he had bought it on impulse as he headed to the inn. Why he didn't get fresh flowers he couldn't say, but as Belle opened the door and stood before him, the flowers were all but forgotten. Harv could not wrap his tongue around a single word, or his mind around a thought, except how beautiful Belle looked and how she caused his middle to flip. Her heart-shaped face and delicate features swelled his tongue and all he could do was poke the bouquet in her direction.

"How wonderful! A perpetual bouquet! That is so thoughtful!" Belle said as she received the flowers, examining every inch. "I'll take them with me when I leave, and they'll always remind me of Nantucket... of you."

Blood drained from Harv's face. She had to go home when she remembered, sure, but, but… what if she stayed? Maybe she could make a new home with him and Walt. It was too much to consider and selfish, to boot. Harv covered his emotions with a single word, forced past his paralyzed vocal chords. "Leave?"

Belle set the vase on a table just inside the door and joined him on the porch. Harv took her small hand in his, watching her face.

"Yes, when I remember, I'll have to leave," Belle said softly and all around them, night stole over the dusk.

"Don't go." Harv managed those two words but he wanted to shout so many others. He wanted to say, *stay here! Now that I found you, now that I'm no longer sleepwalking through life, you can't possibly leave!* But he didn't. Her next response indicated she read some of it in his eyes.

"You can come with me," she said low, looking at the light reflecting off the stones.

"Where would we be going?" Harv asked just as quietly. Of all the things Walter disclosed about his and Belle's conversations, Harv still didn't know where she was from. But then again, the reason Walter had learned so much about her was because he wasn't afraid to ask questions. Maybe Harv could do that, too. He decided to try. "Where do you come from? Have you remembered?"

"No, but it's somewhere far away," she said and looked up at the stars flickering to life. She gave a tiny laugh. "Also, I feel that my life involves a lot of travel."

"You traveled a lot before the crash?" Harv asked helping her navigate a particularly bumpy section of cobblestones.

"No, I don't think so. It's more along the lines of there's a lot of travel in my future. I'm sure of it, actually."

Harv considered her answer with a slow nod. Then asked, "Where will you travel? Across the country? Across the sea?"

Belle lifted her arms wide, her face to the night sky. "I feel like... like I'm going to travel the entire world!"

Before Harv could digest her assertion, they were in front of the restaurant. The scent of rich foods wafted out as someone opened the door.

Harv gestured with a knuckle to the establishment, its sign framed by two mermaids the same shade of Belle's flowing dress.

Once inside, they were immersed in the sounds and scents of the intimate world of fine dining. A snappily dressed maître d' chauffeured them into a room where tables were topped with exquisite tile, supporting menus that reflected only the most sophisticated selections. Before long, they found themselves in the middle of dandelion salad with poached shrimp and blood oranges, not even remembering that they had ordered. Long flat ribbons of tagliatelle with lump crab came next and Belle sampled each food with a smile.

"This is such a treat!" she said finally, savoring her current fork-full.

"What do you normally eat?" Harv had asked wanting only to know more about her, about what she liked, what she enjoyed. He hadn't realized until he said the words that a question might help her remember more of her origins.

Belle smiled. "Miss Tabatha and I make grilled cheese sandwiches every night. Sometimes we split a tin of tomato soup." She swiped her crusty bread through the sauce and made a new noise of pleasure at the flavors.

Harv shook his head. "No, I mean back home."

"Oh, much heartier things than that, for certain. Heavy stews, huge burgers… It's so cold there that we're always eating substantial things, meat and potatoes…"

Harv and Belle stared at each other. Then she said in a small voice, "That's it. I'm from somewhere cold." Her gaze turned for the floor-to-ceiling windows across the dining space. "No wonder this weather doesn't faze me and... at my wedding... all that ice. It makes sense."

"Maybe we need to do a missing persons report in cold climates," Harv offered. "We think it's English-speaking, right?"

"I think so…" Then she said to the side, "That gives us a lot of possibilities." Belle gave a nod and looked off. "The coldest countries are those like Antarctica, Russia, Greenland,

Iceland, Finland, Kazakhstan—"

"Kazakhstan? You really know your geography," Harv marveled.

"Hah, I guess I do," she said in a giggle.

One glance revealed that their plates were empty and the server dropped off dessert fingerfood samplers. Harv bit into a sesame seed butter bar and crunched. Belle paused her list to taste along with him.

"I think I used to travel with my guardians for practice." Belle's eye narrowed in thought. "On my first practice run, we crashed." Belle stopped, her eyes coming to Harv's.

"Sounds like a family business," he offered.

"Yes! It is a family business, and I am meant to take over." Belle sat down her cookie. "And I need help." She leaned closer. "Will you help?"

When she turned her big brown eyes his way, Harv knew what his answer would be. "Of course, I'll do anything I can to help you. Anything."

With that, Belle released a sigh and relaxed backward. She sipped her wine and gave him another warm smile. "Now all I need to do is remember what my family business is."

"Sounds about right." Harv nibbled at a toffee macaroon and watched her lift the same type on her end.

"This is delicious," she said. "I wonder how they make them..."

As she spoke, husband and wife chefs, Bob and Brenda, stopped at their table. "You're the new baker at Magee's shop?"

Harv watched her compose her reply.

"Yes, I am," she said with a blush rising to her cheeks. "But I only bake cookies and they're nothing like this." Belle took another bite into the chocolate tidbit. "My heavens! My elves would work overtime for these!"

Bob and Brenda chuckled in unison. "We can't get our elves to work for cookies, never mind work overtime." With that, they wandered off to visit at the next table.

"Your elves?" Harv asked in a chuckle. He reined in his humor when he saw Belle was serious.

"Yes, back home I bake cookies for elves," she said without a hint of a joke.

Harv lifted his brow. "You're serious?" he asked gently.

"I know it sounds ridiculous; it does to me, too. But I only need to find more pieces to the puzzle."

Belle nibbled her lip and Harv's face softened. Maybe she worked in a kitchen at a preschool and referred to the children as elves. She was certainly good with Walter. He ran down a few more sensible explanations as the server delivered cups of strong coffee to accompany the last of the sweets.

Too soon, their dinner date was coming to a close. After paying the tab, Harv pulled back her chair. He would walk her home and that would be a nice few minutes. Then he considered her comfort.

"I should have thought about you walking so much in those beautiful shoes," Harv offered but Belle only smiled wider and displayed her toes after lifting the hem of her dress to reveal her ankle.

"Thank you but these are so comfortable. I borrowed them from Miss Tabatha, and you'd think they were made especially for me."

"Thank goodness," Harv said and stepped her to the sidewalk. "How about I take you past some things you haven't seen yet?" When she gave a sweet smile, Harv turned them toward the dock. The two of them held hands and watched the water, now put to bed for the night, looking as if it wore its own glass blanket.

"This is where I come when I play Santa," Harv said and pointed to an area off to their right.

"On the Coast Guard boat," Belle replied.

"That's right," Harv whispered as a breeze stirred between

them and fluttered in her long hair. He slipped an arm around her back. "Are you cold?"

Belle shook her head. "There is something so right about you being one of Santa's stand-ins." She had said the phrase softly, as if more to the night than to her companion.

Harv was charmed. "There is?"

Belle nodded. "Do you bring anything with you when you play Santa?"

"Sure, I've been making extra toys all year round. I have a gigantic red velvet sack that I bring them in." Harv smiled thinking of all the wooden boats he'd made and all the doll beds. "I've made everything that's great for our island children."

"How do you know who gets what and what they'll like?" Her question was so sincere and serious that Harv answered forthrightly.

"Nantucket is a small island and I know just about everyone. Once you know somebody, you learn what they like. No one ever asked me that before, but I've always found it very easy to know what people would like for Christmas."

"Just like that?" Belle asked still serious. "You make it sound so easy. I mean, Chris really struggled with it."

"Chris?" Harv asked. That was the name of her husband. Harv did not want to admit that he did not care to learn anything more about him anyway.

Belle did not seem to have heard; her sentences again had been fading into the night as if merely thinking aloud. They were walking now back toward the village and Belle remarked on the crisp evening air and the beautiful aroma of the oceanside at the open of winter.

Belle paused at the shop window of Trianon, the island's most elegant jewelry store. A citrine pearl and diamond bracelet sat on a piece of velvet. Next to it dangled a golden-brown topaz on a slender silver chain.

"That is the color of the sky at night right when the sun leaves off," Belle remarked in a wistful manner.

"I was thinking it's the color of your eyes," Harv replied. "Also, of the sea when it is stirred up. I see your eyes when I look at this stirred-up ocean even now." Harv had not meant to say all that out loud but he had. Belle did not respond but he could see that she was smiling.

She turned from the window and met his eye. "Can I help you with the toys?"

"I'd like that," Harv said and reached out his hand which she took. He started them walking again and said, "I have a doll cupboard for little Ruthie that needs painting. Can you paint?"

Belle laughed a beautiful sound. "I don't know but why don't we find out?"

Harvey felt the pressure lift in his spirit at the thought of his beautiful new friend working side by side with him in his cozy toy workshop. Her painting over there, him hammering together a rocking horse over here.

"This is going to sound rather odd," Belle said and he turned his eyes to hers, "but it seems to me that every day is its own little miracle rediscovering something about myself and the world around me. I wasn't sure if I would like crab. You'd think a person would know that sort of thing." She gave him a wink. "Turns out, I love it." Belle laughed again, pure joy in her face.

"You know what," Harv said, "under the circumstances, you have an amazing attitude. I don't know how I would've handled all this." Change was hard for Harv, as was the unknown.

Belle turned serious. "Oh, Harv, you've handled so much more than I have, and you're doing great. Walter is so wonderful and..."

Harv cringed disgusted and reflecting on his behavior the past few years since his wife's death. "I haven't handled it at all.

I've just muddled along."

"And that isn't handling?" she asked in a soft voice. "Taking it as it comes and making the best of it?"

"Ehh," he said with a shrug, not ready to agree. "I worry about Walter…"

"You must see that he has come along so great. He has your kindness, and he has a charming sense of humor. He also has a great sense of adventure; he's not afraid to try anything."

"He's had no choice," Harv said choking on the words.

"Don't be so hard on yourself. You're both the most special people I have ever met."

"Even with your memory problem?" Harv prompted with a twinkle of humor.

"Oh, I'd remember if I had met anyone more special than you and Walter."

Belle had spoken with such sincerity that Harv believed her. It seemed the only thing for him to do just then was to lean in and give her a kiss, so he did. Gently, sweetly, and once begun, he did not want to let go. Belle responded and pulled away only when he did. Without another word, they turned as one and walked quietly back to the inn lost in their thoughts. At one point, Harv glanced behind them and Belle's seafoam dress seemed to trail moonbeams. In that moment, the island felt like their own little oasis.

At the Tuck You Inn, Miss Tabatha had left the porch light as a beacon and they headed to it.

"I'd like to see you," Harv started, uncertain what to say next.

"I'm right here," Belle replied indicated the door behind her. "Otherwise, I'll be at the bakery."

"For now." The words caught in Harv's throat as he remembered the sadness in his past. He did not want more goodbyes in the future. As if she read his mind, Belle placed a delicate hand to his cheek.

"Why don't we see what happens? After all, you're really good at handling things, right?"

He gave her a kind smile thinking maybe it wasn't such an impossible situation after all.

"Besides," she said as she opened the front door, "who knows what I'll remember next? You'll want to be around for that, right?"

She was right and Harv did not leave the porch until she was well inside.

nine

BELLE AND HARV CONTINUED TO SEE EACH OTHER, cautiously at first and then more carefree. One morning at breakfast, Belle sat with Miss Tabatha over a plate of stuffed French toast when the subject came up on its own.

"I keep remembering bits and pieces, and when it all comes together, I don't see how I won't have to leave." Belle wanted to stay now more than anything, but it hadn't been so long ago that remembering was the only thing on her mind.

"Honey child..."

Belle continued before Miss Tabatha could get a word in.

"My feelings for Harv and Walter grow deeper every day, yet I know in my heart that I'll be leaving soon." Belle played in her syrup, not eating.

"Well..." Miss Tabatha stopped. She then topped off their coffee and changed the subject. "How are the toys coming?"

Belle smiled wide. Making toys with Harv had become a huge part of her life. She worked at the bakery each day until 4:00 and then walked Walter home where she helped Harv make toys for the famous Christmas Stroll which would occur when Santa arrived.

In answering Tabatha, she said, "I love it. Harv is so creative, and even Walter has the knack. I'm surprised how much I love working on the toys." Her mind ran across all the pieces she lovingly painted for the children.

"I know you've come a long way from painting doll beds and doll cupboards," Miss Tabatha said with pride in her voice.

"Thank you, I think so, too. Ever since Magee loaned me her sewing machine, I've been making dresses for all of the dolls." Belle's joy swelled as she discussed the toys and the children who would get them. "After Santa arrives and gives out the toys... well... I'll miss the time we spend together, Harv and me." Belle inhaled; after this project ended, they would need to decide where to take their relationship.

"It doesn't have to end."

Belle sighed. "No, I guess not, but right now we have this project and it's a great excuse to be together."

Miss Tabatha raised an eyebrow. "I think Harv will want to still spend time with you after that."

"You know, you and me, we're like a little family. We eat supper together and visit and you help me a lot," Belle said, her voice tender.

"I know, I know," Miss Tabatha responded and pat her hand.

"But over everything else, I feel like I have an urgent project of some kind and I need to leave. If I leave..." Belle said no more and left it hanging. Miss Tabatha did, too.

The Nantucket Historical Association sponsored the Festival of Wreaths every year. Merchants and artists donated over one hundred wreaths to be bid on at a silent auction at the Nantucket Whaling Museum. Belle had convinced Magee they needed to enter one. "I mean you are a very important business here on Nantucket," she asserted to begin her campaign.

Magee rolled her eyes. "I'm a bakery. People want real wreaths, you know, evergreens and flowers, and all that."

Belle did not allow that refusal to hold her back, and as she and Walter worked on their cutout cookies, she had an idea.

"Walter, our cutouts are so beautiful, what if we made dough art cutouts and put them on a wreath?"

Walter's face lit up. "And Dad could spray it with poly so it would last."

"Yes!" Belle beamed.

The two of them began sorting their favorite cookie cutters, trying to decide what would be best. When they finally narrowed it down to Santa, a reindeer, the bell and the Christmas tree, Belle booted the computer and found a dough art recipe. From then on, the afternoon was lost in creating their masterpiece.

Deep into the project, Walter asked casually, "Do you know why someone's name would be on a list?"

"A list?"

"Yeah, a big list of names." He set his chin as they cleaned up their project and the fake cookies baked to hardness.

"Well, let me think." Belle noted the strain on Walter's face. "It could be for any number of reasons." The topic nagged at the back of her mind. Why did it sound familiar? She shook her head, unable to bring it to the surface.

"Let's put it this way, what kind of lists would you have if you had some?" Walter persisted, his tone growing speculative.

"I'd have my grocery list. My list of cookies we would be making each week. A list of people I want to make gifts for."

"What people?" Walter pressed in the same tone. "What kinds of gifts?"

Without thinking Belle said, "Children, and what toys I think they'd want."

"Would you list the toys?"

"This is going to sound funny, but you know how your dad *just knows* which toys the village children will love most?" Walter nodded. "I would just *know* like he does."

"You would?" Walter asked, eyes wide.

"Sure. Take you, for instance. I know what you want most." She gave him a tiny smile.

"What?"

"Now, it wouldn't be fair if I told you."

"But you know?"

"I think I do."

"Belle," Walter began, his five-year-old face so serious, "my dad makes toys, so I know there's not a toy out there that I want."

Belle's heart softened. "It doesn't have to be a toy, does it? Come, let's put this wreath together," she said and returned to their work. Walter did, too, and the back of her mind wondered what brought all that on.

ten

IT SEEMS EVERYONE IN NANTUCKET FOUND THE cookie wreath a charming addition to the Festival of Wreaths. Belle proposed they decorate a Christmas tree in cutout cookies for the Festival of Trees, November 29th. When she said so to Walter, his jaw dropped.

"Won't that be a ton of cookies?"

Belle gave a 'we can do it' grin. "It'll be fun; I'm used to doing things on a big scale." Belle considered what she just said and went with it. "We put little holes in the tops before we bake them so we can thread ribbons to hang on the boughs."

"And we're going to decorate *all* of them?" he asked with emphasis. "Won't we need a hundred-gazillion?"

Belle laughed and pecked his cheek. "Let's go for ten of each style. We'll have a little Santa's assembly line going."

Once Belle's helper was on board, they started with the stars, which would only need gold sugar once they were iced. They were using royal icing which set like cement. From stars they went to wreaths, because they would be iced green, and then M&M's would go on as the decorations. Belle and Walter both rationalized these were the easier ones, along with the reindeers made of gingerbread dough-art and required a simple red hot on the nose. Finally, they moved to the more complicated cookies. Santas coming out of chimneys took a bit more decorating skill and time, as did the standard Santas. The

Christmas trees were on par with the wreaths, but they added white frosting loops as garland. Each time they finished a style and set it out to harden, they would stand back to admire their work.

"We did this!" Walter exclaimed one day before they left, looking at trays and trays of beautiful artificial cutout cookies.

"Indeed, we did! I couldn't have done any of it without you!" Belle meant the words and he raised his eyes, unsure, probably since cookies were her thing. "I mean it. We make a great team. Who else could have pulled this off?" She waved her arms to take it all in. "*Plus* keep up with Magee's regular baking? It would have taken a team of elves working day and night to get this done," Belle said beaming with pride.

By the end of the week, cookies were on every surface drying and waiting. They had managed to stay on top of the regular baking for Magee's customers, too.

"Are we decorating the cookie tree tonight?"

Walter's face said he couldn't wait and Belle agreed. The cookies were ready and the trees were all set up. It was finally time for their masterpiece to come together.

She gave him a nod. "Magee and your dad are going to help."

"At the Whaling Museum?" Walter asked, his eyes like saucers.

"Yes, sir."

"This is the best Christmas ever because I've got to help from the inside!" Walter said busy cutting lengths of thin ribbon for the stringing.

Belle nodded in agreement. "It's always more fun to work from the inside. That's why I love Christmas so much." Then she stopped. What did that mean? It must be important because of the way it rolled off her tongue. Still, she had things to do and she would think about it later.

The cookies were transported while still on the cookie sheets. They had allowed the cookies to harden after they decorated them right on the sheets. It seemed to be the easiest way to keep them from breaking. Belle and Walter joined a museum full of townsfolk, merchants, and artists as all got to business decorating their trees. Harv stopped to get Miss Tabatha, knowing she'd want to join in.

"Miss Tabatha, you can't eat the cookies!" Walter was mortified as Miss Tabatha nipped a corner off a Christmas Tree.

"Oh, honey lamb, I think there's plenty." She pursed her lips. "Salty, though."

Walter pealed out a high laugh. "These aren't real cookies! We made them out of dough-art so they would last. I will help Belle make you a batch of real ones," he assured. "You'll always have cookies long as we're around." Then he stopped, a decorated bell cookie in hand midway to the tree as his eyes clouded. A fat tear snuck out.

"Oh, honey…" Miss Tabatha swooped him in her arms. "Don't think about what's not here yet. It's the Christmas season, a magical season, anything can happen."

Walter snuffled. "You think?"

"I do," Miss Tabatha said. "Why don't you ask your dad if you and Belle can ride in the Coast Guard boat Sunday?"

"You think he'd let us?" Walter asked seemingly forgetting all about Belle leaving. "No one but Santa rides on it ever…" Walter's voice faded, his tiny face thinking hard.

"I don't see why not. Santa stand-ins need helpers. Besides Belle has her red velvet cape she could wear." Miss Tabatha's eyes twinkled.

"You're right. I bet he'll say yes." Walter's face brightened.

The cookie tree was so spectacular even Magee and Belle were impressed. No matter where you looked on the tree you saw a beautiful cookie. It was non-commercial, and it made you want to curl up in front of the fire with a plate full of cutouts and a glass of cold milk.

"We're doing this every year!" Magee announced.

"I'm going to make one just like this for the elves!" Belle proclaimed. It dawned on her then that she would be gone. She wondered in the back of her heart if she'd be able to return. But before she could make herself upset, she forced it away as to not take anything away from their festive mood.

Afterward, they ended up at Captain Toby's Chowder House for steaming bowls of clam chowder and fried clams. Everyone involved was too pumped to call it a night and all of them were hungry.

"Can I have onion rings?" Walter asked his dad. "Belle, you're gonna love these; they're the best in the world."

Belle agreed to try one and Walter grinned ear to ear.

Everyone ate in comfortable conversation, marveling at the spectacular array of trees for this year's event.

"I bet there's never been a cookie tree," Walter snuck in. Magee assured him it was head and shoulders the best tree there.

Walter sat between Miss Tabatha and Belle holding an onion ring that could have been a bracelet it was so huge.

"Miss Tabatha," Walter whispered, "Ask Dad about *you know.*"

She gave him a wink. "Harv, you know this has been such an unusual year what with the Cookie Tree and everything else." By *everything else* she meant Belle. Harv spooned his thick chowder nodding absently. "Belle tells me the three of you have been burning the midnight oil making all those toys for the island children."

Harv's features softened. "That's true, the toys this year are really great. I couldn't possibly have done it all without Belle and Walter." He ripped a packet of oyster crackers open and tumbled them into the end of his chowder.

"Wouldn't it be a great idea," Miss Tabatha began, "if Sunday when you arrived on the Coast Guard boat you had them with you as your helpers?"

"My helpers?" Harv raised his brow.

"Sure. As you know, Walter has worked harder than anyone." The old innkeeper's eyes twinkled. "Regular elf he's been."

Walter gave a proud thumb's up at Miss Tabatha's assessment.

Harv gave a slow nod.

"Belle could wear her red velvet cape, kind of like Mrs. Claus," Miss Tabatha added with a new grin.

"Mrs. Claus?" Harv choked out.

"Sure! A beautiful Mrs. Claus stand-in, on the ride with Santa's stand-in, handing out gifts!" Miss Tabatha winked at Walter.

Belle listened on and then her mind suddenly went far, far away. She was on a sleigh with her husband Chris going for a trial run, a practice run on their wedding day.

Because...

Belle's heart grew too big for her chest.

My guardians are Santa Claus and Mrs. Santa Claus!

Only, they were retiring. Santa's knees were bad and Mrs. Claus … wait, they had names.

"Nickolas and Nicole," she said under her breath and those beside her turned.

"What, honey child?" Miss Tabatha asked.

"My guardians, I remember their names. Nickolas and Nicole." She looked from one eager face to another, afraid to tell them what else she remembered.

Everyone talked at once. What had triggered this? What else did she remember?

"I'm not sure," she lied. She hated to, she'd go on the naughty list for sure, but she couldn't tell them. Not now. Not this. *I remember everything! It's all flooding back!*

She lived at the North Pole. Her guardians were Santa and Mrs. Claus. They had adopted her, and loved her, and raised her as their own daughter. They taught her to bake. They brought Chris to the North Pole for her to marry and continue the tradition when they retired.

I am next in line to be Mrs. Claus!

But she hadn't loved Chris—not like …

Oh, my goodness, I love Harv! And Walter! I love Harv and Walter! When did this happen? Why hadn't I seen it coming? I love them and I'll have to leave! That's why I'm never cold! And why I only bake Christmas cookies! And love to travel!

Belle looked at Walter who was offering the last onion ring in the basket to Magee.

That's why I love children! Her heart grew too big for her ribcage.

The deer at my wedding! They were reindeer! Santa's reindeer! Rudolph … Prancer … Dancer … It's November 29th! Oh dear! I shouldn't be here. Who's making cookies for the elves? Helping with the toys?

Panic bubbled up and she grew dizzy.

I'm meant to carry on. I'm Mrs. Claus now. I'm Belle Claus. But … Chris is dead!

I …

Need…

A …

Husband!

I …

Need …

A …

Mr. Claus!

Belle looked at Harv who was carefully wiping Walter's face with a paper napkin.

"I'll do it!" She broke into the conversation around her.

"I'll be Mrs. Claus on December 1st! I can do it! I know I can! And Walter, you'll help me! And we'll both help your dad!" Her eyes gleamed. From there, she would have to find a way to share with Harv the rest of the truth.

Harv marveled at Belle's face, glowing as if from within. She had more to say, he could see it in her expression, but maybe the crowd of people prevented it. Maybe she wanted to share more about her feelings for him and for Walter. Maybe later when they were alone, she would be able to open up.

He considered her request and Tabatha's suggestion, to have the two of them arrive with Santa. Why not? He could see it, Belle by his side, her red cloak caught in a breeze, Walter between them, holding their hands, his face beaming. They would head in together to give gifts to the island children, gifts they had worked on together with love and care.

Harv broke the silence. "Yeah, we'll start a new tradition. We'll all come in on the boat!"

Those at the table agreed and Magee lifted her coffee mug to toast the idea. Harv turned his gaze to Belle who was speaking now to Walter, fully involved, giving him 110% of her attention. She was wonderful, truly, and that alone gave him a tiny fright. The more Belle recalled, the closer they grew to her departure. He no longer denied that he had grown to care for her very much. He might even be in love with her, but he shouldn't allow it. She would leave soon. Now that she remembered her guardians, she had to go home, right? By the New Year, she'd be gone. Gone from Walter, gone from his workshop, no more soft looks from her big brown eyes.

Harv needed to get through the rest of the evening and not let his feelings weigh everything down. He would act as cheerful as possible. It was the Christmas season and everyone who knew him depended on him to bring the correct spirit—after all, he was Nantucket Island's official Santa stand-in.

With great effort, he shoved his trepidation deep down and around the corner. He would face it again after Christmas. Yes. For now, they'd play Mr. and Mrs. Santa Claus, a role that seemed so very perfect if he could forget it was only pretend.

eleven

AFTER THAT, IT WAS AS IF THEY'D DONE IT EVERY year. The toys were finished and wrapped, and Belle had made paper tags with her pinking shears to tie each package. Each child's name was lovingly printed in gold glitter. Harv's toy sack was loaded and by some Christmas miracle, they were able to cram in gifts long after the bag seemed full to the brim.

"Where do they keep going?" Walter asked pushing in the last few.

"That's the magic of Santa's sack," Harv said so naturally that Belle was taken aback.

They certainly looked the part. Walter wore a fisherman's sweater with a red and green striped scarf, Belle wore her wedding clothes, and Harv the village's vintage Santa suit. He did not have a fake beard or a padded stomach, although he did wear a Santa hat slung over his shaggy hair.

"I'm young Santa," he said with a chuckle. "Everyone in the village knows it's me, so I don't see any reason to change that," he told Belle but she had not questioned a thing, dazzled by the young sexy Santa he had become. "I like to think I'm Santa at various stages of his life."

Belle absorbed it all marveling at his wisdom, when she wasn't totally distracted by his looks, that is.

Miss Tabatha helped them load into the boat. "We'll have hot chocolate at the Whaling Museum when you get in."

The drill was the boat took them out early and idled in place, awaiting the signal. Around noon, the entire village will have gathered at the wharf for their arrival. A makeshift parade including the island's two squad cars and the fire engine paraded to the Museum. Residents with vintage cars followed in the procession with huge wreaths on their grillwork or red and green streamers. The ceremony of children sitting on Santa's lap was omitted since Harv already knew what they wanted. Once the Coast Guard dropped Santa to the shore, Harv would ride to the museum in an old farm wagon, which was as close to a sleigh as practicality afforded. He especially loved the ride, pulled by two white and gray dappled draft horses with gigantic wreaths about their muscular necks and dainty silver bells tingling from their traces.

For the moment, they were at sea awaiting noon. Walter was so excited, he could barely sit still and it was Captain Toby from the Chowder House who distracted him now and then with tales of how he came in command of the Coast Guard Boat seven years back when Captain Billingsley fell over the side drunk the week before the event.

Harv shook his head with a wry grin as Captain Toby began a new tale and asked Walter if he wanted to see the wheel. Belle sighed beside him standing at the rail, aft deck, looking over the water toward the island. The clothing she'd worn fit the occasion perfectly and Harv allowed himself to memorize tiny details of the beaded bodice, appearing to be made of glitter and magic, and how fragile and feminine every inch of her appeared to his eyes. Two thick side strands of her honey-blonde hair had been employed to tame the balance, clutched behind her head with a sparkling clip. But the length of it flowed free, and only when Walter laughed nearby did Harv realize he had been mesmerized by the sight.

"I'm glad you're here," he said finding his voice and she turned to meet his eye.

"Me, too, really," she said over the sound of the waves against the boat.

"Having you here feels as natural as seafoam on the shore. I mean, I never heard of Santa coming in with helpers, but I never want to do it without you."

Belle gave a demure chuckle. "I agree a hundred percent."

"A ga-zilion percent!" Walter said having zoomed close and overheard their conversation. Belle touched his head and he took her hand, grinning like the luckiest boy alive.

Overhead, the clouds were puffy, the sky a brilliant turquoise. And the sea was calm as glass, seemingly for the three of them alone. Harv reached over his son's head to touch Belle's shoulder and she raised her gaze to his.

"Walter and I have come to love you," he said and between them, Walter craned his head back to watch their movements on his either side. "*I* love you and I don't want you to leave. You fell into our lives and nothing has been the same."

Still holding Belle's hand, Harv got down on one knee. Walter clapped his hands and stepped out of the way making tiny yips and watching the adults' faces.

"Marry me, Belle. Marry me and Walter. Make a life with me. Make *toys* with me. Let's have a million Christmases together. I don't care where you're from, but we'll make it work if you'll only stay with us. With me." His words choked and he had one more thing to say. "I promise you will never regret it."

Belle's eyes swam with tears. Slowly, carefully, she nodded a tiny yes before her smile escaped for real and nodded with abandon. "Yes! Yes! Yes!"

Harv opened his arms and Belle fell in, allowing her happy tears to spill full bore.

"You won't regret it," Harv repeated in a whisper as he held her close. "I will make you happy. I promise."

Belle pulled back in the circle of his arms and looked into his sky-blue eyes. "Harv, I love you so, and Walter…" She opened an arm and pulled him into their embrace. "I love Walter so much."

"It's not too much? A ready-made family?" Harv asked hating the question that need to be asked.

Belle brushed back tears of joy and hitched Walter onto her hip. "No, it's the perfect gift."

Walter's pudgy arms wrapped around her neck and he wept, his face nestled in her long blonde hair and the hood of her red velvet cape. Harv leaned in on her free side and kissed her cheek, his heart peaceful for the first time in forever.

How should Belle tell her final secret now that he had proposed? Her heart burst with love for him, but what if he didn't believe her peculiar life story? Some of her worry showed on her face for he asked if she was okay.

"I'm so happy and I love you so much," she said and hugged him again. "It's just the things I remembered… now I know my life is, well, complicated. I'm afraid I'll scare you off with the whole tale."

"Be serious!" he said with a kind shake of the head. "I don't care what you say about your past, I can handle it. *We* will handle it together, Mr. and Mrs. Claus today, and Mr. and Mrs. Nichols as soon as possible!"

Belle's grin was genuine, but she still worried. Her gaze fell over his shoulder as the waves broke and dipped. She swore she saw a mermaid dip out of sight, causing turquoise and gold glitter to rise from the wave.

"Do you believe in magic?" she asked Harv in a whisper.

"I believe in *you.* The way you came to us, found me, and changed me. It was as though you landed here *for me.* If that isn't magic, I don't know what is."

"Will you promise me that no matter what you learn about

me, that you'll stay?" She worried her bottom lip because he would be tested as soon as she said the words, *my parents are Santa and Mrs. Claus… for real!*

"Nothing about what has gone before can make me leave. I love you, I'm *home* with you. Me and Walter, both, are *home.*"

The boat was arriving at the harbor as they sealed their love with a kiss. The waiting crowd went wild. They loved Harv and had suffered his sorrow for years. And they had adopted Belle not knowing a thing about her, needed no more than witnessing that kiss to know their own Santa had finally received the ultimate gift of happiness.

The next little bit became a blur as in a blink, they were moved to the old farm wagon, assisted into the seats by Miss Tabatha and the mayor. Three Coast Guard members carried the gigantic red velvet sack of toys and gently set it in the back of the wagon. Then the parade began!

The high school's marching band began on cue, the crowd waved, and the children danced in anticipation, but Harv and Belle only had eyes for each other. Walter was speechless with joy, overcome with his love of Belle.

They passed the Weezie Library for Children with its banner, "Welcome Santa, Mrs. Santa, and Walter," and then on to the museum. Most of the locals were there, ready and waiting. Three wing chairs had been placed in anticipation of their arrival. The decorated trees for the Festival of Trees were in all their glory, including Belle and Walter's cookie tree. Christmas carols floated on the breeze and happiness rode everyone's shoulders like a cozy cloak. Harv, Belle, and Walter headed into the museum like visiting royalty while the crowd cheered on. The mayor took the microphone to open the ceremony.

"Welcome, Nantucket's own Santa, with Belle and Walter! Let our Christmas season officially begin!"

The Coast Guard placed the sack of toys at Harv's feet and the children gathered around, anxious for their treats. They tried not to fidget or fuss, yet their anticipation was contagious.

The buffet line had formed, and the hot chocolate and eggnog tables were crowded with people selecting beverages. The children formed a line all their own, eyeing Santa's enormous toy sack.

A grinning Harv picked up the mic from the stand.

"Merry Christmas, everyone. I want to thank you for showing up and for this wonderful potluck supper!" The people cheered and he continued when they settled down. "Thank you to everyone who helped make all this happen."

Harv looked out at the crowd and saw the ladies from the Cottage Hospital who had helped save Belle, Magee and Jay who had always been his friends, Billy in line with his parents off to the side, camera on the ready. And there was Miss Tabatha, someone the island had never quite taken the time to know even though she had become part of their community by sheer determination with her Tuck You Inn. He gave the elderly dame a salute and continued addressing the crowd.

"As you know, this Fall we were lucky enough to have Belle fall into our lives." Everyone laughed kindly at his play on words. "Slowly, with your help and encouragement, she is bit by bit regaining her memory." Belle blushed to the color of her red cape. "She has also fallen into my heart." There was a collective 'aah' from the crowd, but Harv boldly went on because he was so happy. "And she has agreed to marry me and become our own Mrs. Claus!"

The crowd cheered louder than ever and some who knew Harv and Walter best were moved to tears.

"I have some special treats," Harv said to the gathered children. Belle reached into the sack and handed him a gift.

"Ruthie!"

Little Ruth Sharp came up and hugged his leg and then scampered off with a beginner's gardening kit. Dolls and doll beds, wagons and mini rowboats were handed out and the children got busy opening and exclaiming. Walter also helped to hand out gifts, giving little Barbara Welsch hand-painted garden markers he'd worked on for her junior garden. Billy got a sled—Walter still wondered how it fit in his father's bag—and Billy was ecstatic.

When the last gift was given, the tissue, wrapping paper, and ribbons lay in shreds. Belle and Harv looked over at the happy children, consumed in their new toys, and they shared a look that said all those hours had been worth it. The painting, the building, the wrapping. For the first time since becoming the Santa stand-in, Harv had someone to share it with, and he couldn't imagine doing it any other way.

Over the next ninety minutes, the island folk ate, children played, and the overall clatter of a great day filled the museum and grounds. Belle and Harv headed to the buffet joined by Miss Tabatha, her eyes brimming with joyful tears for their good news.

"I am so happy for you two! And Walter, as well!" She reached a hand to both of them. "I don't know when you are planning on getting married, but I'd like to open my inn for your reception."

"Oh, no, that's too much!" Belle and Harv both proclaimed.

Magee cut in line. "I will make the wedding cake!"

"Oh, no, Magee, absolutely not, it would be too much work!" Belle sputtered, aware that Magee struggled with wedding cakes as their specialty was artisan breads, cookies, pastries, and pies.

Magee squinted. "And let someone else have the honor! I think not! I'm making the cake! Chocolate, or white? Or maybe candy cane?"

Harv said chocolate as Belle said white.

"We'll alternate the layers. End of conversation." Magee lightened up. "What about a dress? What will you wear?"

It was implied in her comment that Belle wouldn't want to wear what she had on and she dropped her gaze to her first wedding clothes.

"Huh. I don't know," Belle admitted, looking down.

"We'll stop at Gwyn's tomorrow and start looking." Magee took charge. Gwyn's was a tiny boutique of upscale dressier clothes. "If anyone has anything special on the island, it'll be Gwyn."

"We haven't set a date," Belle said, afraid to look at Harv. She didn't want to wait and really *shouldn't.*

Thankfully, Harv jumped in. "I say the sooner the better. I can see no reason to wait. I'd like to start the New Year with you as Mrs. Harvey Nichols." He beamed down at Belle's upturned face.

"A New Year's Eve wedding?" Magee threw out. "It will be a great way to kick off the New Year!"

Everyone turned to Belle with expectant eyes.

"Um, well ..." She looked up at Harv. "You're sure about this? I mean, you want to marry me even if I remember some odd things?"

"Belle!" Harv swooped her in his arms as they reached the macaroni salad at the beginning of the buffet. "There is nothing, and I mean *nothing,* that can make me change my mind. I love you. That is everything we need to know."

Magee and Miss Tabatha sighed.

Belle blushed with a gentle smile. "Then I would like to get married the weekend before Christmas Eve."

"But that's so soon," Magee began as if panicking about the preparations.

"It's really no sooner than New Year's Eve." If she was going to do it, she needed to get on with it. Belle had no choice; too much depended on it.

Magee paled, her eyes darting as she worked out a rushed plan.

"We don't need a fuss. We will make it simple," Belle turned to Harv, "A small and simple wedding so we can be married as soon as possible."

"Then I'm the luckiest man alive. Saturday, December 19th it is!" he said with a smile.

They continued from macaroni salad to lobster rolls and on to king crab legs with plans being made with every entre.

* * *

By his father's side, Walter did not hide his joy at finally seeing his dream come true – Belle as his mom. For the first time in his life, he didn't care about a cake, or presents, or the party, or anything else, but a wedding. And oh, December 19th couldn't come fast enough!

twelve

MAGEE RETURNED TO THE KITCHEN FROM THE front counter to find Belle piping royal frosting on a gingerbread cookie shaped like a tiny Cape Cod cottage.

"Gwyn called, she got a new shipment and thinks there might be something you'll like."

"Oh?" Belle said lifting her frosting tube.

"Why don't you take a break and run over there?" Magee and Miss Tabatha had burned the midnight oil on the phone. There was a lot to get done, and every minute of every day was important.

"Okay. I'll finish this batch of frosting so it doesn't harden. Aren't you going to tell me about my cake?" Belle asked.

Magee laughed. "Then it wouldn't be a surprise!"

As soon as Belle was out the door, Magee began melting chocolate for the molded tiny Christmas packages that would cover the cake.

Belle walked along the cobblestone sidewalk, wondering how she was going to tell Harv her last secret. No matter how she looked at it, it sounded crazy. They had been inseparable since the day at the Whaling Museum when Harv asked her to marry him. Since then, they talked all the time, about the food for the wedding, about the guest list, about if they should write their own vows. They talked about how she could move into his cottage, about whether or not there would be enough room. Maybe she wanted something bigger and grander, but she had laughed and told him in all seriousness that his Cape Cod cottage was her dream house.

"Because it is yours and Walter's. I already feel home there," she'd assured him and the topic closed.

Yes, they talked about everything except the thing she was afraid would scare him away. Yet it was the thing he needed to know to save Christmas. Belle's mind went round and round and didn't notice he had come out of nowhere and was walking next to her.

"Hey, Mrs. Claus, can I walk with you?"

Belle turned and couldn't speak for a moment. He looked, well, *wonderful,* and her stomach filled with butterflies. She finally managed a *hi* gazing into his aqua eyes. "Where'd you come from?"

"School let out early and when I looked for you at The Bake Shoppe, Magee said you were headed to Gwyn's."

"I am," she said with a huge smile and took his elbow. From there, they walked along, Harv oblivious, Belle torn. "Miss Tabatha said Chantelier is one of Nantucket's premier restaurants and they will cater our reception."

"Fancy," Harv said and slipped an arm around her waist. "Do we get any say on the menu. I'm not very frou-frou. Are you?"

Belle laughed and his rhyme. "We'll let them decide with this short notice, eh?" she asked teasing and he shrugged.

"Snails are delicious this time of year," he said looking off.

Belle laughed again. "How's your guest list coming?"

"I think the whole village wants to come," Harv replied and then said more serious than before, "I need an address for Nickolas and Nicole."

"The North Pole," Belle said, allowing it to slide out without planning.

"The North Pole, North Pole?" he teased and then laughed. "But really, where do I send their invitation?"

"The North Pole," Belle repeated and stopped walking. Here it was, time to tell the truth. Her scalp crinkled with fear of his reaction, but she barreled on in a gentle tone. "I've remembered more details that I've been reluctant to tell you."

"Reluctant?" he asked, his head tilting to the side. "Why?"

"I'm *afraid* to tell you." An artic chill blew past her spirit and Belle shivered.

"Belle, stop that. I love you. You don't have to be afraid to tell me anything." Harv looked at her as though he meant it.

Belle hemmed twirling a long strand of her windblown hair. "Even if I told you something that would change your life forever?"

He put both hands to her shoulders. "You've already changed my life," he said tenderly. "Go ahead. Tell me about Nickolas and Nicole."

"Claus."

"A clause?" He gave her a quizzical look.

"That's their last name."

"Whoa! What are the chances? I mean, other than Santa Claus, I've never met a *Claus*."

"They *are* Santa Claus. Santa and Mrs. Claus." Belle rolled in her lips and waited. There it was. The impossible truth released to her beloved's ears. But Harv's eyes were crinkling with humor.

"Good one, Belle."

Belle gave it two ticks and added, "My guardians, Nikolas and Nicole, are Santa and Mrs. Claus." She watched his eyes and they grew narrow in increments.

"Belle," he said finally pacing his words, "I know you have amnesia but…"

"*Had* amnesia. I remember them perfectly and there is no doubt: my guardians are Santa and Mrs. Claus. But they're retiring. Nickolas has bad knees and I am meant to take over for them. Me and my husband… the next Santa."

"Belle, you know I love you, I adore you …" There was humor in his voice. "But you have to stop. You're scaring me. Is this a movie we're playing out? Is this a prank?" he asked looking around as if for a camera crew.

"Harv! Pay attention!" Belle barked with a budding anger at being disregarded. "I am the new Mrs. Claus!"

Harv shook his head incredulous. "So that makes your husband, Chris—he was supposed to be the new Santa Claus?"

"Chris Cringle, and yes, my husband, my *dead* husband. Harv! You need to listen. My new husband will be Santa. That's why I need to get married before December 24th, to save Christmas!" Belle's voice had hyped and she couldn't control her tone. He wasn't believing, he wasn't even trying. And he was no longer laughing. On the contrary, his eyes had narrowed as if she was being dishonest.

"Why are you doing this?" he said his voice low. "If you don't want to marry me, just say so. This crazy story isn't necessary—"

He'd said the word. To him, her facts were crazy.

Belle turned and ran.

He thinks I'm crazy! He loves me as long as my past makes sense to his small understanding! He pretends to love Christmas but can't even believe there is a Santa Claus and that Santa might have a knee problem!

Belle's thoughts ran like this the entire way and when she looked up, bleary-eyed and eyes puffy, she had reached the wharf. Dropping onto a cold metal bench, she allowed the dam to break, tears fell in rivers and her thin shoulders shook with pain and grief.

In her heart, she apologized to Nikolas and Nicole—they didn't deserve all that, this waste of time and energy when they needed her most and she had chosen the wrong man.

With that horrible thought, Belle fell into an entirely new season of sobbing and she hoped her guardians understood how much she loved them.

Harv wished he could laugh. Staring off the way she had run; why didn't he chase after her? Take her into his arms and ask her to explain? Why had she made such preposterous claims? What was her angle? And wasn't that the thing? Belle didn't come across as a woman who would work an angle on anyone, much less the man she said she loved.

So, then what was all that about Santa Claus? Is she insane?

Harv remained on the cobblestone walk, facing the sea, although from his vantage, he saw only rooftops and powerlines.

Maybe she did something to her head when she crashed. But if that was so, why did she seem so normal up until today?

Harv huffed. "Unbelievable," he muttered, his mind going over everything she claimed before running away.

Her guardians are Santa and Mrs. Claus? That is like saying there is a real Santa Claus!

Harv stopped cold. Was there a Santa Claus? For years, he'd played Santa's stand-in never questioning the legend with any cognizance. He loved Christmas and Santa Claus was simply a part of that. Now this beautiful young woman falls into his life, sees him making toys and then finally, dressed the part. Did he fit into her delusion so well that he broke her mind with his Santa suit?

There were no answers to be had for the moment, standing alone, staring into space.

I love her. I'll get help figuring it out. I'm not going to lose her over this. If she needs counseling, I'll get her the care she needs.

Harv turned for home, lining up what he might say to the women in Belle's life for advice.

Belle wept until there was no more hurt to seep from her tender heart. She lowered her head to crossed arms and rocked gently back and forth. Why had she told him?

Because I had to. Nickolas and Nicole and all the children in the world are counting on me.

Just then, Billy and Walter rode near on their bikes singing "Joy to the World." Seeing her slumped forward on the bench, they stopped short.

"Belle! Are you okay?" both voices clamored dropping their bikes as they scurried to her side.

Belle didn't raise her head. Not yet. They shouldn't see her in such a state. "I'm okay," she managed but they would hear her voice was wrong.

"Somebody hurt you?" Billy asked and one or both of them patted her head as if she was a dog in need of a calming and gentle hand. In a way, that's precisely how she felt.

"No, I'm okay," she said muffled and then sat up, unable to disguise her blotchy face, wet cheeks, and red eyes. The boys jumped back at the sight.

"Somebody beat her up!" Walter said. "Let's get Dad!"

Belle made an effort to pull it together. "I was crying, that's all." She sniffled and smoothed her long hair, and then she reached an arm out to each of boy who allowed themselves to be hugged.

"You sure?" Walter asked sounding so much older than five.

It occurred to Belle anew how much she loved him and wanted to be around to see him turn six, and then seven, and on and on. She hugged them closer. "I'm remembering more, that's all."

Walter patted her hand and Billy copied the action on his side. "But that's a good thing, we wanted you to remember."

He sounded like a miniature Harv just then and Belle's breathing hitched at the thought of him and his face when he didn't believe her truth. She couldn't cry anymore, not in front of the boys. She had to get up, go back to the inn, talk to Miss Tabatha. She needed advice and her new friend at the inn was the wisest person she knew in Nantucket.

"I need to get home."

"To the Tuck You Inn?" they asked.

"Yes, to the inn," she said brushing off her skirt.

"Are you coming over for supper?" Walter asked as if sensing all was not right.

Belle's heart cracked but she couldn't face Harv. If he wanted to see her, talk to her, *believe her,* he knew where to find her.

"No, tonight, I'll have a bite with Miss Tabatha and maybe lie down and rest." The sadness she felt radiated in her face.

"She's sick," Billy whispered.

"Yeah," Walter agreed in a sad tone. "Gots a cold maybe."

Belle shook her head and gave both boys a new hug. "I'm not sick, honest, I'm tired. That's all." When they relaxed into the hug, she knew they believed her. "Come on. You two gentlemen can walk me home."

"Gentlemen, we are!" Billy announced and puffed his narrow chest. Walter took a position on the opposite side and once they interlaced their elbows with Belle's they marched her properly toward town, leaving their bikes behind. They'd run back for them later, and Belle allowed it. Having them close dissipated her sadness and by the time she reached Miss Tabatha, she was ready to share and listen with the best.

thirteen

DAD WASN'T IN THE WORKSHOP SO WALTER WALKED into the cottage and called out. No answer. He was about to holler louder when he caught a glimpse through the oceanside window of his father walking the beach.

"Dad, I'm home!" he called, running at top speed to join him on the sand. His father said nothing and didn't turn, looking gray and distant to Walter's young eyes. "Dad? Somethin' the matter?" he asked and fell in step.

His father surfaced but did not look over. "Wrong? No, nothing's wrong."

Walter knew that wasn't true, he wasn't a new guy. "Belle was crying," Walter tossed out to get the ball rolling.

"You aren't getting too attached to Belle, are you?" his dad said in an odd low voice.

Walter huffed a breath and tried not to say, *duh.* "Well, yeah. I mean, I found her, remember? We bake cookies together. She taught me how to mix the dough and make candy canes. She's going to be my new mom." Walter's eyes shrank. "Is this a trick question? She's gonna marry us."

His dad grimaced and Walter stopped dead in his tracks. The fear washed over him at his father's now shaking head. "You're backing out?"

"No, I," his dad said and stopped talking. He dropped his eyes and Walter snorted.

"You're backing out! And that's why Belle was crying! Because you don't want her anymore! Well, I want her! I love her! She's my mom! I wished for her! And you're not going to ruin it! You promised! You promised you'd never leave! I heard you. You said it over and over again. You said it in front of everybody! The whole town!" With that, Walter tore off down the beach, tears falling free.

Walter ran until his lungs burned and a stitch stabbed his side. Where was he going? He had no clue. His stubby legs carried him with a mind of their own. He was so winded he had to stop, lean over, and throw up.

Oh no! Miss Tabatha's hydrangeas!

He couldn't clean that up, make it disappear, there was no way. Walter started to cry all over again, blubbering that he didn't want Miss Tabatha or Belle to come out and see him or the mess he made.

I gotta hide! he thought and crept to the back of the inn. In all his five years, he'd never been back there. Turns out it wasn't so strange, or dark, or scary. He found another great porch, decorated with rugs made of seagrass and accentuated with hanging baskets of fading roses. Sniffling, he crawled into the seat of an old metal glider, the gentle rocking soothing and petting his frazzled mind. A breeze off the ocean arrived and the fevered sweat dried on his forehead.

"I can't let this happen! I won't!" he whispered under his breath, completely exhausted by his current fit of emotions. Before he knew it, he put his head down on the striped cushion and fell sound asleep.

It took him too long to holler for his son and Harv was ashamed. His little boy had scampered off, bawling like he never seen, and Harv had let him do it. As he shook off his selfish grief over Belle and her behavior, he headed down the beach in the way Walter had run. Calling his name, he continued all the way back to town, leaving the sand for the cobblestone alleyways, his eyes peeled for the angry little boy he had so greatly disappointed.

His search took him in a circle, ending back at his own cottage, entering the front door and calling his name. Walter's bedroom was empty, as was the kitchen, and the rest of the small home. Harv felt a twinge of distress. Where was his son?

Belle! He would have gone to Belle!

Harv raced to the Tuck You Inn. Once there, he pounded the door harder than he should have, but his mind had brought panic with every bad thought of what might happen to a sad little boy running mad.

Miss Tabatha answered the door, flustered at his noise, wisps of white hair floating about her face as if she raced to his ring.

"Harv! Goodness!" she said, jerking her eyes over his shoulder as if he was chased.

"Where is he?" Harv he asked and pushed inside.

Miss Tabatha allowed it, standing aside before they made contact, her famous giant mug of cocoa expertly balanced as she swiveled. "He or she?"

"He! Walter!" Harv barked crossing to the edge of the foyer to look around the landing and up the stairs.

"Walter? What is wrong with you? You're hysterical!"

"Walter's missing. I thought he'd come here, you know… to see Belle."

"Oh, dear." Tabatha closed her eyes, "Walter."

"We were walking along the beach and he got mad and ran away." Harv did not want to admit the reason Walter ran but Miss Tabatha raised an eyebrow. He sighed. "He got mad at me. We were fighting."

"About Belle?"

Harv nodded running a hand through his disheveled hair.

"Oh, Harv," Miss Tabatha *tsked*, shaking her head. "Belle's asleep and Walter has not been by tonight. Come inside. I'll call Magee, see if she'll sit at your house and watch for him. You call the station and get the boys to drive around in the patrol car."

These were all good ideas, and he calmed a bit, Miss Tabatha's peace affecting him. He followed the old innkeeper into her kitchen. The room seemed cold; after all, Belle had nothing in the oven. No scents of warm cinnamon buns baking, no trays of cookies awaiting frosting. No potpourri simmering in a bowl, wafting its sweet floral scent.

Wrong, it's all wrong.

Tabatha removed two mega-mugs from the cupboard and poured hot steaming coffee for them both. Then she opened the cabinet over the fridge, pulled out a bottle and tossed a generous dollop of Grand Mariner in both cups. In the last, a pantry opened and she snagged a roll of McVities Digestives biscuits and added them to the tray with the enhanced coffees. She carried the trove to the loveseat and indicated with a crook of her head to Harv.

"Sit, drink, dunk, talk."

Harv did as instructed and told her about the conversation he'd had with Belle, as well as about the horror he felt at worrying for her sanity. "I love her, Miss Tabatha, I do. I just can't understand why she'd say all that stuff…" He took another gulp of his laced coffee. It burned his mouth, scalded his tongue, and somehow helped. "She seemed so perfect. I just…" His voice disappeared as it threatened to choke him up.

"Harv," Miss Tabatha said, her voice gentle, "maybe she is perfect."

"But did you hear what I just said? She thinks she's Mrs. Claus." Harv couldn't say more, his heart breaking all over again.

"I heard you, all right. I mean it, maybe she is perfect for *you.* Specifically. Harvey Nichols."

Harv looked up; a digestive biscuit mid-dunk broke off, sank, and dissolved.

"Have you ever thought to take Belle's story at face value?" she asked as serious as the weather.

"Are you nuts?" he slipped and apologize. "I mean, what are you saying?" *Oh, help me,* he said inside his heart, *she's as crazy as Belle!*

"I heard that!" Miss Tabatha snapped with a cluck of her tongue.

Harv jerked up. Had he said that aloud? He must have because she heard it.

"Young man, listen. Life is often complicated, disturbing, and mysterious. I don't understand how those people get in my TV, or where the sun goes when it sinks into the ocean."

"But Miss Tabatha … come on… Santa Claus? There is science behind those things. Santa is a story. A wonderful story for children of all ages to remind them of the wonder of Christmas…"

Tabatha leaned close where they sat adjacent on the long, upholstered couch and placed her palm gentle to his cheek. "You want my advice? Open your heart. Anything's possible."

"Even the impossible?" he whispered.

"Especially the impossible."

The inn's landline phone interrupted with its shrill ring and they both startled, getting to their feet.

"It's Magee," Miss Tabatha said before even picking up the phone. After initial greetings, she held the phone out so Harv could hear. "Has Walter shown up there?" she asked Magee.

Harv listened with a keen ear and sighed audibly when the baker said no. Tabatha launched into explaining their plan and when Magee agreed to go to Harv's house in case Walter went home, Harv walked slowly to the large square of the entryway, his eyes subconsciously traveling to the upstairs railing.

Belle was up there. Beautiful, funny, kind, interesting.

And maybe nuts.

Then a familiar form appeared at the top. She met Harv's eye and gave him a concerned tip of the chin.

"Everything okay? Is Walter okay? I thought I heard his name."

"Belle…" Harv stuttered and focused on the immediate need. His son. "It's Walter. He ran away. I thought he'd come here, but no one's seen him."

"Oh, dear," Belle said and started down, her movements so graceful she might have been a dancer. "We have to find him." She turned to Miss Tabatha. "He's so small and it's dark outside."

"Go, you two. I'll keep an eye here." With that, Miss Tabatha piled a thick sweater over Belle's shoulders and pushed them out the front door.

At the foot of the porch, they faced the street lit by the glow of evenly spaced hook lights. A breeze rushed past, icy-edged and threatening snow, and Harv peeked to see if Belle was suitably dressed. The coverup appeared to be cashmere and she wore slacks and boots. Her delicate form made him think of long hugs and snuggles under a quilt before a roaring fire. She turned her face in response to his attention.

"Where to?" she asked, her bright eyes hoping he had the answers.

"After home, here, and the bakery, what's left?" Harv asked.

"The Toy Boat?" Belle suggested and he led the way, reaching for her hand as they navigated the bumpy cobblestones.

At the shuttered toy store, the bench in front was bare, and when they looked around back, they found nothing but a grumpy alley cat having a bath.

They wandered up and down the lanes calling his name, fear gripping their hearts. They reached the Whaling Museum where they'd all been so happy not so long ago.

Nothing.

Next up, they found the entrance to Captain Toby's, open late and serving dinner to anyone still out and about.

"Booth or table?" Toby asked his normal jovial self.

"We're looking for Walter," Harv blurted as a reply.

"Haven't seen the little guy. You try Billy's?" Captain Toby asked.

A couple of diners overheard and expressed concern. One of them spoke without thinking. "Good thing Nantucket is such a small island. Not too many places to go except the sea."

Suddenly Belle crumbled and Harv shot close to hold her up.

"Oh Harv! Walter is so small! What if?" She didn't finish but covered her mouth with both hands.

"Call the Coast Guard," Toby said with authority, but Harv waved him off.

"No, guys, no," he said meeting every concerned eye, Belle's last, but with warmth. "He won't go near the water. Trust me."

Harv thanked everyone and led Belle into the night. They faced the road and looked up and down as far as the eye could see. A notion arrived then, deep in Harv's heart, or maybe his mind, but he sensed something.

"Let's walk this way. I'm having a feeling." Her small fingers intertwined with his once more and they resumed the trek, parallel to the ocean down an interior street that would eventually meet back at the Tuck You Inn. "He's along here somewhere…" Harv had her duck and peek at every nook they passed, each time they found nothing, they sighed and moved to the next shadowed hidey hole.

"He's so small," Belle said low, her voice full of motherly concern.

Scanning left and right, Harv agreed. "I remember when he was even smaller." His memory traveled to Walter as an infant and then toddler. "He was such a sweet baby. Always so happy."

"You were raising him alone, too," she said commiserating and Harv gave a heavy sigh.

"Almost from the beginning." Harv shook his head. "I was depressed for so long, he practically raised himself."

"But he's fine, he's wonderful. You sound like you think you failed him, but you didn't. He's quick to learn anything I show him, and kind to everyone he meets. He won't step on an ant."

"Yeah, he's funny that way. He loves animals. He's wanted a dog forever." Harv *humphed.* Why hadn't he ever gotten him a dog? "Belle, when I find him, I'm getting him a dog."

"He can have my dog Sprinkles; she's still a puppy." Belle stopped speaking when Harv inhaled. Then she softened her voice. "It's not impossible, what I told you. People *do live* at the North Pole. I'd like to take you there, show you, and get Sprinkles for Walter."

"We couldn't take your dog," Harv said, dismissing most of what she was saying. How could he take it seriously? "No, I'll get Walter his own dog." Harv set his chin.

Belle twirled a strand of her long hair as they continued along. "How's your feeling coming? I think you're right. I think he's right around here somewhere…"

Harv called Walter's name, more softly now that it was late and folks were no doubt sleeping. His fear for his son had been dissolving the past fifteen minutes and he gave a slow nod, peeking under an overhang and straightening again beside Belle.

"What sort of dog would he like?" she asked, calming as Harv was.

"Something big like a shepherd. He had a stuffed dog when he was small and it was a husky, I think. I dismissed a lot of that stuff I should have been paying attention to." Harv didn't like facing it, but he had missed a lot of great stuff in his self-pity.

"Like an Alaskan Malamute?" Belle suggested.

"Maybe," Harv sighed.

"Nickolas and Nicole have Samoyeds—I call them Sammies. They're such a joy." She giggled a precious sound and Harv glanced over, her beauty hurting his heart. She continued, facing in the way they walked. "Sammies are glorious, huge, white, fluffy, and ever so gentle. They can pull sleds." Belle laughed. "Sometimes the elves ride them like ponies."

Harv's skin prickled at the last sentence. He covered with a quick placation. "You have an incredible imagination; I can almost see it."

"Come with me," Belle said her tone intense. "See for yourself. Don't give up on us just because you don't believe in Santa." She lowered her voice to a whisper. "Come see my home and then decide."

Harv pressed his lips together and got them walking again. "Let's find Walter. I can't think on anything else until he's in my arms."

Belle didn't argue. She marched along, the wind more wicked as the night progressed into pre-dawn. Since neither spoke a long while, Harv's memory looped everything Belle had said about her guardians and then what Walter shouted at him on the beach. It sounded as if his son believed in Santa Claus and elves and magical flying sleighs. And what of Miss Tabatha's responses? She wanted Harv to believe Belle. Why? Was she saying it was true? Was that odd old bird indicating her inn guest was the new Mrs. Claus?

"Walter believes in you," Harv said under his breath, not really wanting Belle to reply.

She did, though. In a soft voice that petted his spirit, she said, "He believes in you more, Harv. And he believes you can believe if you want to."

Tiny slivers of light were sneaking through, breaking up the darkness, creating a soft gray pall.

"I want to believe," Harv said to the dawn.

"You can," Belle said as they walked into morning, hand and hand, both of them thinking of the little boy they loved most in the world.

fourteen

"WE NEED TO DO SOMETHING, HON, AND QUICK. I'M going bananas waiting for the punchline."

The cookies had cooled, but the frosting had not melted down the sides this time. Nicole touched her fingertip to the green icing and gave it a taste.

Her husband gave a jovial huff. "You need to believe in miracles, my dear. Believe in miracles. I'm sure I do."

Nicole didn't roll her eyes, but she wanted to. She counted to ten and forced herself to be patient.

When Walter awoke his neck hurt and he was cold, curled into a ball on the glider. He dreamt he'd been cradled in a wooden shoe, lost at sea, looking for Belle, rocking on the waves. He kept calling out her name, but no one answered, no one came. As his tears fell into the water, they turned into the ringing of a million tiny bells.

Walter wiped the sleep from his eyes and looked up to see a crystal wind chime tinkling in the morning breeze. Sun sparkled off the glass shards, sending prisms of light bouncing off the walls of the porch. Walter wiped both cheeks, the previous night returning to his mind, every detail. He brought his knees to his chest, hugged them tight, and looked out at nothing. He had to fix everything. But how?

Miss Tabatha had fallen asleep with her cell phone clutched in her hand. All night long, no sign of Walter, neither had Harv and Belle returned. Morning had broken and she needed to get some go-juice in her gullet for the new day.

Once she padded to the kitchen and hit her Russell Hobbs to boil water, she decided on cocoa over coffee. She scooped her special concoction from the snowman shaped ceramic cannister. Hershey's cocoa and white sugar were a given, but her secret recipe wasn't really magic at all, it was a pinch of cinnamon and splash of vanilla extract.

"Oh! And the elves' pillows!" she said in a sing-song whisper, dropping in a handful of miniature marshmallows. The water poured over her chocolate and she snagged one of Belle's candy canes to use as a stirrer.

She headed out the back, the weathered door slamming behind her. Normal morning sounds brought the customary grin—the sea lapping to the shore, the periodic call of a water-loving bird that didn't mind the chill, and the tinkle of wind chimes.

Wait. Was that a squeak?

The *squeak* was not part of her porch mornings.

Tabatha watched as a tiny foot dipped down off her swing reaching for the slatted floor. Toes made contact and the swing went into a smooth glide.

"Walter?" Tabatha said gently as she walked forward.

"Miss Tabatha?" a tiny voice replied.

Miss Tabatha set the cocoa to the porch railing and scooted forward. Grinning wide, she gathered Walter into her arms. "There you are! We were so worried!"

"I'm sorry," He clung tight, pudgy arms around her neck. "I was mad at Dad and I ran away."

"I know," she replied and settled into the glider. A rough afghan sat on a stool within reach and she grabbed it to flip around his tiny form. She set them into a slow back and forth, the boy in her lap facing out and sighing. "You've been here all night?" she asked.

"Uh-huh," he answered and wiped a runny nose.

With a little stretch, she reached her cocoa and handed it to Walter, stopping the swing with a slippered toe. He took a sip, dodging the marshmallows that hadn't yet dissolved. "Come on. I'll make us some waffles."

"Yeahhhh," he said and slid to the floor, cocooning the blanket. "Can I have chocolate syrup instead of maple?" he asked as he scampered behind her into the house. Miss Tabatha laughed and followed him in.

Soon after, true to her word, she passed Walter the Hershey's syrup and watched him squeeze it into the little pockets on his waffle with precision.

"We need to talk, young man." Miss Tabatha poured Vermont maple syrup on her own waffles and peeked at him until he looked up. It took a long moment.

"Um… what about?" he said stumbling over his words as if she was mad with him.

"You're not in trouble." Reading his mind, Miss Tabatha topped off his cocoa. "I know you're mad because your dad backed away from Belle."

Walter looked up, holding a forkful of waffle over the rim of his plate, chocolate dripping on the table.

"The story's not over," Miss Tabatha began. "He's just confused."

"He changed his mind. He said he wouldn't but he did."

"It's because he's scared," Miss Tabatha said.

Walter stopped working his breakfast. "My dad's not

scared of nothing. He can solve anything, do anything."

"Anything he *knows,* honey lamb. He can do anything he knows, solve anything he knows. He doesn't know this. It's new to him, that's all."

Walter sat very still and listened.

"Belle is remembering everything, and your dad is confused by what she's telling him."

"You mean that her guardians are Nickolas and Nicole?" Walter asked. "So what? She was adopted. She was going to adopt me. What's the big deal?"

Miss Tabatha patted him like the honey lamb he was. "It's about Nickolas and Nicole, where they live, and what they do."

Walter waited for more, his fork hovering over his plate.

"They live at the North Pole." Miss Tabatha said watching for his reaction. His face lit up without delay.

"Like Santa Claus!" Walter beamed. "If we go there to meet them, we might see Santa Claus, too!"

"What if I was to tell you that they *are* Santa Claus. Belle's guardians are Santa and Mrs. Claus."

"No way!" Walter's eyes lit up, his grin so wide.

"Yes, way."

"That's great! More than great! Think how lucky I am! My new grandparents are going to be Santa and Mrs. Claus!" Walter released his fork to plop into his syrup. "That means the little people Belle made cookies for were Santa's elves! That means I get to go to Santa's workshop! The real Santa's real workshop! I've gotta tell Billy! I can't believe it!"

Miss Tabatha nodded with a twinkle in her eye.

Walter caught his breath. "Are… Are you making this up?"

Tabatha shook her head. "Think about it. You said you couldn't believe it. Your dad can't believe it either. That's why he's confused."

Walter's face fell, his young brain working it out. "But Belle said it was true. She wouldn't lie."

"That's right."

"Then, what do we do?" Walter nibbled his bottom lip.

"It is very difficult for your dad because no one has ever seen Santa or Mrs. Claus."

"Sure, they have." Walter was confident now. "How else would we know what he looks like?"

"Some people think it's a legend."

"But someone must have seen Santa to know. Someone knows." Walter opened his eyes wide. "Belle knows."

"You think so?"

Walter huffed. "Of course, she does, Miss Tabatha! She told Dad." Then he started to look panicked. "Don't you believe? You have to believe in Santa Claus, or Belle sounds like she's telling a story." His face started to crumble.

Miss Tabatha wondered how a five-year-old could piece all this together. "Of course, I believe, honey lamb."

"Dad doesn't believe?" he asked just above a whisper. Before Miss Tabatha could answer he went on. "He's been a Santa stand-in forever. He *must* believe."

Miss Tabatha closed her eyes and sighed.

Exactly, she thought, *and that's where the problem lies.*

fifteen

WITH WEARY HEARTS AND WEARIER FEET, BELLE and Harv found themselves back at the Tuck You Inn. Before either could ponder whether she had heard anything, boisterous noise from inside revealed it all. Harv pushed open the door to see Miss Tabatha and Walter at the piano playing Christmas carols.

"Dashing through the snow!" Miss Tabatha belted out and then pointed to Walter who took over.

"In a one-horse open sleigh!"

Miss Tabatha was quick with her next line. "Ore the fields we go!"

And Walter waved his arms as he sang, "Laughing all the way!"

"Bells on Bobtails ring!" Miss Tabatha was laughing now as she tried to sing.

"Making spirits bright." Walter was shout-singing.

Then Miss Tabatha started to lose it. "Uh da da da da da!"

And Walter caught the fun. "Da da da da tonight!"

Then they joined together for the chorus, still laughing, Miss Tabatha pounding out the chords.

"Hello," Harv called out.

The singing stopped, the music along with it.

"What's going on?" Harv asked with an edge.

"We're brushing up on Jingle Bells!" Walter proclaimed.

"Only we can't remember all the words, so we fake it!" He swallowed a giggle. Belle smiled but stole a look sideways at Harv and forced it away.

"I've been up all night looking for you!" Harv told him.

Belle cleared her throat with a demure ahem. "Don't you me *we*?" But Harv didn't hear or chose not to.

"I've been worried sick!" Harv went on.

"Umm…" Walter looked to all three adults in turn.

"We just finished our waffles," Miss Tabatha broke in. "Why don't we head to the kitchen and I'll whip up some more. I'm sure you two are famished. Walter, you crack the eggs."

Walter climbed off the piano bench and followed Miss Tabatha to the kitchen.

"I am hungry," Belle agreed and slipped past.

Walter had already cracked the eggs in the bowl and Miss Tabatha was pouring in milk.

"Walter only got as far as my inn and fell asleep on the back-porch swing. That's where I found him." Miss Tabatha looked at Walter and gave him a quick wink. "He's fine and he agreed never to run away again."

Harv had no anger left. He opened his arms and Walter fell in. "Don't ever, and I mean *never ever*, scare me like that again. Anything could have happened to you!" He rocked Walter in his arms as he spoke. "Haven't we always been a good team?" Walter's head bobbed up and down. "Haven't we always managed?" More bobbing. "And we *will manage,* Walter, you and me. We'll do fine."

Belle heard that he excluded her. Miss Tabatha caught her eye and tried to give her the *it's okay*, sign but Belle was shattered anew.

"Don't you want to go home?" Harv asked Walter. "Sleep in your own bed? I'll tuck you in, it's you and me, Walter. You and me forever."

Miss Tabatha shook her head. The boy needed a mom, but

before she could think one more thought, Harv lifted Walter from where he stood at the counter and headed out the door without a word.

Miss Tabatha and Belle stood in the kitchen, the waffle iron smoking. The front door slammed and they were alone.

Miss Tabatha pulled an overdone waffle free with a fork and unplugged the iron. She held her arms open to Belle. "Oh, he didn't mean it. He wasn't thinking. He …"

Belle felt a thousand years old. She was tired. The fear for Walter had evaporated and exhaustion filled the void. She pulled away from Miss Tabatha and picked up the plate with the crispy waffle. Sitting at the kitchen table, she poured the Hershey's syrup.

"The important thing is Walter is okay. He's safe." She ate absently, not even tasting, burnt bits and all.

"Yes, dear, but you're important, too. That lad needs you, not to mention Harv." Miss Tabatha's face held a lifetime of concern.

"That may be the case…" She looked at her empty plate realizing she'd inhaled the waffle. "But until Harv knows it, it won't happen."

Miss Tabatha hummed. "He'll come around."

Belle was now awake, fed, and serious. "Harv's not a child, he's a grown man. And sure, he lost his wife, which is horrible, but that was years ago. Everyone tiptoes around him and it's doing him no favors." She sighed, knowing full well what she was talking about. "Harv has built up walls so he doesn't get hurt again."

Miss Tabatha took a seat. "You're right, you are."

"Circumstances pushed him along. If I had never landed here, he wouldn't have left his comfort zone, wallowing in self-pity."

"Aye. I agree."

"Now he's frozen in fear of the unknown. He won't go

forward. You heard him tell Walter they were a good enough team by themselves."

Miss Tabatha cringed.

"And he can't go back, even though he wants to." Belle pushed back her long golden hair and looked straight at Miss Tabatha. "It isn't Santa Claus Harv doesn't believe in. It's me. He doesn't believe in me." The reality stung worse when spoken aloud.

Miss Tabatha released a breath she hadn't realized she was holding and opened her arms. "I'm sorry, honey…"

"I love Harv and Walter, but I have a huge weight on my shoulders. Harv could take *forever* to decide if he can handle a relationship with me. I don't have that kind of time. Call the island airport and then Logan."

"Wh … what do you mean?" Miss Tabatha asked.

Belle carried her plate to the sink. She turned to face Miss Tabatha. "I'm going home."

"But … but … but … how?"

"I live at the North Pole. I'll fly up there and figure out the rest on that end." Belle began mentally tossing stuff in a suitcase.

"But the wedding, the caterers, I've paid them. The cake, Magee's been slaving on the sugared trim." Miss Tabatha stuttered. "Harv will never decide if you leave. What do I tell Walter?"

"Have a party. It's time the village folk all knew how wonderful you are." Belle helped her wash up the dishes and jogged upstairs. Her heart hurt from so much turmoil, but seeing her guardians again would make everything manageable, if not heal her altogether.

Within the hour, Belle was packed into the Island's single-prop plane leaving the island for Boston's Logan Airport. She wore her red velvet cape, taffeta plaid skirt, and fur-trimmed sweater. Her velvet backpack carried a seashell Harv had given her, the menu she'd kept from Neptune's, a picture of Walter that Miss Tabatha had taken, and a cell phone Miss Tabatha had pressed on her last minute.

Logan was jammed with travelers; she'd never seen anything like it. She stopped at the newsstand for a paperback novel to pass the time reading, and on impulse got an atlas so she could look for the North Pole and anything that sounded familiar.

Belle changed planes so many times she'd lost count, but now she was finally landing at a tiny airport as far north as Miss Tabatha and she could figure out when they had called. The airport itself was caught in a time warp, wrought-iron lattices and old-time carved benches were everywhere. The crisp air glowed with the glitter of snow crystals. She inhaled deeply as she stepped off the plane, cool air filling her lungs.

"This feels right." At the last step her mind whirled. *Now what?*

The station's roof was dome-shaped with huge glass windows criss-crossed with iron gridwork. Iron lanterns lit by gas jets swayed under the overhang. She'd lost the day in travel, so it was twilight, and the snow glistened like diamonds on every surface. Belle clutched her backpack and headed into the building. Her magazine had been loaded with recipes that she wanted to try for the elves.

Or Magee, if I ever return to Nantucket…

Belle cleared her mind and forged into the terminal.

Inside, the airport was maxed out in Christmas trees. She stood in awe, gaping all around, taking in the twinkling lights, inhaling the scent of pine, smiling with a growing peace.

"Can I help you, Missy?" an old man in formal uniform asked stepping up from behind. A silver pin clipped to his lapel read North Pole Airport and a candy cane hung looped in his breast pocket.

She turned and her full skirt and cape swung out behind her. "I'm not sure," she said and looked one more broad scan. "So many Christmas trees. It's so *beautiful.*"

The man followed her gaze with an agreeing nod. Belle looked out the huge window; the runway was gone, covered in snow.

"You'll be needin' the train, Missy," the man offered and pulled a huge brochure from his candy cane pocket. It was bordered in vintage baby dolls, train sets, and fire engines. "One's coming up just about—" He pulled out a pocket watch in the shape of a jumbo chocolate chip cookie. "Now!"

He snapped the watch shut and bits of gold glitter danced in the air. The man took her elbow and led her out the front double doors. Sure enough, Belle heard a steam engine coming down the track.

She exhaled, perplexed even though since she arrived, her troubles had all but dissolved from her spirit.

"Yes?" he asked noticing her expression.

"I don't know where I'm going."

"Of course, you do." As he sent her a new wink, the train came to a halt. Another ancient, very bent man in uniform popped out and plopped a small iron stool below the last step. Together they each took an elbow and helped Belle up the steps.

Once in place, she turned to the airport attendant. "Thank you. How will I know where to get off?"

Both men laughed until their small round bellies shook. "Why, Missy, this is the Candy Land Express and it only goes one place—to Candy Land."

Then the man disappeared, and the train door banged shut.

"The Candy Land Express," she whispered in wonder. This was something she should remember. Something she forgot in the crash. Belle relaxed her mind to allow it to return.

I'm going home. I'm safe. I should be able to remember everything.

"Yes, Missy," the conductor said with a grin. His uniform was covered with shiny brass buttons, red-and-white fringe epaulets at his shoulders, and an elaborate embroidered crest with a C and L cross swords under it. On closer inspection she saw it was a cross of candy canes.

"All aboard!" he called although Belle sensed she was the only passenger. This, too, was something she shouldn't find odd and she let it happen.

Let it all come back…

The train whistle blew, and she felt the chug-a-chug of the train starting forward. She turned her attention to the aisle. The interior of the train was a step back in time to a long-ago forgotten era of luxury. Ornate brass shelves hung from the ceiling above each puffy red velvet tufted seat. She slid into one of these, realizing how tired she was. She'd been up all night hunting for Walter, and then traveling well in to the day to get this far. The lull of the train relaxed her further and Belle found herself enjoying the ride.

Peeking past black brocade curtains out the window she watched snow-covered pine trees dash past. Among the pines stood out one gigantic tree—why, it looked to be made of gingerbread! Then it was gone, and the pines returned, only to change into a forest of … peppermint sticks as big as towering oaks … and then the peppermint forest gave way to mountains. The sun bounced off the sugary surfaces that if she wasn't mistaken were giant gum drops. As bright and cheerful as they were, the train then shook through a dark forest of black twisted trees. Belle leaned to the glass to see more of the outside when a shimmy rocked the train-car.

From somewhere behind her, the conductor hollered out, "Lord Licorice! I'll get you yet! Keep that licorice off my tracks!"

From there they burst back into sunlight and Belle could have sworn they were riding through a cabbage patch. She pressed her face against the window and found it was not cabbage plants she spied; a hand painted sign read *Peanut Acres* and nestled on the green plants were enormous Nutter-Butter cookies. An old lady in a brilliant orange dress topped with a golden yellow apron worked away in the garden, her pockets bulging with Nutter-Butters.

The conductor rolled down his window and waved. "Gramma Nutt!" he called. As she waved back, a Nutter-Butter-shaped dog barked and wagged its tail.

Belle watched it all entranced and delighted. *I know this place! I am going home!* she thought, her joy permeating her entire frame.

The train chugged on, past Peanut Acres and into the Lollipop Woods. The colors were brilliant, blueberry, cherry, lemon, and orange, each shaped as round trees.

This is Candy Land! Belle marveled, and at that, a red-haired sprite in a purple dress waved a red lollipop Belle waved back saying, "Hi, Lolli!"

The Lollipop Woods gave way then to a frosty lake with a skating princess in a pink sparkly dress. She held a snowflake wand and waved it at the train. Sugared snowflakes danced and Belle grinned anew, fully enchanted. The glitter of sugary white gave way to a dark sludge. On second glance, Belle recognized the Chocolate Swamp. Sure enough, Gloppy, a huge human-faced chocolate glob, was spotted doing the back stroke. Fudgesicles edged the swamp like garden hedges. Gloppy tossed a handful of chocolate chips up in the air and caught them in his open mouth. Belle laughed and felt better for it.

The sunlight turned rainbow and she looked ahead to paths made of M&Ms that led to a castle made of candy. The train slowed as her adrenaline amped.

Candy cane arches! she thought and spotted a caramel fountain that gave way to gumdrops and Starbursts forming brick and stone patterns. Necco Wafers formed the tiled roof, the shutters were made of ice cream cones and pink cotton candy topiaries flanked the front door.

The conductor motioned to the train exit. "Missy, we're here!"

Smiling, Belle edged to the step, her happiness overflowing. The conductor helped her to the platform and she turned to say thank you, no longer questioning where she was going or what would happen. She was in Candy Land at the Candy Castle where soon she would meet King Kandy! Surely, he would help her get home. Belle scooted to the castle doors at a jog, happiness escaping in her laughter.

sixteen

"WHERE'D BELLE GO?" HARV ASKED, SITTING AT MISS Tabatha's kitchen table with a cup of her magic cocoa, barely tasting the rich chocolate. He poked at his marshmallows with one of Belle's candy canes as his eyes fell to the jar she'd left behind. Were those canes replenishing themselves? He was still staring at the cannister when the innkeeper responded, her tone edgy.

"She's gone home, of course."

"North Pole," Harv said not intending the derision in his voice.

"Don't take that tone with me, young man," Miss Tabatha returned waiting for him to look up. "You are a stubborn man, set in your ways," she said shaking her head and her finger his direction. "If you don't watch out, this trap of your own making will be your undoing!"

Harv huffed once not looking at her face. The old woman had him pegged and he felt awful. His hand went to his cheek to scratch and he moved his fingers through his new beard. He hadn't shaved and his hair needed a wash. Five days had elapsed since he took Walter from the inn and turned his back on the woman he loved.

And now she's gone. Is she gone for good?

"That is entirely up to you," Miss Tabatha said as if answering his unspoken thoughts.

Harv raised his gaze; she was an odd one and often seemed

to know what he was thinking. Harv watched her dribble a hit of Grand Marnier into her cocoa.

"Walter won't work at The Bake Shoppe without Belle," Harv sighed. "He still goes in but won't help Jay or Magee bake. It makes him too sad."

"Hmph," the innkeeper said sipping her spiked cocoa and most likely biting her tongue of more things she would like to admonish Harv for.

"Magee lets him sweep—"

Miss Tabatha's silvery-gray eyes came up. "Aren't you home for Christmas break?" Harv nodded once. "Then take care of your son yourself. Do some holiday stuff together. It's not rocket-science…" She muttered the last phrase with a shake of the head, and then mumbled even lower after taking a new swig, *"menfolk sometimes make everything so complicated!"*

Harv made no reply. Even if the liquor added spunk to her spoken opinion, the old woman meant that it was time Harv parented and stopped moping around. Before Belle started with the *Santa is real* schtick, he thought life had finally turned around for the better.

"Have a shortbread candy cane cookie, Belle's recipe," Miss Tabatha said interrupting his train of thought. She opened a tin and pushed it over. "Cookies have a way of making everything seem less serious."

"Do you think she's nuts?" Harv let slip.

Miss Tabatha shook her head. "The question, Harv, is do *you* think she's nuts. I'm not the one professing his undying love before an entire village."

"But what if she is?" He picked up a cookie and absently nibbled, his gaze soft and far off.

"So, what if she is?" Miss Tabatha tossed back. "Besides, I don't think that's the real question."

"What do you mean?" he asked. *If she is?* Was he supposed to ignore that? And what was the real question?

"Take these cookies to Walter. Tell him he can drop by whenever he likes. Tell him I miss him." Tabatha instructed and then stood and crossed her arms. *Time to leave, Harv,* her posture said. He wanted to object, but she turned for the front door and he swallowed down the rest of his cocoa in three gulps in order to meet her at the foyer.

Miss Tabatha handed him the tin of cookies. "Thanks for stopping by."

Harv sighed and started across the porch. He turned back as she was closing the door. "Miss Tabatha, where is she really?"

"I told you already. She's gone home," Miss Tabatha responded and with the soft whoosh of the heavy door, she was gone.

seventeen

"THE SLEIGH LOOKS FABULOUS! I SEE YOU BROUGHT out the ermine throw and polished the bells!" Nicole beamed at her husband.

Nickolas blushed. "It's not every day we get our girl back." Then he slipped in, "Even under these conditions …"

"Now-now, dear, matters of the heart are something even *you* can't control." She laid a plump hand affectionately to his cheek. "Let's go get her."

Nicole climbed into the sleigh settling the ermine throw over her lap and pulling her red velvet fur-trimmed hood around her silver curls. The reindeer stood patient, understanding the importance of the outing, no nudging, no squirming, on the ready. Nickolas dropped into place and as he picked up the reins, Sprinkles, the malamute puppy raced through the snow and leapt upon Nicole's lap.

"You can come along!" Nicole ruffled her fur. "Now, my dear, you think you can drive?"

"I've been doing my knee therapy and anyway, it's not like flying around the world."

Satisfied and a little desperate, Nicole nodded. Nickolas tightened the reins. With a whistle and a wink, they were off. Sprays of snow flew up as they raced along, powdering the air in their wake. Sprinkles crawled under the ermine throw on

Nicole's lap but kept her head out, her big eyes cautious.

"That's a girl, you settle." Nicole rubbed the spot between her brows.

The evergreens they passed were festooned in snowflake garlands and twilight glistened like silver glitter in a snow globe. Nickolas's cheeks were red and his eyes flashing. He looked like his old self—energized, revitalized. The setting sun's rays bouncing off Candy Castle caused a rainbow glow that spanned the horizon. Nicole grinned; it had been a while since they'd seen their old friend King Kandy. The icy roadways gave way to cobblestone made of gigantic M&M's.

As they came up the drive to the huge front door, twinkle lights on the cotton candy topiaries winked. Nickolas reached down to pluck a jellied orange slice.

"Dear, please don't nibble the landscaping." Nicole raised her eyebrows and Nickolas had the decency to look reprimanded. As they walked up to the castle, Nicole spoke again. "And that includes the building."

Nickolas gave a jolly laugh, pulled a candy cane from his pocket, and popped it into his mouth.

Before they could grasp the lollipop door knocker, the door swung in and King Kandy bellowed, "Nickolas! Nicole! Come in! Come in!" It was old friends and good times all over again. "Belle is anxious to see you and get home."

King Kandy was a big man, bigger than Nickolas, certainly as old, possibly heavier. His purple robe was trimmed in white fur and strings of M&M's and candy corn hung about his neck. His puffy purple fur-trimmed crown was enhanced with Starbursts and more of the M&M's he loved so. His red-and-white peppermint scepter was studded with LaffyTaffy and cut rock. On his feet, black boots shone with more cut rock, gum drops, and sprinkles all creating a brilliant mosaic.

Nickolas and Nicole were barely through the door when Belle ran into view and fell in their arms crying with joy. Nicole also wiped away happy tears and Nikolas dabbed his cheeks with an enormous red-and-white striped hanky.

Tearful himself, King Kandy watched on and offered, "Dear friends, Belle filled me in on everything that transpired, from her crash, to losing her memory, to ending up coming home from a place called Nantucket. I suspect you all are anxious to turn that sleigh around and head home, time is short. Time is very short."

"King Kandy…" Belle took his hand. "Thank you for everything. You rescued me through and through with your kindness!"

"My pleasure, my dear. I'll come by and visit before Christmas Eve. Here is a little something for the ride." He passed over a picnic basket made of woven candy canes and lifted the lid to give Nicole a peek. Nestled among the red and green M&M's were chocolate creams, caramels, fudge chunks, and milk chocolate peanut clusters. King Kandy kissed Nicole's hand. "Always a pleasure, my dear." Then he gave Belle a tender kiss on the cheek. "Take care, my child. It will all work out. Have faith." He gave Nickolas a bear hug. "My friend, if it comes to a crisis, you know I can help deliver those toys, but I have a sweet feeling all will work out. Godspeed, before it gets too dark."

Belle and her guardians headed to the sleigh and as they approached, Sprinkles jumped out squealing with delight. Belle scooped her puppy in her arms.

"Sprinkles! You didn't forget me!"

Hardly, the dog went crazy not sure if she should lap at Belle's face, or make happy squeaking sounds, or both. Belle cradled the puppy and gave a quick pat to her beloved reindeer who graciously stood at attention.

Then it was time to go. Belle, Nikolas and Nicole settled into the sleigh, and with waves from King Kandy, they were off in the moonlight headed home.

eighteen

WALTER MISSED BELLE SO MUCH HE ACHED ALL OVER. Why had she left? Didn't she love him? This went round and round in his head. Why couldn't his dad believe her? Why could he have gone most of his life without a mom and when he was so close, lose her to grownup silliness?

Magee tried to console him but without Belle, it wasn't the same. Magee's husband was always behind the eight-ball making bread, rolls, and coffee cakes. Now that he had to add back in cookie-making, he was swamped. Walter usually sat on a tall stool behind the counter to keep Magee company. He didn't really have an assigned chore, but he didn't mind. He kept the waxed bags in a neat stack and occasionally got the broom out and swept up imaginary crumbs. Mostly, he kept his eyes glued on the door in case Belle came back.

"What do you suppose she's doing?" he asked Magee nearby arranging the displays.

"I suspect she's making cookies for the elves about now."

This was his favorite answer because he could picture her doing just that. "Which cookies ya-think?"

"Oh, wow, I guess maybe Christmas tree cutouts, or Rudolph Reindeer gingerbread with red-hot noses."

"Yeahhh." He twirled his ankle with a sigh. "Do you think she's thinking about us?" Walter looked off as though he could see all the way to the North Pole.

"I'm sure she is." Magee said. "Do you want a brownie?"

"No, thanks. I brought an apple." Walter never turned down sweets before Belle left, but now? He didn't feel sweet inside or out.

The door to the bakery jangled and they both looked up. It was Miss Tabatha.

"Hi, you two."

"Miss Tabatha!" Walter said the name like a lifeline. "Any word?"

"Not yet. But she has my extra cell phone. I suspect when she's all tucked in, she'll call." Tabatha inhaled. "Magee, it smells wonderful in here as always."

Magee smiled a thank you and went to arranging a tray of Chocolate Chunkers.

"I'll have a loaf of Portuguese bread." Miss Tabatha pointed to a loaf near the front of the case. "That coffee ring looks very nice." She pointed to a crumbly apple and cinnamon number. "Walter, how are the Chocolate Chunkers today?" She looked at him with kind eyes.

"I don't know…" Walter was so happy to see Miss Tabatha he forgot his sales pitch.

"Why don't I get a dozen and you and I can find out. I've got some takeout chowder from Captain Toby's in the car and thought you might want to come over and eat with me."

Walter's face lit up and Magee mouthed 'thank you'.

"I thought we could stop at the Toy Boat and maybe get a new jigsaw puzzle to work on." As she paid Magee she added, "Don't stop making the chocolate sea shells for the cake or those little chocolate boxes that look like presents."

Walter perked up.

"We may still have that wedding," she said with a confidence that gave Walter new hope.

As they headed to Miss Tabatha's car, Walter wheeling his bike, he asked excitedly, "Do you really think we'll have the wedding, Miss Tabatha?"

She looked straight at him. "We can't give up hope now, can we?" Then she stowed his child's bike in the back seat of her car and they walked together into town.

The streetlights were swirled with Christmas greens and the weather had taken a decided turn. The Toy Boat was busy with people Christmas shopping. The whirl of an electric train greeted them as they opened the door creating an atmosphere like that of being in Santa's toy shop. All displays overflowed with extra merchandise, gameboards were stacked high, baby dolls and stuffed animals everywhere. Children's tea sets filled their assigned shelves and all available stock had been moved from the back for the customers to choose from.

"Pick us out a puzzle while I look around. Don't get us a baby one, you hear?" Miss Tabatha warned.

With an assertive nod, Walter headed off to a display of jigsaws while Miss Tabatha headed to the back room. Harv was putting the finishing touches on a pink dollhouse with a dainty artist's brush in his hand and black paint open on the workbench.

"Miss Tabatha, hello." He stopped mid-action and a droplet of paint fell to the floor.

"Hi, Harv. Walter and I stopped in for a new puzzle. I thought he could come over for a while and have supper with me. Maybe even spend the night, have a little sleepover."

"Uh, sure."

Harv looked bad and Tabatha's concern grew. "Why don't you come by when you're done working and eat with us? I picked up chowder from Captain Toby's. If you stop at home first, you can grab Walter's backpack and toothbrush."

Harv nodded and finally asked, "Any word…?"

Miss Tabatha shook her head no. The paint on Harv's brush was drying but he was a million miles away. With a sad *tsk,* she said goodbye and returned to the sales floor. Walter came close, a gameboard clutched to his chest.

"Miss Tabatha—I found a game. Can we get it instead of a puzzle? I do puzzles at home because I can do them alone. But a game, you need two people."

"Of course, honey lamb," Miss Tabatha said automatically. Her goal had been to get Walter out of Magee's hair, and to see if maybe she could cheer him up. Miss Tabatha's heart broke a crack for Walter's comment, that his father did not play games with him near often enough.

"Miss Tabatha, if Dad finds Belle and they get married and I land up with a mom, do you think they might have a brother for me to play games with?"

Walter was so serious that Miss Tabatha wanted to cry. Instead she sighed, "What if they had a sister instead?"

Walter looked as if he had never considered such a thing. "You mean a *girl* baby?"

"It could happen." On a more cheerful note she added. "You have Billy. Ask him to play some times."

"Nah. At Billy's house we use all his stuff or we're outside messing around." Walter grew pensive. "Miss Tabatha, do you think Belle will come back?"

"I have faith she will. We must be patient."

"What about Dad? Is he not going to try to find her?"

They were now at the counter and Miss Tabatha paid for their game and a deck of Go Fish. On the counter sat a rack of stuffed animals and she snagged a fluffy malamute puppy adding it to her purchases, the counter height preventing Walter's interest.

"I think your dad wants to find her," she said completing her purchase.

"Good. He should." Walter looked hopeful.

"I agree," she said and pat his head.

Returning to the cobblestone sidewalk, Miss Tabatha held the big Toy Boat shopping bag and Walter held her free hand.

He looked into her weathered face. "Miss Tabatha, I think he's running out of time."

Tabatha said nothing, but the boy was right.

Harv had not restarted his painting task since the innkeeper left, his brush still hanging in midair, the acrylic paint dried up and ruined.

Where has Belle gotten off to? The North Pole? Seriously?

His mind traveled to their walks on the beach, how she charmed him with her every glance. He recalled how absolutely fascinated she had been by the seashore, the sand between her toes, the lapping of the water. It was obvious now that she had never been to a beach. Wherever she was from must have been inland.

And chowder. Belle loved chowder…

Miss Tabatha invited him over tonight for some of Captain Toby's delicious chowder.

Belle loved chowder, scallops, crab, and lobster.

She had loved the beach roses and couldn't help but stop to smell them whenever they'd gone for a walk. The hydrangeas he had taken for granted all his life, she adored.

"How can a flower be blue? Where I'm from everything is white," she had said. Harv hadn't questioned it then. Had he even paid attention? Of course, he thought she meant white flowers—not snow. Could she really be from the North Pole? The chilly nights on the island didn't faze her; she wore only a thin cardigan at best. Did people—*real people*—live at the North Pole?

If she's from the North Pole, that could explain why she loves Christmas so much...

Harv had always been obsessed with Christmas himself. There was something about that magical time of year that made him feel good, warm, like eating one of Belle's cookies right from the oven.

"Belle… Heaven help me, but I miss her so much."

Harv dropped his brush in a jar of water, got another one out and went back to painting. His gloom was turning into despair with every tick of the clock.

nineteen

"NICKOLAS! NICOLE! I HAVE SO MUCH TO TELL YOU!" Belle said as they zoomed toward home.

The sleigh ride through the frosty pines gave way to a settlement whose red-and-white striped sign simply read, *Santa's Village*. Belle's heart quickened at the sight. The elves had laced it with evergreen boughs and silver balls, and adjacent a makeshift sign read, *Welcome Home Belle!* in silver glitter.

Belle sighed, holding Sprinkles close. "I feel as though I've been gone a very long time."

The sleigh pulled under candy cane arches onto a street cobbled in red-and-white peppermints. The pine trees were decorated, their twinkle lights winking. The elves wore their finest green-and-red felt waistcoats, britches, and striped socks. Their pointy caps sat at jaunty angles and their faces shone with excitement. As the sleigh pulled onto Main Street, they cheered and chanted Belle's name. Tears rose in her eyes as they rode through the village. You would never have known it was late; everything blazed with light or bustled with activity.

The Cocoa Bar with its peppermint swirl chairs and tables was open. Several elves sat under the striped awning enjoying steaming cups of hot chocolate. The roof was shaped like a white mug with swirls of steam coming out and a huge candy cane stirrer standing tall.

The Candy Shoppe was the front for the Candy Factory that made all the Christmas favorites from cut rock to candy ribbon.

They came to the elves gym where they worked to stay in shape. Everything was smaller than you would expect from the red-and-green tiny treadmills to the silver sparkled recumbent bikes.

Next was a building whose roof was covered in every size chimney known to man. This was Santa's practice area. Inside was Santa's gym to keep him chimney-fit.

"That's where I've been doing all my knee therapy," Nickolas told Belle pointing as they passed.

The Gift Wrap Shoppe and Factory was next, followed by the Ribbon Shoppe and Factory, and the Tag Shoppe. The sign for the tag shoppe was, of course, a gigantic carved wooden tag.

They came up to Santa's Post Office where all the letters children sent to Santa were received and sorted for Santa to read. Lights were on, reminding Belle that this time of year, the postal elves were working round the clock and they would not allow a single letter to go un-opened.

Shoppes and eateries gave way to the Toy Workshop. It looked like a rustic lodge but upon closer inspection, one could see a gigantic rocking horse on the peaked roof. Nickolas pointed to a newer building that looked like a life-size dollhouse.

"Requests have been so great we've opened a dollhouse factory. We've had to also step up our dollhouse furniture production, which has its own building behind," Nikolas gestured proudly.

A 1/10-scale train ran behind and between the buildings with brightly colored train cars painted like packages. Elves popped on and off at different locations.

"Are you behind?" Belle hated to ask but had to.

"No, my dear, production is right on schedule, although shifts have been working round the clock."

Belle looked off to her right to the elves' cottages. Some were lit; others were dark, where she knew they were resting.

Nickolas didn't mention Christmas Eve, and Belle was too exhausted and too excited to bring it up.

Nicole patted her lovingly. "My dear, once you're rested, we'll have plenty of time to talk."

Belle released a sigh and stared at the familiar sites she loved and had so missed. The movie theater that only showed Christmas movies had its marquee shining bright. She smelled the Sugar Plum Shoppe and Factory before they even reached its façade. Gigantic rainbow sugar plums covered the roof and sidewalk, animated to dance and spin. An elf ran up to the sleigh and handed her a box.

"Thank you, Higgins!" she said and the elf bowed and blushed.

They passed the Naughty and Nice Archives, the library of all Christmas books, and finally, Santa's chalet loomed before them. It was split logs with a massive porch. Off a bit and behind was a colossal log barn for the reindeer. Another carriage-house structure held the sleighs. Nickolas had broken out his favorite to fetch her from King Kandy.

"We've built a new flying sleigh," Nicolas said. "Supercharged and hopefully crashproof. I'm sorry, my dear, for all you've been through."

"I'm sorry, too, so very sorry. I've made a muddle of everything." Belle brushed at a tear. She'd replayed it a million times. Could she have prevented it? Taken control before they went down? The speed of the crash had been overwhelmingly fast, caught her by surprise, and probably Chris, too. For the millionth time, she hoped he hadn't suffered.

"Nonsense, my dear," Nicole chimed in. "Odds and probabilities, you know. Why, we have not had a crash in a thousand years! We were due! We are heartbroken about Chris, but none of this was your fault." She patted Belle's arm. "Fate has a way of working everything out without our input."

Belle swallowed hard. "Why was I spared?"

"Because better things are round the corner for you!" Nicole answered. As they pulled up to the chalet, Nicole got serious. "We picked Chris for you and he wasn't good enough. We wanted him to be, and he was close, but in matters of the human heart, it simply must run its own course. The only guiding hand can be fate itself. We interfered with that. If anyone is to blame, it is us."

"Please don't feel responsible," Belle pleaded. "Besides, you know Chris was a daredevil and this is the way he would have wanted to go out." Belle jumped out of the sleigh and held a hand for Nicole.

Nicole disembarked from the sleigh. "My dear, you are so young but also so wise."

The three linked arms and headed onto the great porch. The front door was massive and carved to look like Santa's sack of toys. When one grasped the silver cord tie of the sack, you entered into another world. The scent of gingerbread greeted them along with the warmth of home. The spacious foyer gave way to a great room with an endless stone fireplace. The stockings were hung, the logs blazed. The hooked rug in a patchwork pattern suddenly reminded Belle of Claire Murray's handmade rugs on Nantucket. *Nicole would like one of Claire's rugs for the kitchen,* she mused inside but cleared her mind.

The oversized red leather chairs sat grouped by the fire. A log coffee table was set with a red-and-white striped cocoa pot and matching mugs. Nickolas's spare eyeglasses sat next to a pile of letters waiting to be opened, read, and sorted. Bookshelves spilling with volumes, and fur throws on massive sofas for snuggling added to the room she loved and missed. She ran to the cathedral window to take in the pines always lit with twinkle lights and stopped short, her mouth ajar. She pointed, her eyes wide. Construction was underway for what looked like another chalet. It was set back and nestled under the graceful hemlocks.

"What is this?" she asked in wonder.

Nicole and Nickolas came to her side. "My dear, we've started a house for you."

They didn't say Chris's name, but Nickolas picked up the ball.

"Someday, you're going to want your own home with your own family."

"And my husband?" Belle whispered as Harv returned to mind full force. She missed him so badly that her heart hurt. When she could hold it no longer, she allowed a new round of sobbing, her first breakdown since arriving at the North Pole.

"Come on, my dear, why don't you get some rest, it's been a very long day," Nicole said and led her to her old room.

Belle agreed and walked, leaning into her adopted mother's embrace the whole way.

twenty

"MISS TABATHA! I GOT THE GAME SET UP. YOU READY?" The Tuck You Inn hummed with energy as Walter carefully cleared the coffee table of the various fragile knickknacks and arranged Candy Land with all its game pieces.

"I'm getting the popcorn," Miss Tabatha called and appeared with a huge bowl and a roll of paper towels.

"I can't believe I'm five years old and I've never played Candy Land!" Walter was already fascinated by Lord Licorice and the Licorice Forest. "Do you think Lord Licorice is evil?" he asked studying the images on the board.

Miss Tabatha looked hard in the same area and shrugged. "He looks evil enough."

"Would those licorice trees be as big as telephone poles?" Walter moved forward to the Gum Drop Mountains. "Do you think those mountains are real mountains covered in gum drops or they are gum drops all the way through."

Miss Tabatha moved her gingerbread game token. "Ummm…"

"Do you think Gloppy ever comes out of the Chocolate Swamp? If he did, he'd make a mess I'm sure!" Walter giggled at the picture in his mind of the character leaving a chocolate trail everywhere he went.

"Well, I suppose," Miss Tabatha said and she didn't sound like she knew for sure.

Walter continued his observations, mostly enjoying his

own voice. How could she know unless she'd been there? He cut her some slack and added, "If he stays in the Chocolate Swamp, he must only eat chocolate, unless Lolli brings him food now and then. I wonder how big the castle is. Do you think King Kandy really lives in it? And if he does, is there candy furniture?"

In the game, Walter and Miss Tabatha made it to the castle in good time and it was still early.

Walter gave her an eager look. "Wanna play again?"

Miss Tabatha tightened her lips and then her eyes widened. "I have an idea. Let's make gingerbread!"

Walter frowned and leaned back in his chair. He didn't want to bake without Belle. Besides, gingerbread wasn't even a cookie as far as he was concerned. He didn't say anything, but Miss Tabatha seemed to have read his mind.

"Not just *any* gingerbread. Let's make a gingerbread castle and decorate it with candy. It can be the Candy Castle."

Walter brightened. "But won't that take a really long time?"

"Yes, it will. We'll make up a big batch of dough and while it's chilling, we'll run to the store for the candy."

"Can we bring the board, so we get the right stuff?" Walter's mind spun with possibilities.

"Absolutely! We'll put it in my tote bag and prop it up in our grocery cart at the store."

So, in short order, side-by-side, Miss Tabatha and Walter cracked eggs and measured brown sugar. An hour later there was enough dough in the refrigerator to make a dozen castles he thought. They headed to the car with the board game tucked into Miss Tabatha's tote and as they drove, Miss Tabatha mapped out the plan.

"After we get the candy, we'll need to sort it on the counter."

"Open it all?" Walter asked excited, picturing this being as much fun as Halloween. Of course, he'd have to try some, to make sure it was good enough for their castle.

"Uh-huh." Miss Tabatha smiled. "And tomorrow morning first thing, we'll start baking, so by lunchtime we'll be ready to decorate. Now, don't let me forget to get lots of powdered sugar and extra eggs."

"What for?"

"We'll use the egg whites and the powdered sugar to make the plaster and the snow drips, and to glue the candy to our castle."

Walter's eyes gleamed. "This will be like when Dad and I build things, only we can eat parts of it."

"Exactly!"

Once in the grocery store, they first loaded the bottom of the cart with bags of powdered sugar and set the eggs in the baby seat. Next, they headed to the candy aisle with the board open leaning on the egg cartons.

"Licorice!" Walter called as he ran to get a bag. "For the licorice trees! We'll put a few outside our castle, only we'll use red licorice for good trees."

They found Necco Wafers, and gumdrops, and M&M's first and Miss Tabatha got a few extra bags for eating.

"What should we use around the bottom?" she asked.

Walter looked and labored and finally decided on caramels because they looked like rocks. They chose tiny peppermint sticks to outline the windows, chocolate chips to use as more stone foundation, and Starbursts for rainbow building blocks. Anything that had a cute shape or was a great color, they threw in their cart. Fruit Life Savers, Teddy Grahams, candy corn, Jelly Babies, Swedish Fish, Gummy Bears, jellied orange slices, Ring Pops that looked like gigantic diamonds, Non Pariels, and some red licorice pipes which Walter was sure Santa would like.

"My goodness!" The checkout girl exclaimed when they reached her counter. "It isn't Halloween!"

"We're making a Candy Castle!" Walter proudly explained.

"The one from Candy Land!" He showed her his board.

"I'd like to see that," she said smiling and Walter gave Miss Tabatha a look that said she had come up with a great idea.

In the end, they had sixteen bags of candy. Once back at the inn, Walter helped lug them into the kitchen and place the bags so none would be on top of each other.

The eggs went into the refrigerator before they could begin sorting. When the last bag was set in line to be opened, Walter realized he was hungry.

"I am too!" Miss Tabatha replied and dug around in the refrigerator for the leftover chowder. Once it was heated, she and Walter ate while planning their castle.

"Hey, what's this?" Walter asked when they had put their bowls in the sink. It was a stuffed Malamute puppy forgotten on a chair.

"Oh!" Miss Tabatha said with her hands to her cheeks. "I thought you might like to have it."

"Is this what Sprinkles looks like?" he asked thinking now of Belle's dog. One day, he'd get to see it in person. Or at least, part of him believed he might.

"I think so," Miss Tabatha assured.

Walter liked that, pretending he had Belle's puppy with him. Maybe he was taking care of Sprinkles while Belle was on her trip. Maybe she'd be back soon and they would be reunited.

When Miss Tabatha directed him to brush his teeth and go to bed, Walter took Sprinkles with him, one red licorice pipe in his free hand, and his mind running over their big plans to work on the castle in the morning.

Belle lay very still. Why couldn't she hear the soft lapping of the ocean on the shore? What about the call of seagulls? Where was she? Panic reigned for a moment until she opened one eye and looked up. Overhead, a lace canopy crocheted in a snowflake pattern.

"I'm home," she breathed.

Belle pulled her red-and-green tartan quilt under her chin and tugged, her blanket weighted by a sleeping Sprinkles. Noticing she was awake, the pup inched up to find her hand for a pat. The matching curtains had been left open and the morning light filtered through snowflake lace sheers, throwing patterns on the walls.

Belle was safe and secure and where she belonged, but the cursor that blinked of what (and who) she left behind prevented 100% joy. Nonetheless, she *was* happy.

Stretching, she swung her legs off the side of the bed finding her red shearling slippers. Pulling on her tartan robe, she scooped Sprinkles and padded to her bathroom. A gigantic clawfoot tub sat in one corner and a diminutive potbelly stove sat in another. She was too energized for a calming soak, so she popped into the shower, singing, "Santa Claus is coming to Town," ready to get on with her day.

Soon after, girl and pup danced down the split log stairway to the main floor following the aroma of breakfast. In the vast kitchen, Nicole was turning sausages in a cast-iron skillet and batter dripped from the seam of a steaming waffle iron.

"Just in time, my dear. Are you hungry?" Nicole asked singsong.

"Famished! Other than some toffee at Candy Castle, I can't remember when I ate last." Belle sat at the huge round maple table and Sprinkles curled underneath in her fluffy red doggy bed. The Samoyeds, forming a cozy white dog pile, were asleep by the kitchen hearth where a cheery fire crackled. "Have you eaten?" Belle asked Nicole.

"No, I waited for you. Nickolas has been in the workshop for hours." When Belle looked concerned Nicole waved it away. "We're on top of it but he likes to keep his finger on everything. It keeps him busy so he doesn't think about …"

"Christmas Eve?" Belle stopped pouring their cocoa and met Nicole's eye.

"Christmas Eve," Nicole nodded, dividing the waffles. She slipped crispy sausages on each plate. Before she sat, she slipped a bite under the table to Sprinkles. Belle raised an eyebrow, but Nicole explained before she could object. "I took to spoiling her a little while you were gone."

Belle softened, grateful. "Again, I'm so sorry about Chris on many levels, not the least of which is Christmas Eve." Belle bit her bottom lip not sure what else to say.

Nicole drowned her waffles in syrup. "I'm sorry he's gone, but for the multitudes still here, we need to look forward."

Belle released a slow breath. Maybe that was all the talk of Chris that they would require. She remembered now; she *had* liked him. He was funny and cute and outgoing. But only when her heart pointed toward Harv did she realize there was a deeper emotion available. Was it love? Belle truly believed it was.

Why did it end up so awful? Belle nibbled the delicious burnt end of her sausage and sighed. Nicole gave her a smile.

"Spill," she said, also biting the charred ends first.

"I was just thinking… When you met Nickolas, was it easy?"

"Goodness no, my dear, Nickolas is an opinionated and stubborn man." Belle raised a questioning brow and Nicole continued. "Don't get me wrong, he is kindness personified, the perfect Santa. But he can be very trying."

"But…" Belle began and Nicole waved one hand.

"Oh, I love him—he's my world. And when I fell for him, I didn't know what hit me." She laughed at her thoughts. "I think our courtship was more a struggle than anything. He knew he had a brilliant future ahead of him, he was ready to do great things, and being Santa Claus is that. But he often forgot the small things, the humble things. He was very caught up in the bigness of his future, the glamour, even the power. It's a very powerful position you know. Dating was emotional, not cut and dry, and it didn't fit on a tidy schedule like Christmas. It was very tough."

Belle looked closely at Nicole. "Yet, today he is *so perfect.*"

"You called it—*today* he's perfect." Nicole laughed. "Today's Santa took shaping and compromise on both our parts to find the balance and partnership we enjoy today."

Belle translated everything she said to imagining herself and Harv. Even though he rejected her, something deep inside assured he was the one. How to make that happen, she had no idea.

Nicole's face softened as she continued. "Nickolas knew he loved me, but the balance escaped him." She held up both hands, palm down and raised one higher than the other as a scale. "Romance and relationship… Santa and a world full of children." Nicole's palms alternated up and down and Belle watched, thinking this made perfect sense. "He's a bit of a steamroller in case you hadn't noticed," Nicole added and they both laughed. "Maybe it was harder for him than a more moderate person to allow himself to be vulnerable, to accept love."

Belle inhaled; Nicole had touched on her matter perfectly.

Nicole waved it off. "Matters of the heart are their own animal, but they work themselves out one way or another."

It seemed time to speak of Nantucket and Belle began in a soft voice. "I met a man…"

"Harvey Nichols," Nicole finished with a knowing nod.

"Yes, he goes by Harv. You knew?" Belle's eyes grew wide.

"A little. Our sight only goes so far," Nicole confessed.

"Ah… well, you see, he lost his wife in a tragic accident," Belle began, her voice soft and her heart daring to crack. "And he had to raise their son on his own…"

"Walter?"

Belle gave a gentle nod. "I love them so much… It's as though my crash was guided specifically to *them.*"

"That is very possible, my dear. I've seen it many times in my long life. A crash you couldn't avoid landing you, perhaps, where you belonged."

"Everything was perfect until…" Belle set down her fork, her appetite all but erased with heartache. "I overwhelmed him. I think he's afraid. Not of being Santa, but of giving his heart away. I think when all was said and done, he freaked and used my Santa destiny as an out."

Nicole's eyes said she understood, and she changed their topic to joyful Christmas Eve planning. By the time Nikolas came in to eat, Belle was able to smile and mean it. No matter what happened, she was home, and the two people who loved her most would help her sort the rest.

twenty-one

HARV COULD NOT CONCENTRATE. THANK GOODNESS school was out for the holidays. He needed to get a grip; he had been wandering in a fog for days. He was behind on his Toy Boat projects and he was snapping at Walter—

Walter's at the Tuck You Inn! Where's my head?

When the old innkeeper invited him to come by after work, he had fallen into despair even further and begged off. Instead, he left the Toy Boat at 9 PM and went to the cottage alone. He had poured a double and hit the hay. Now it was morning and the woman probably would enjoy a respite from babysitting such an active child. It was time to collect him and maybe Harv should buy Walter a treat since he'd been so cranky.

Heck, maybe something for Miss Tabatha for watching him.

On the way to the inn, Harv stopped at the Fast Break and grabbed a bag of licorice. Noticing a display of miniature poinsettia plants, he nabbed one of those as well. Pouring a cup of strong convenience store coffee, he headed to the checkout.

What was it about Belle that got under his skin? It went without saying that she was beautiful. Was it her eyes? They looked *right into him,* she saw who he really was and liked him anyway. Whatever she saw when she looked at him, he missed that expression of selfless love when their eyes met. And didn't she make every tiny thing seem new again? It wasn't because she lost her memory, it was more than that. Everyday things fascinated her and brought her joy. Things he overlooked or forgot about. When he was with her, he saw them, too, and appreciated them all over again. From butterflies to seashells, she helped Harv see the beauty in the mundane that he took for granted. And she excited him; true electricity radiated between them from the start. Harv wanted to marry her, have her with him for life, have those feelings buzzing around him all the time. Granted, she was different but also unique, special, and irreplaceable. He missed her sweetness and tenderness, this moment, right now, as he was about to drive to the Tuck You Inn and face Walter, the boy who blamed him for Belle's departure, reportedly, to the North Pole.

Harv scoffed and then frowned deep.

Come on. No one lives there…

He walked to his car. He was afraid of the "what-ifs". What if he decided to believe her and was made a fool? What if she turned out to be a bonafide nut case? What if she returned and was committed to an insane asylum? Was there even one nearby? Certainly not on island.

What if she's telling the truth and I'm too hardheaded to open my ears?

What if he hadn't opened his heart for so long that he wasn't able to love her the way he wanted? The way she deserved? What if he let her down? But he knew, as he slumped into the driver's seat, if he didn't try, he'd never know.

"Hey, Harv! What's the scoop? Is there still a wedding?"

Harv looked up. It was the editor of Nantucket Magazine, interrupting his thoughts.

"Tabatha Tucker told Magee who told her husband who told my sister at the drycleaners that there was going to be a party regardless if the young woman makes it back in time."

"Oh, huh," Harv mumbled, managed a nod and closed his door. What the guy would think of him, he couldn't guess. He headed for the inn hoping his rudeness would be forgiven.

Hadn't the townspeople been forgiving him for years? They may as well continue doing so.

If Tabatha and Magee planned on going forward with the reception, he understood. The plans and preparations could not be cancelled at such short notice. Harv hated to be the cause of such consternation but could figure no way to fix it.

Once at Tuck You Inn's porch, Harv knocked on the front door. When no one called out or came to let him in, he entered, calling hello as he crossed the threshold. Still, no one answered, but then he heard voices from further in, and one of those was his son.

"Quick! Quick! Miss Tabatha! More glue! The back tower's breaking!"

Walter's aggravated plea caused Harv to rush in only to find the two of them dusted with flour at the kitchen table. Miss Tabatha held a pastry tube oozing white frosting and Walter was busy bracing an enormous gingerbread house with his palms to the sides. They both looked up at his appearance for the moment ignoring the escaping frosting.

"Dad!"

"Harv!"

"What's going on?" Harv asked with a crooked grin. The kitchen looked like a war zone. The mist of powdered sugar hung in the air like smoke and the aroma tickled his nostrils with its sweet strength. Cookie sheets armored every surface scattered with mis-match puzzle-bits of gingerbread, open bags of candy decorated the counters spilling contents to the tile floor, and glops of frosting speckled every surface, including the two bakers. Harv grinned at the chaos. "What are you making?"

"A gingerbread castle!" Walter sang out. "From the Candy Land game!"

"So, I didn't just interrupt some sort of cookie battle?" Harv jibed cheeky and chose a scrap of gingerbread to drop onto his tongue. He diverted his attention from the frosting in Miss Tabatha's silver hair and focused on the edible structure Walter still braced with sticky hands. "This is really impressive."

"Thanks, Dad!" Walter belted out his excitement evident. "Did you see the stained-glass windows? We took fruit roll-ups and rolled them flatter with a rolling pin to make the glass!"

As he spoke, Miss Tabatha returned to gluing the walls to prevent collapse and Walter watched her with a supervisor's eye.

"Careful!" he said and turned to grin again at his dad. "Don't eat the shutters, Dad!"

Harv chuckled. "I won't, I promise."

He scooped a few M&Ms from an open sack and popped them in his mouth. The castle was covered in candy, from the caramel-and-M&Ms base to the pink-and-lavender Necco wafer roof. Harv marveled at the fountain constructed of a chocolate cup with red Swedish Fish carefully positioned in blue cotton candy "water". The landscaping included tiny topiaries of pink cotton candy with pretzel trunks, sitting in peanut butter cups with everything glued into place with same-colored icing. The masterpiece was enormous and sat upon the largest wooden baker's board that Harv had ever seen. Coconut was tinted green for the grass and with his hands free from holding up the near wall, Walter began laying an M&Ms path toward the doors.

"All those M&Ms will stay in place that way?" Harv asked watching his son with pride. Walter nodded and made a big show of dipping the bottom side of each candy into frosting to cement it into place.

"This will weigh as much as a castle when we're done," Miss Tabatha said and Harv agreed with a new chuckle.

"If we made smaller ones, I bet Magee could sell them," Walter said, his eyes on his job and planning ahead.

"Oh, my! That's an idea!" she said and stood up straight

from her work with a swipe to her brow. "But we do have a ton of expense in the candy."

"She could charge a ton for each one! I know they would love them. Look, Dad – it's fantastic! Don't you think so?"

Harv backed to view it all at once and gave a new nod. "I sure do. It's quite remarkable and so detailed." Harv forgot his own misery and smiled.

"Maybe we can make the gameboard, too," Walter said not ready to stop, but Miss Tabatha was worn out, which Harv could plainly see.

"I think I'll fry up some burgers," Miss Tabatha suggested. "Aren't you hungry?"

Walter admitted he could eat one and maybe some Tater Tots.

"Harv, can you eat one?" Miss Tabatha called from the freezer where she pulled out meat patties. "I've got Munster and Swiss for cheeseburgers."

"Sure, but Miss Tabatha, you don't need to feed us. You've done plenty," Harv said, still admiring the castle.

"Pish-posh," she said heating up a skillet. "I hate to eat alone. And anyway, Walter and I have more work to do on the castle."

Harv conceded with a lopsided grin. "Okay, if you say so. What can I do to help?"

"Good man! Gather up the gingerbread scraps and I'll use them in an apple cobbler."

Harv got to it and as the burgers sizzled, Tabatha dug the Granny Smiths out of the fridge to come to room temperature. Since the kitchen table held the castle and candy, she suggested the living room table and carried out napkins and silver to set the places. Then, as they ate, Walter and Miss Tabatha told Harv about building the castle.

"I wanted it even bigger," Walter said motioning with both hands, one holding a cooling tater tot. "But Miss Tabatha said we had limitations. Limitations!" he repeated with flashing eyes at both adults. "I told her life has no limitations!"

Miss Tabatha laughed. "And what did I tell you? I said, that may be, but gingerbread castles *do.*" She shook her head with a smile. "Trust me, it is already far bigger than I had planned."

"Did you notice the landscaping? I got to do the M&Ms cobblestone path, and-and-and … did you see our fishpond?"

Harv nodded yes, getting into the spirit.

"Now that you're here," Walter said, "you can make streetlights out of candy!"

Harv took another bite with a slow nod, putting his thoughts on it. "I guess I could."

"Yay! Soon as we're done eating!" Walter held his hamburger with two hands and tackled it with new fervor.

"We could use a hand, Harv," Miss Tabatha snuck in as she pushed a stray strand of frosting-coated hair off her cheek.

The next thing Harv knew he was molding LaffyTaffy into an elaborate bracket from which he had mounted a Hershey Kiss.

"Okay, let's glue 'er to the pretzel stick," he said, an oversized pretzel rod in one hand. Miss Tabatha plopped the gooey pastry bag of frosting in his other. The frosting started oozing out of the back end almost immediately. "Oh, hey, a little help here?"

"Naw, Dad—you can do it," Walter assured as he worked on a tiny flag for the tower. "It's just frostin'."

Tabatha chuckled low. "Yeah, Harv, castle making is messy, just like life sometimes," she offered with a quick glance, busy fashioning a gum drop over a marshmallow on a toothpick.

"But I don't want to make a mess," he whined.

Miss Tabatha and Walter broke out laughing. "Look around!"

Harv exhaled and looked left and right, and as he did, his

pretzel snapped. "Oh."

"Eat it, Dad," Walter chirped. "We've been eating our mistakes."

Harv dipped it in a glob of frosting and popped it in his mouth.

"See, Dad, it's a bonus! We can't eat our mistakes in your workshop." Walter pulled a pretzel out of the bag and joined his dad. Finally, two streetlights were successfully mounted in front of the castle in globs of frosting glue.

"This looks pretty good," Harv said and called them over to inspect. "What do you think?"

"They're great! How about a Hershey's Kiss over the door, like a matching light?"

"You're on." Harv dug out a LaffyTaffy for the foundation.

"Do you think we need a hedge?" Miss Tabatha asked as she held a silver dragée[iv] with tweezers and put it in the center of her gumdrop flower.

"Sure. What self-respecting castle doesn't have a hedge?"

"What should we make it out of?" Walter asked.

Harv scrutinized the candy carnage. "What do we have left?" He poked at the bag of marshmallows and tumbled a few out. "How about you tint some coconut green and we can glue it to either the marshmallows or graham crackers?"

And that is how the afternoon proceeded, with dripping frosting, eaten mistakes, one spectacular castle, and no talk about anything that wasn't related to sugar or Candy Land. When there wasn't room for even a single additional Lifesaver or gumdrop, the architects leaned back from their work with a communal sigh of satisfaction.

"We are geniuses," Walter said with a giggle.

Miss Tabatha agreed with a laugh and rose to clean up. All three hauled things to the sink, scraping bowls, spatulas, and pastry tubes. The trash can overflowed with castle-making refuse.

Walter gathered empty candy wrappers and put the few leftover pieces in a crockery bowl. "You know, so people can eat these and not our castle."

"Good idea!" she assured him with a wink. "T'would be a shame to see it nibbled down by a hungry visitor!"

"I'll mop the floor," Harv said and added, "then I'll order pizza. Anyone want salad, too?" Not too strangely, Walter and Miss Tabatha said yes, anxious for anything not made of sugar.

"Miss Tabatha, can I take a shower?" Walter asked, holding his arms out from his body, covered in frosting, mashed gumdrops, and chocolate streaks.

"Sure, honey lamb. Let me find a clean T-shirt and you can make do with your other clothes." She headed up the stairs and came back down with a red-and-white striped T-shirt. "Wear this, Belle said it looks like an elf's shirt."

"Belle wore it?" Walter asked, his eyes shining. He took possession and hugged the item as he listened for Miss Tabatha's reply. Harv looked away, afraid to awaken his pain and the old innkeeper sent his son up to bathe.

"You are a great helper, just like your son," Miss Tabatha said when she reentered the kitchen. Harv turned to see her studying their masterpiece.

"It is amazing," he marveled. He lifted his cell phone and snapped a photo of the creation. "Belle would love it," he said low, not sure if he meant to be heard or not.

"She would." Miss Tabatha remained on task, putting away the bowls and covering exposed candy with plastic wrap.

"I miss her," Harv allowed. The fun of castle-building had ended and Harv's frazzled demeanor crept back in. He ran a hand through his shaggy hair catching here and there on globbed frosting.

"We all miss her," Miss Tabatha replied just as quietly.

"Is she coming back?" Harv asked.

"I don't know. She's probably swamped with work."

"Swamped with work?" Harv's eyes narrowed. "With what?"

"Christmas is right around the corner," she said as if he should have figured that out on his own. "I imagine Nickolas and Nicole are happy to have one more pair of hands to help."

"You can't be serious," he mumbled, watching her face for any sign of a joke. It sounded like she was saying…

"I can't even imagine what all they have to do. Nickolas had planned to retire, something about his knees."

"Retire? You mean you believe—"

Just then, Walter clamored down the stairs breaking what was about to be very awkward. "Dad!" Walter hollered. "Can we play Candy Land while we eat our pizza?"

"Uh, sure." Harv's eyes had gone soft in thought. When there was a sudden knock at the door, for a second, he thought it might be Belle.

"It's the pizza guy!" Walter cheered rubbing his middle.

While Harv paid the delivery driver, Miss Tabatha set three settings at the kitchen table this time, as it had been cleared of mess, save the castle which hogged the entire center. Miss Tabatha brought out extra paper towels as they set up the board to play as they ate.

"Dad, it's your turn," Walter said and snagged a piece of pizza.

Harv drew a card. "The Licorice Forest! I remember this. When I was a kid, I was certain it was a real place." With a nostalgic grin, he moved his gingerbread piece.

"I think it *is* a real place," Walter said with a nod.

"No, son, it's only a game." Harv picked up another piece of pizza.

"It could be," Walter mused.

"Maybe it is based upon something real," said Miss Tabatha. "Does it say anything about that on the box?"

Walter dutifully wiped his hands and left the table at a

sprint for the box lid. Harv gave Miss Tabatha a look but she only shrugged.

"It can't hurt, and besides, he needs things to believe in."

"Even if they aren't true?" Harv asked with an edge.

"You don't know that," Miss Tabatha countered.

But before they could debate further, Walter was back. "It says based on Candy Land, North Pole." Then he squinted. "Is that a place? I mean a real place, on a map?"

Harv rolled his eyes.

"Go to the computer and find out," Miss Tabatha encouraged.

Walter booted up Miss Tabatha's kitchen computer and typed in *Candy Land location.*

"Dad—look." Walter gave Harv sad eyes until he rose and looked at the monitor. "Read it," he said turning a happy face to Miss Tabatha at the table.

Harv sighed and adjusted the angle of his head for the screen. "Candy Land was fashioned after a town in the northern regions of the North Pole near Santa's Village where King Kandy lives in his castle. It is a quiet place, unless Lord Licorice causes trouble or Gloppy becomes stuck in the Chocolate Swamp. Visitors are few as there is only one train to Candy Land with a limited schedule." Harv stopped reading, his shoulders drooping, weary of the game.

"Can we go there? We could go get Belle. We could meet Gloppy and Lolly and and-and-and bring Belle home!" Walter exclaimed. Despite his exuberance, exhaustion tinted his eyes.

Harv rubbed his son's head. "Let's go home. It's time we got some sleep."

"But can we go to the North Pole?" Walter persisted.

Harv picked him up as though he was still two or three, and as they headed out, he said, "We'll see."

Once they waved goodnight to Miss Tabatha, they began the trek to the empty cottage.

twenty-two

"THE ELVES LOVE THOSE CHOCOLATE CHUNKERS," Nicole said to Belle eating a third enormous sample. "And your sketches for rocking row boats for babies, very clever. We will add them to our line."

"Thank you," Belle responded to both compliments.

"Your sewing is really coming along on the doll clothes. I can tell you've been practicing."

"Thank you," she said again but this time she set down the bowl of cookie dough she was mixing, "You don't have to cheer me up. Honest. Besides…" she shrugged, defeated. "It's not working."

"I'm sorry, my dear." Nicole said, her face filled with concern.

"Do you think he'll come looking for me?" Belle asked, a little short of desperate.

"He might, my dear. We can hope. How about that?"

"He doesn't have much time," Belle said and tried to remain calm.

"No, but Nickolas assures me that he has one last run in him. It'll be fine."

Belle didn't believe she was as confident as her words. Flying the biggest sleigh was hard work, and a long, long night of it. His knees simply couldn't take it. Without forethought, she asked, "Do you think you and I could fly the sleigh?"

"Oh, my dear! What a picture! Belle and Nicole zooming

across the sky!" she said with her hands coming together at chest level. She gave Belle a kind smile. "In reality, we probably *could* fly it, but we wouldn't be Santa Claus. We'd be two Mrs. Clauses. What if a child awoke and saw us? There's too much at stake."

Belle hummed with a nod, thinking. "Could we go along—in case he needed us? I mean it would still be Santa."

"I don't know." Nicole worried her bottom lip.

"That's not a no?" Belle asked.

"No, no it's not, but there is still time to hope."

"For Harv?" Belle asked.

"That would solve a lot of problems," Nicole conceded.

"Yeah, it sure would." Belle sighed and they both sat down to a platter of Chocolate Chunkers, the bowl of dough forgotten.

"Dad, I'm not tired, honest." Walter gave it one last shot, barely able to keep his eyes open.

Harv knew what was happening. His son *liked* having his dad back to his happy self and did not want to risk in the morning, the sad and cranky dad would be back. "It's okay to hang it up," he told him. "We will do something fun tomorrow."

"Promise?"

"I do," Harv said with a pert nod. "Now go do some serious brushing of those teeth."

By the time Walter was in his PJs, Harv turned down his bed.

"I forgot Sprinkles," he said with a yawn.

"Who is Sprinkles?" *Other than Belle's dog …*

"Miss Tabatha bought me a stuffed dog that looks like Belle's puppy, so I named it Sprinkles." Walter started to get that look in his eyes, the one of a much younger boy about to cry missing his security blanket. “I need her! I can’t sleep without her! I can’t!”

“Sure, you can, guy, we’ll get her tomorrow,” Harv said but Walter couldn’t settle. “How about Sock Monkey?” Harv pulled him off the shelf and tucked him under the covers, but Walter remained upset. “Let’s add your bear and your blue dolphin.” Harv added the toys and reached for more. “And your football and … and my autographed baseball?”

He went to his own room and came back with the baseball, then snagged the football off a shelf, and tucked them in with all the stuffed animals. Walter gave a tired nod and reached up for a hug and kiss.

“Good night, big guy.”

“Dad, will we figure it out?”

“Yes, we will.” He turned out the light. “I’ll leave the door open.”

“Night, Dad.”

“Night, Walter.”

Harv carried a stack of long ignored mail to bed and began sorting it in piles. He heard the steady rhythm of his son’s breathing and he knew Walter was asleep.

He was dozing off himself when he heard Walter thrashing and crying out. Harv rushed to his room. The blue dolphin, football, and baseball went off the bed. Walter continued to call out in his sleep.

“Walter, Walter, it’s a dream.” Harv sat on the edge of the bed and cradled his son, rocking him gently. He brushed the hair off his forehead, “It’s just a dream.” His son awoke halfway, his eyes watery. “Go back to sleep and you’ll have good dreams. Dream about Candy Land.”

“Dad, will you get Dolfy and baseball? I think they fell.”

Harv scooped up the blue dolphin and tucked him in next to Walter. “I’ll get the baseball and the football. Good night, Walter.”

"Night, Dad."

Harv crouched low and felt for the football. Once that was securely beside his son on the covers, he leaned lower and searched for the baseball. He felt it with his fingertips as he stretched his arm underneath the boy's bed. It rolled out of reach and Harv pushed further in, grasping the ball that had lodged against something immoveable set center. With the baseball in his possession, he grew curious at the unknown item. After all, he was the one who put heavy things under beds, not his son. Then he saw what it was. A book. After rolling the ball behind him, Harv grasped the book with both hands and slid it into view. It was too dark to see what it might be, so he lifted it and quietly tip-toed to his own room to drop it on his bed. Harv turned on his bedside lamp and considered the book he'd lugged from under Walter's bed. The cover read simply, "The List." His curiosity growing, Harv crawled upon his covers, dragged the book onto his lap, and ran a hand over the embossed letters.

What a curious title, he thought. Harv turned to the first page. It had no table of contents, title page, or dedication and no publishing data. One large and ornate capital letter A sat at the top, followed—true to the name on the cover—by a list. Specifically, a list of names. Tons of them. Starting with the letter A. *Abby Smithson, Adam Wolke, Andy Jones, Ashton Kramer,* and on and on. Name after name, page after page.

"I don't get it," Harv mumbled, turning the pages in slow motion, his mind scrambling to make sense of it. Eventually, he landed on a page with an oversized capital B at the top. Neatly under this, more names began again and Harv scanned them. *Bernard Griffin, Bertram Whitehouse, Brenda Keller…* There was nothing after the listed name and they weren't divided male and female. Harv paged on to the 'Cs', 'Ds' and, 'Es'. He skipped to the 'J's and read. *Jim Hart. Joyce Hart.* Out of curiosity he flipped to the 'Hs' for his own name, holding his breath as he ran a finger down the list. He wasn't there. Harv wasn't sure if he was disappointed or relieved.

No, I'm tired… Exhausted, really…

With care in respect to the odd item, Harv closed the book and set it on his nightstand. Then he turned off his light and sank into sleep.

…He was lost in the pages of a gigantic book. Had he shrunk or had the book grown? The names were now four feet tall and he stood in front of them able to read the bottom three. He was still mystified by the names with no clue as to who they were or why they were listed. He walked to the far right and grasped the bottom of the page with both hands, tugging with all his might. The page separated from the rest and as it swung to the left and turned, he was knocked over. Dream-Harv crawled to his knees and leaned into the page to pull himself up. As he pressed his hands onto the paper, he heard a crackle and then a pop. The sound seemed to come from where his hands connected with the name, Marlene Pierce.

"Hey!" Suddenly, right next to him was a little girl of six or seven with long blonde hair and hazel eyes. She pushed her curls off her face. "How'd you do that?"

Harv stared in amazement. Where had she come from? "Who are you?" he countered.

"Marlene Pierce!" She gave him a *duh* look.

"Marlene Pierce …" Harv he looked at the page where he'd leaned. It didn't make sense.

The girl reached a hand out to him but Harv backed away, tripping on his own feet. Still, he caught himself, his fall broken by the book. A crackle of electricity sizzled through the air and then a pop, like a champagne cork … Then there was another child, a little boy this time the same age with black hair and a round face.

"Who are you?" He hated to ask.

Two people answered, the little boy and Marlene. "Marvin Henderson."

Marvin Henderson was the name in the book on the page across from Marlene Pierce. Who were these two and why were their names in the book? Were they trapped? Harv was too worked up to think clear. His heart hammered and he felt cold and clammy. Without an express plan, Harv began to run.

"Hey! Wait for us!" Marlene and Marvin shrieked. "Come back!"

But there was no stopping Harv. As he ran, the pages skittered under him flapping open as though he were on an amusement park ride, running as pages slipped behind him, getting nowhere. As he raced, and flailed, seeking traction—more children kept appearing. Each page he kicked up brought another child and every single one of them called to him to wait. Harv screamed, aware that they would catch him. Even now, he felt their little hands grabbing his shirttail.

"Dad! Wake up! You're having a nightmare! It's morning!" Walter sobbed at his bedside, jabbing Harv with balled fists.

Harv surfaced in increments until there weren't hundreds of calling children. Only one, crying, and shaking with fear.

Walter realized his dad was awake and jumped on top of him hugging and crying in gratitude. Then he said with urgency, "You always bring me water when I have a bad dream. Hang on! I'll bring you a cup of water!" Walter scampered off and raced to the bathroom, flipping the taps, filling the Tupperware glass that sat next to their brushes. "Drink this," he said shoving the water near.

Harv sipped and his head began to clear. He looked around his familiar bedroom and then hugged his son. Walter patted him as he had so often been patted himself. Then his eyes fell on the book: *The List.* He froze. Harv felt him tense up and his eyes followed to the source of his nightmare.

"Walter," he said, "What is that?"

His son hemmed and touched the cover. "It's a list."

"I can see that." Harv ran the fingers of both hands through his hair and scratched his scalp. "Where'd it come from?"

"Under my bed."

Harv raised one eyebrow and his son spilled more truth.

"It's Belle's."

"Belle's?" Harv raised the other eyebrow.

"Uh-huh."

"How did you get it?" Harv wanted answers.

"I found it."

"Found it?"

"When I found Belle." Walter dropped off the bed, ran into his room, and returned clutching a red velvet tote bag. "It was in this." Walter held the bag out with reverence.

Harv examined at the tote made of the same fabric as Belle's backpack. "I didn't see this."

"After they took Belle away in the ambulance it was there, so I put it in my bike basket and took it home to keep it safe."

"And?"

"And then in all the excitement, I forgot about it."

"And?"

"When I remembered, I thought I'd get in trouble for keeping it."

Harv rolled in his lips but there was more. "And?"

"When I finally looked inside and saw the book, I got scared so I shoved it under my bed."

"Until …"

"Until I could figure it out."

Harv looked in amazement. "And then I found it," Harv volunteered.

Walter nodded, relieved, "Now we know what it is."

"No, we don't," Harv admitted.

"But you know everything, I know you do…"

Harv appreciated his son's loyalty, but what was he getting at? "No, Walter, I don't have a clue. What do you think it is?"

Walter's expression dropped and he looked away.

Harv pat his shoulder. "Let's take it to Miss Tabatha. She'll know what it is."

Walter brightened and skipped to his room for his clothing.

Miss Tabatha was enjoying a half-coffee/half-cocoa, debating if she wanted an omelets or a bowl of Frosted Flakes. The eggs would give her the protein she needed to jumpstart the day, but she still couldn't give up those childhood cereals. Her ponderings were interrupted by a rapping at her door. Tabatha heaved herself upward, leaving her coffee/cocoa on the table. She overheard Harv and Walter debating something at the door.

"What brings you lads 'round bright and early?" Miss Tabatha asked blinking her eyes at the morning sunshine.

Before Harv could make small talk, Walter pointed. "This."

Harv held the heavy book out sitting atop the red velvet tote, presenting it like a cake.

"Oh, that!" Miss Tabatha exclaimed and then covered with, "Have you eaten? Come inside." She held the door as they assured her hey had not had breakfast. "Omelets or cereal?" she asked as the three headed into the kitchen. The Candy Land castle sat proudly on the kitchen table, greeting them like old friends.

"Would you make waffles?" Walter asked.

"Absolutely, with chocolate syrup."

"Yes!" Walter ran and gave her a pint-sized hug.

Tabatha gathered ingredients on autopilot and in the blink of an eye, the iron was sizzling, and she was beating eggs into her batter. "Harv, get the juice out of the fridge, would you? And some glasses from the cupboard over the sink."

Harv was still holding the book and he set it to a clean counter to do as requested.

"Anyone want bacon?" Tabatha asked as if there wasn't a weird old book beside her mixer.

Walter said crispy bacon would be great, but having set out the glasses, Harv stood lost in his thoughts.

"Harv, get that white plate out of the cupboard and put some paper towels on it," Tabatha nudged. "The bacon's in the fridge crisper. Grab us six slices and lay them on the paper towels." She was pouring batter now into the iron as she spoke, ivory droplets running down the side. The sweet scent of waffles filled the air. Harv hadn't moved. "For goodness sake, Harv, get the lead out. We should start that bacon."

"I'll do it, Miss Tabatha," Walter volunteered. "Dad's upset."

Miss Tabatha stopped, she set her bowl of batter down and turned to Harv. "Honey lamb," she said to Walter, her eyes on Harv, "take that first waffle out. I know you can do it, use a fork." She touched Harv's arm. "Harv …"

Harv resurfaced and lifted the huge book again, holding it to his body.

"Set that down and eat. You need food and caffeine. Eat a bit and then we'll talk." She guided him to a chair and then literally pried the book loose. "Walter, bring me that first waffle and grab the syrup."

Walter already had it on a plate and carried it to the table. He climbed on a stool to a cupboard and brought down the Mrs. Butterworth's and gave it to Miss Tabatha. She dumped tons on the waffle and handed Harv a fork.

"Eat this and then we'll solve whatever needs solving."

Harv ate mechanically, lost in thought.

"Miss Tabatha, I'm pouring the next waffle." On the tall

stool on folded knees, Walter carefully covered the waffle grid with more batter and closed the lid.

Miss Tabatha poured a mug of coffee for Harv and set it before him. Then she had Walter find a seat at the table where she fetched his finished waffles and handed them over on a plate.

"Hershey's!" he belted with a grin and Tabatha smiled despite herself. She snagged the chocolate syrup and handed it over.

Next, she poured batter in for herself, and while it sizzled, she put out the orange juice. There was enough batter in the bowl for maybe half a waffle. She took her golden brown one out and scraped the bowl clean to make the last partial to get Harv to eat a little more. Then she poured him a tumbler of O.J.

"Now, go ahead," she told him. "Tell me what's going on."

"We have a book of Belle's," Walter jumped in before his dad.

"Okay. What else?" Miss Tabatha pressed allowing him to speak on his father's behalf for now.

"I found it when I found Belle, and I hid it and forgot it. Then Dad found it and it scares us 'cuz we don't understand it." Walter was eating the end of his chocolate syrup with a spoon.

"Let me see it. I'm sure it isn't anything to be afraid of."

Neither Harv nor Walter made any effort to pick it up and give it to her, so she left her seat and walked over to the massive book.

"The List," she whispered and opened it. "I know what this is. I'm one-hundred-percent sure." She smiled warm as a pan of cinnamon buns.

Walter and Harv looked at her warily, yet with a glimmer of hope that Miss Tabatha would have answers.

"I'm certain." She turned to the first page, her finger to the first name and then heading down the column. "It's a list of all good children." Miss Tabatha's smile was touched with tears of joy to behold this very special book.

"What?" Harv and Walter asked, stunned.

"It's a list of all good children. Were you in it, Walter?"

Walter nodded.

Harv turned to him surprised; he hadn't thought to check for Walter's name.

Miss Tabatha had already paged to the W's and fingered down to find him. "There you are, honey lamb."

"Is Dad in there?" Walter asked in a high voice.

"Of course, not." She smiled and continued. "Harv is no longer a child. This is Santa's list, his list of good children."

"Santa?" Harv managed but Walter had warmed to the idea instantly.

"Oh, wow!" he exclaimed leaning his upper body onto the tabletop looking at the book sideways.

"Santa keeps a list of who is naughty and who is nice. This is his list of good children. If Belle and Chris were doing a trial run in the Santa sleigh, I'm sure they took a copy of The List with them."

"A copy of the list?" Harv mimicked, but with very little venom.

"But it doesn't say what anyone wants," Walter said eyes wide.

"It doesn't have to. Santa knows what the children want for Christmas, just the same as your dad knows what the island children want—only this is in a bigger way since it's the entire world."

"But Belle crashed," Walter whispered. "The List is here. Don't they need it?" Then he spoke up. "They need it. I know they need it!" Walter grew panicked. "Christmas is coming, and we have Santa's list!"

Tabatha pat his head with a smile. "Each Santa has a list.

Chris was supposed to be Santa so he had Santa Chris's list. Nikolas still has his," she said with confidence and Walter seemed relieved.

Harv fingered the ornate cover. As sometimes happens since her youth, the young man's thoughts trickled past sounding something like, *"It could be. It could be just what Miss Tabatha said. It's crazy but life is sometimes crazy…"*

Finally, she thought, *Harvey Nichols has decided to open his eyes, ears, and heart to a truth that he tamped down long ago...*

Harv leapt to his feet, his eyes blazing. "I believe you!"

"Fantastic!" Miss Tabatha clapped her hands.

"You believe?" Walter asked incredulous with a careful half-smile.

"I do! I believe this is Santa's List. And I believe Belle." His eye flicked to the front door. "I have to go find her!"

Walter and Miss Tabatha cheered.

"Help me book a flight to the North Pole!" he said heading for her computer on the counter. And a happy commotion broke out in the kitchen of the Tuck You Inn.

twenty-three

NICOLE SET THE TABLE IN THE SPODE CHRISTMAS tree china. A roast simmered in the huge old oven, and popovers sat in a basket on the table, popped to perfection. There were mashed potatoes, fruit salad, and the Chocolate Chunkers Belle had made. Belle and Nicole lit the red-and-white striped candles and waited for Nikolas.

"What do you suppose he has to tell us?" Belle finally asked.

"It could be anything," Nicole said with a sigh. "I stopped trying to guess anything related to Nikolas years ago."

"Do you think it has to do with Christmas?" Belle absently twirled a strand of her long blonde hair.

"Everything has to do with Christmas," Nicole replied.

Belle's stomach was tied in knots, but Nikolas bounded down the stairs, humming a jolly tune and barely favoring his knees. He gave Nicole a snuggle and patted Belle on the head as if she were twelve.

"Something smells delicious and I'm starved!" he bellowed with a huge smile.

Nicole brought out the roast and Nikolas carved, noting aloud that it was perfect, crispy on the edges and juicy in the center. The potatoes circulated and the rolls were loaded with butter. Nikolas ate it all, ravenous, but Nicole and Belle only pushed their food around. After his third roll, Nikolas spoke.

"My dear! You have a magical way with popovers!" He

gave his wife his famous Santa wink. "Now, I have an announcement. I'm going on a little trip…" His eyes twinkled as he reached for a Chocolate Chunker.

Nicole and Bell's mouths dropped open.

"To the Land of Nantucket!" Nikolas roared, pleased with himself.

"Why?" Nicole asked eyes wide.

"Why else? To get Belle's young man," he said and turned to Belle. "You love him, don't you?"

Belle nodded but could not speak.

"And he loves you. He told you repeatedly. Isn't that so?"

Again, Belle nodded.

"Very well. I'm going to meet him and introduce myself," Nikolas said. "We do not have time for him to become a believer on his own. I have a feeling he's close, *very* close." Nikolas gave out a few ho-ho-ho's. "By jove, if need be, I will yank this young man back by his ears! Anything to make my Belle smile again."

Belle was speechless.

"After we eat, I thought you ladies could drive me in the sleigh to Candy Land. From there, I'll catch the Candy Land Express and after a few connections, land in Nantucket."

Nicole found her voice. "You're flying commercial?"

Nikolas grinned like a child. "I've always wondered what it would be like to let someone else do the flying!"

"But the ferry? It's offseason," Belle stammered.

"No hill for a climber," Nikolas said with a new grin. "I booked myself into the Union Street Inn. Lovely people. A young man named Ken is picking me up at the airport."

Nicole shook her head in wonder. "How did you find this inn?"

"The Internet, of course! Everything is there. All you do is type in your request. It's very much like Santa Claus without the lap!" he laughed. "Nice chap, this Ken. I told him there was an emergency and could he help an old gentleman have a perfect Christmas. He didn't ask any questions. Simply said he'd have a room for me as long as I needed, and he would drive me wherever I needed to go."

"Well, that's… that's…" Belle whispered in awe.

Nikolas continued. "Seems Ken knows your young man, he knows of you, and of course, of Miss Tabatha and the Tuck You Inn."

"There would be room there for you," Belle offered.

"No… I want it to be a surprise! Ken knows the word is mum!" Nikolas pulled foil from the cupboard and made himself a package of the remaining cookies. "I'm ready whenever you are."

Nicole considered her husband's attire. He wore black suede trousers over his ample girth and a crisp white shirt. His shiny black boots could have been from any western store. If it weren't for his red-and-white candy cane-striped braces, one might think he was simply a portly older gentleman traveler with a huge white beard.

"We will tidy the kitchen later," Nicole said and reached for her husband's shearling. "Let's be off!"

Throwing on their capes, the women followed Santa Claus out the door to the one-horse open sleigh.

When Harv awoke he was cramped, his back hurt, and his knees were stiff. Where was he? As his head cleared, it came back: he was on his way to get Belle. He had changed planes what seemed a dozen times; thank goodness he only had a single carry-on. For the moment, he did not know where he was other than on a very small plane headed north.

Harv reached into his pocket for a mint and found one of Belle's candy canes that Miss Tabatha had forced upon him as he left. Before boarding a puddle jumper off the island, he had stuffed them in his pocket. Unwrapping the cellophane, he pondered his current time zone. No matter; his stomach said it was time to eat.

The plane touched down and bounced on the runway. Harv realized then that he was the only passenger. When had everyone else disembarked? When and how had he gotten on this plane, anyway? He had been so exhausted and anxious that he could not remember boarding the smallest plane of all. As he snagged his duffel from the overhead, he wished he had picked up a gift for Belle. Maybe he could get her some flowers in the airport. He paced toward the terminal and thought he had arrived at an old Victorian movie set. He slung his bag over his shoulder and walked onward.

Next, Harv pulled out his wad of ticket information wondering how much further he had to go. The iron wrought grillwork on the terminal doors formed the shape of crisscrossed candy canes. After noting that with a hum, Harv rummaged through his pocket for some change. Maybe he would find a vending machine. When he pulled open the heavy door he stopped and stared. The entire space was filled with Christmas trees. Colored lights twinkled from every angle, filling him with a sense of magic and wonder. The scent of fresh cut pine hit his senses and Harv's fatigue evaporated.

"I love Christmas!" He hadn't meant to say that aloud, but it had bubbled out on its own.

"So do we, sir," a tiny porter said appearing out of nowhere in full uniform, including red-and-white braided epaulets. His cap sat at a jaunty angle and his waistcoat barely covered his round belly.

Harv jumped back startled.

"Begging your pardon, sir," the ancient porter said clearing his throat. He slid his feet back and forth in an apologetic shuffle. "You would be wanting your connection to Santa's

Village, correct?"

Harv raised an eyebrow. How did this little man know when he didn't even know where he was headed?

"We have been expecting you, sir," the man said with pride and pleasure. Harv couldn't help but smile. "Your luggage, sir?"

"Traveling light," Harv said pointing to his duffel. "But I'm hoping I'll be bringing a lot more back with me."

"As are we," the porter said under his breath. "This way."

Instead of leading Harv to another gate, the porter led him to the front entrance and held open the ornate iron and glass door.

Harv took a last look over his shoulder at the splendid Christmas display and then walked outside to see a train track and an ornate waiting bench, complete with a candy-striped canopy. Before another second passed, a train chugged into view and Harv stared in new amazement. The train was ancient, yet gleamed with polish, its grillwork boasting a huge crest of "C.L.E." He turned to the porter his eyebrows raised.

"You will be traveling by train, sir," the man informed as with a hiss of steam, the locomotive came to a full rest. Another smallish porter hopped down from the train car, turned and dropped open a decorative stool on the bricks.

"Mr. Nichols!" the train Porter beamed. "All aboard!"

Harv climbed the steps with a smile, studying the little man as he passed. The porter picked up the stool and boarded on his heels.

Moving down the aisle, Harv had again traveled back to a long-ago era, the décor of ornate brass hat racks and deep red velvet tufted seats. The windows sported thick tapestry curtains tied back with sparkling gold ribbon.

"Am I dreaming?" Again, he hadn't meant to speak out loud.

"Not at all. This is the Candy Land Express," the porter said with pride.

"Just like in the game... imagine that." Harv shook his head. "Naming a train after the game. I can't wait to tell Walter."

"Begging your pardon, sir. The game was named after Candy Land."

Harv raised both eyebrows and the porter offered a bow. He asked if he would like a bite to eat. And Harv couldn't recall his last meal; he said yes and settled into one of the tufted seats. Very soon after, the porter arrived with a tray topped with a bronze dome that sported candy cane handles. Harv lifted the lid to find a red ceramic plate holding a warm roast beef sandwich, a slice of dill pickle, a mound of still sizzling waffle fries. With a rumbling stomach, Harv spread wide a red-and-white striped napkin to his lap and grasped the mammoth sandwich. He took a huge bite, instantly feeling better. Harv inhaled his fries and watched the passing scenery, the towering pines shifting to form a forest of… peppermint sticks? Surely not, but...

"Porter? Porter?" Harv called and the little man appeared from nowhere holding another tray.

"Ready for dessert, Mr. Nichols?"

"No, well, yes, I mean... are those peppermint sticks?" Harv gestured to the window.

"Yes, sir. That is Gumdrop Mountain and we're coming to the Licorice Forest."

The gumdrop mountains and their brilliant colors disappeared and the train's lights turned on as they tunneled through a dark forest of black licorice. Harv stared in amazement at the sinister trees, exactly like those from the game. Just then, the prickle of fear he had as a child when he would land in the Licorice Forest while playing the game came back as if he were five years old again.

Then also, as when he was young, the train moved on to the Peanut Acres, and the fear rolled away with the movement of the train. He grinned to see Gloppy wave in his direction, dripping with chocolate. Before Harv could wave back, they had moved on, and he could hardly believe his eyes at what he saw ahead: Candy Castle! *Exactly* like the one they had made it Miss Tabatha's, only now it was bigger than life. The sun shone off the Necco Wafer roof and the caramel fountain bubbled gaily to the side. Harv was speechless as the train came to a halt and the diminutive porter reappeared.

"Is this Santa's village?" Harv sputtered.

"No, sir, we have arrived at King Kandy's Castle at Candy Land. I'm surprised you don't recognize it."

Harv recognized it but had been too embarrassed to say so.

"King Kandy will be taking you from here," the porter said.

Harv followed. "Thank you for all of your kindness and thank you for dinner."

"No problem, sir. I suspect we will be seeing a lot more of you and master Walter."

Harv grinned. "Walter would love this place. And I will have to bring Miss Tabatha. She would flip!"

"Do you mean Miss Tucker, sir?"

"Yes, Miss Tabatha Tucker."

"Ah, what a dear. Is she still running the Tuck You Inn?"

Harv nodded.

"She knows this place well, but of course, you would know that," he said with assurance.

Harv did not *know,* but when he imagined Miss Tabatha in this place, he could see her fitting right in. Harv took one last look at the train, memorizing it for his son before a booming voice called out from the Castle, "Mr. Nichols! Mr. Harvey Nichols!"

Harv turned to see a resplendent king approach wearing a purple crown trimmed in peppermints. His purple robes flowed with drama and his swashbuckling boots were a mosaic of gumdrops and Lifesavers.

"Have we met?" Harv asked.

"Many, *many* times. The first time, when you were five," King Kandy boomed.

Harv inhaled. "When I got my Candy Land game from my Nana!"

"Yes!" King Kandy beamed.

Suddenly in his heart, Harv knew everything was going to be okay.

"Shall we get going?" King Kandy suggested lowering his chin. "I believe I know where you would like to go."

Harv gave a nod. "I would like to find Belle."

"That's my boy!" King Kandy said and let out a sharp whistle. A candy covered sleigh appeared pulled by two white reindeer. "Hop in! I will take you to her!"

And Harv did, ready to see Belle again. To tell her he was sorry. To say he should have trusted her. A god's-honest reindeer was pulling them along with a king dressed in candy! Harv kept his mind on the positive and hoped she would forgive him.

twenty-four

EVERY TIME NIKOLAS CHANGED PLANES, THEY seemed to only get bigger. When he finally reached Boston's Logan Airport, a kind porter escorted him to the next plane, this one exceptionally *small.* Nikolas couldn't help but remark on its size.

"It is our commuter, sir. It will take you to Hyannis, and from there your plane will be even smaller."

With a chortle Nikolas thanked him and boarded. As it turned out, the man at Logan had been correct; in Hyannis he was faced with an even smaller plane.

"Why, this looks like a toy, young man!" Nikolas said to the pilot.

"It is!" the pilot said with a twinkle in his eye.

Then they were off. Nikolas held on tight, but the up and down was so quick that he had no time to reflect. Once they landed, the pilot helped him off the plane and congratulated Nikolas with a clap to his wide back.

"You didn't do too badly! Not much one to fly, eh? Come back next season and take the ferry."

Nikolas grinned thinking of all the flying he had done in his life, but his thoughts were interrupted as a young man approached, his pleasant face marked with a wide grin.

"You must be Nikolas. I'm Ken from the Union Street Inn. Welcome to Nantucket. Can I take your bags?"

Nikolas only had one Gladstone that Ken threw over his shoulder.

"Would you like to go to the Inn straight-way, or perhaps have a bit of a drive around the island first? Perhaps you would prefer to take a walk and stretch your legs?"

Happy to see he had chosen well when picking this young man and his inn for this trip, Nikolas gave him a happy chortle. "That all sounds good. Can we go to the home of the Chocolate Chunkers?" he asked with a huge smile.

Ken laughed. "The Bake Shoppe, it is!"

They were off in a jiffy and Nikolas openly marveled at the cobblestone streets and the lovely clapboard and shingle buildings.

"Is this your first time on the island, sir?" Ken asked noticing his attention out the window.

"Call me Nikolas, everybody does. And no, I've been here many times but..." He caught himself. "Only by air, ho-ho-ho!" Nikolas laughed.

Ken continued driving with a new smile at his passenger's joviality.

When they reached the bakery, Magee was out front placing a cookie wreath on the door. Nikolas jumped ahead of Ken and mowed forward with gusto causing her to jump back.

"You would be Magee?" he asked.

"Yes, I am," she said, catching her breath but smiling at their eye-meet.

"The creator of the Chocolate Chunkers?" Nikolas added.

Magee laughed. "Yes, that's me."

"Wonderful! I am Belle's father!" he bellowed. "Nikolas Claus!"

Magee's cookie wreath crashed to the ground slipping through her fingers. After a few seconds of surprise, she threw her arms around his wide body.

"Welcome to Nantucket!" Then she added with a worried

tremor. "But Belle left already. She went home to you and Nicole."

"That's right, my dear. Right as can be! And we could not be happier!" Nikolas did not stifle a new ho-ho-ho.

Belle had pre-warned him who in Nantucket knew he was Santa, and who only knew they were from the North Pole. The baker smiling in front of him would soon learn who he was, so he let everything play out as it would. He swiveled to catch her eye anew.

"On second thought, I think I could even be a little bit happier if I had a sack of those Chocolate Chunkers in my paw!"

Maggie dashed inside and excitedly called to Walter helping behind the counter.

Nikolas followed. "Walter is here?"

Walter had been standing on a wooden stool reaching something on the shelf. He turned and saw Nikolas and his eyes widened.

"You came for us!" Walter shouted with joy and dove into Nikolas's arms.

"You bet I did, my boy! You bet I did!"

Ken stood by in awe watching the tender meeting.

"You're exactly as I pictured you," Walter said with tears in his eyes, clinging tight, his pudgy arms around Nikolas's neck.

"And you are exactly as I knew you'd be!" Nikolas replied. "I've come to help you get what you want for Christmas!"

Ken whispered to Magee, "What does he want?"

Nikolas answered aloud. "A mom, young man! A mom! Isn't that right, Walter?"

Walter was crying full now and he nodded his head. "I didn't tell anybody 'bout that."

"You didn't have to tell. Santa Claus always knows!"

Ken's jaw dropped and he stood looking at all the faces wondering what each thought was going on. He and Magee exchanged a happy *whatever!* expression and played along.

"Does Miss Tabatha know you're here?" Walter managed

"Not yet. I've just arrived."

"Did you bring your sleigh?" Walter asked and finally crawled down. He stood on the floor looking up at the mammoth old man.

"Nope. Flew commercial and what an experience it was!" Nikolas laughed until his round stomach shook.

Ken and Magee stood in shock at the information unable to decide if the visitor was admitting to be a Santa stand-in or something else entirely.

"Why don't we grab those Chocolate Chunkers and go see Miss Tabatha?" Nikolas suggested and turned to Magee. "I'm a little short on cash but you'll find that new Hobart mixer you've been wanting right there on the counter."

Suddenly with a pop and a crackle, the appliance appeared on the counter surrounded with red satin ribbon.

Magee did not see it materialize, but when she turned and saw it sitting there, she inhaled with happy surprise. "What? How? Jay!" she called as if her husband made it happen.

Before her husband responded, Nikolas bellowed, "Let's go! Who's with us? Ken, my boy, you drive!"

Once Magee set Jay to the task of watching the store, she, Nikolas, and Walter piled into Ken's car. Then, they were off.

Ken hadn't spoken so Nikolas interrupted his thoughts.

"Concerning that roof you've been needing on the Union Street Inn…"

At that very moment, Ken's cell phone rang. When he answered, his wife blustered on about how she went to the porch and looked up and saw a brand-new roof on their building. Ken flipped his eyes to Nicolas in the rearview mirror.

"What?! How…?" he managed his mind spinning. "How did you?" He shook his head. "How exactly did you find our inn?"

"The Internet, dear boy! I liked the look of your rooms. Those oversized canopy beds, ho-ho-ho!"

All the way to Miss Tabatha's house, Walter was beside himself with questions and he bounced around unable to be still.

"I want you to call me grandpa," Nikolas told him when the boy paused from excited questions to take a breath.

"You do?"

"I sure do!" Nikolas beamed. "You are going to be part of the family very soon."

"I am?"

"I am certain!"

"And... and Belle will be my…?

"Yes, yes, yes, to all of it!" Nikolas chortled and slid a comforting arm around Walter shoulders.

At the Tuck You Inn, Miss Tabatha sat in her kitchen absently stirring her mug of cocoa with one of Belle's candy canes, her gaze soft. What was going on with Belle and Harv and would it really work out like she hoped? Miss Tabatha took a sip, barely noticing it had gone cold, her gaze landing on the wedding folder at her elbow. Would there be a wedding? Would she go through with a party if the wedding did not happen? The Episcopal minister was off-island due to a family crisis, although he promised his single nephew, also a minister, would be around if they needed him. Miss Tabatha forced herself to look at the small picture, two people in love, fighting their feelings for each other.

A stern wrap on the door interrupted her reverie, followed by the peal of her doorbell. Tabatha pulled herself to her feet, her bones old, but her back strong. With a faint ho-ho-ho from the porch, Tabatha's grin approached. Had she heard that right?

She crossed to the door and put on her most cheerful attitude for whomever came to call. When she opened the door and swung it wide, she spied a small crowd. Walter, Magee, and wasn't that Ken from the Union Street Inn? Now this other…

"Ho-ho-ho!" the old man said with a grin in his eyes. "Give us a hug, sis!"

"Sis?" Magee squealed her eyes going between the two.

"Oh, don't start that!" Tabatha laugh-talked and hugged his neck. To her he was Santa Claus a mere twenty-four hours a year. The rest of the time, he was the wild and shaggy clown her twin sister married a zillion years ago.

"Miss Tabatha! Is Nikolas your brother?!" Walter yelled at the top of his voice.

Tabatha gave him a hush gesture, ushering the crowd of four into the house. "Of course not, honey lamb, he's only joking." Whether or not her guests believed that little fib, she couldn't attend. The crowd ambled in and shook off the chill.

"What a wonderful surprise," Miss Tabatha burbled inviting them into the foyer. "Nikolas Claus at the Tuck You Inn!"

"Where is he?" Nikolas boomed looking over her shoulder.

"Wait…" Magee said, flitting her gaze from Tabatha, to Nikolas, to Walter. "Wait a minute."

Everyone looked her way, mouths ajar, wondering at her odd tone.

"You're Belle's father, Nickolas Claus? As in Nick Claus. As in… Ken's roof and my mixer?"

Nikolas let it happen, but when her eyes fell in his, he gave the wink all people expect from Santa Claus.

"You're…?" And that was it. Lights out. Magee collapsed, falling into Ken who eased her to the rug in surprise.

"You're really…?" he whispered in Nikolas's gaze and he gave a new wink for the young man who smiled a crooked grin, reminiscent of the one he had at five when he once caught

Santa putting out presents. Nikolas recalled that night and although adult-Ken pretended it never happened, right now, he let it be true.

Magee opened her eyes from the floor, Tabatha and Ken helping her regain her feet. She had collapsed on a Claire Murray mermaid rug in the foyer and because of Ken's quick thinking, hadn't hit the shipmen's chest when she went down.

"Oh, me! Nicole tells me I am too bold for my own good!" Nikolas had gone white, even his rosy cheeks had faded in his dismay. "Magee, I apologize. I am a rude, rude old man."

Magee composed herself, back on her feet, and thanked her helpers. She patted down her hair. "I'm fine, just… just… I'm glad I came to work today, that's all." She smiled, ear to ear and grew quiet to listen.

Tabatha patted Magee's back and turned to Nikolas. "*Tsk-tsk,* you are no such thing. You are a *father,* and you are worried about your daughter."

"Correct!" Nikolas swept her into a bear hug lifting her off her feet. When he set her back down, he scanned the room and down the hallway. His eye took in the furniture and the tapestries and his gaze finally landed on the picture window facing the ocean.

"How magnificent!" he announced, walking closer. "And you see this every day! I bet it never grows old! How marvelous!"

Miss Tabatha assured him that she enjoys it new every day. Ken and Magee also looked at the ocean, mesmerized, as if viewing it for the first time. Something about being around Nikolas made everything more amazing than before. Walter asked then for some cocoa and Miss Tabatha inhaled with a grin.

"Goodness! My manners, yes! Everyone, in the kitchen." Tabatha turned to Nikolas. "Are you hungry? Let me get you something to eat."

"I'm always hungry!" he said with a hearty laugh bringing Tabatha a brand-new grin at the thought of cooking for Santa Claus.

She placed a portion of takeout chowder from Captain Toby's on the stove to simmer and started the cocoa. As it heated through, Magee and Walter set the table and Tabatha warmed Portuguese buns and tossed a lobster salad for lobster rolls. Nikolas didn't see nor hear any of these preparations. He and Ken stood in front of the Candy Land Castle.

"Amazing! Simply amazing!" Nikolas said shaking his head. "It is perfect!"

Ken agreed. "That is the best gingerbread house I have ever seen!"

"No, son, you don't understand," Nikolas said and he gestured to the game box on the countertop. "It is not simply a gingerbread house. It is a perfect replica."

"Of a game?" Ken asked

"No, son. Of King Kandy's Castle at Candy Land!" He turned to Miss Tabatha. "Where did this come from?"

Walter stepped forward. "We made it, Grandpa. Me and Miss Tabatha and Dad helped, too!"

"It is perfect!" he reiterated as Tabatha entered with mugs of cocoa. He leaned in to eyeball the details and gave a new ho-ho-ho. "All the way down to the caramel fountain!"

Walter's eyes popped as Miss Tabatha dished the chowder. "Tell us about it, Grandpa. How is Gloppy?"

"Gloppy is good, my son, very good!" Nikolas said with glee.

"Is he stuck in the swamp?" Walter asked with all seriousness.

"Goodness, no! He glops out when he wants to, leaving a trail of dripping chocolate behind him every time. King Kandy had him over for a gumball croquet game just the other day!"

At that, everyone settled in to hear about Candy Land and

King Kandy while they ate, gobbling up the stories even more than the lunch. In a break from his tales, Nikolas complimented Tabatha on her chowder.

"It is magical! Hearty, yet soft and creamy. Nicole would love it. And what did you call these? Lobster rolls? They are delicious. Can we make them at home? Nicole would die for them."

"Some things are best local. Why don't you bring Nicole and I'll make more?"

"Indeed, a fine idea!" Nickolas turned to Magee. "And you, missy, you're the inventor of the Chocolate Chunkers! I take my cap off to you and your factory. I must meet your elves. They are obviously stupendous."

Magee giggled into her hand. "I don't have a factory and my elves are Walter and my husband, Jay."

"Jay! He was the sweetest little boy! He once left me a sesame seed butter baguette with a note saying sometimes Santa might like some bread!"

Magee giggled. "That sounds like him!"

Nikolas gave her a serious head tip. "I must admit, I am amazed such an amazing cookie came from such a tiny bakery. You have a gift for pastry."

Magee glowed under his compliments as everyone finished off their meals.

"You and Nicole need to come for a vacation. Enjoy Nantucket. The island has so much to offer," Tabatha said sincerely.

"By Jove, we'd like that! We will come." Lowering his spoon, he caught her gaze hard. "Now, where is the young man, Harvey Nichols?"

twenty-five

COULD THIS REALLY BE HAPPENING?

All Harv knew for certain was that he was going to see Belle and his heart swelled with anticipation. King Kandy led the sleigh across the snow at speed and all around them, the landscape grew denser, the fir trees bigger, and the snow thicker. King Kandy kept a lively conversation going, mostly about Christmas. But his conversation was practical and business-like, revealing how closely he and Nickolas worked together on Christmas candy production.

Harv took the conversation seriously. After having taken the train ride through the Licorice Forest and to Candy Land he could believe anything, so he nodded along, wishing he could contribute to the topic. Then he remembered Belle telling him about Nickolas's medical issue.

"How are Nickolas's knees?" he asked.

King Kandy turned in his seat scowling. "He had to have both knees replaced. The therapy almost killed him which took its toll on Nicole. He struggles to walk long periods of time. He can't kneel, can barely get up from the ground when he is sitting in the snow. His flexibility is minimal. You can imagine his difficulty maneuvering a chimney." Kandy shook his regal head. "Sitting too long is painful and his knees stiffen, so as you can imagine, sleigh rides around the world are out."

"Poor guy," Harv offered, not realizing until now how dire it was.

Kandy gave a new sigh. "Nicole is worried sick and Nikolas won't slow down until Belle's situation is settled. The future of Christmas literally hangs in the balance."

"The future of Christmas?" Harv asked not grasping the enormity.

King Kandy shook his head, "Do I need to spell it out?"

Harv's mind raced. What was he trying to say? The man was filled with emotion on the topic of his friend, Belle's father, Santa Claus, but what was he not saying?

King Kandy leveled his gaze. "Nickolas has great hopes for you. That is, once he got past your name."

"My name?"

"There has never in history been a Santa named Harvey!" King Kandy said with aplomb.

Harv was dumbfounded. It sounded like Kandy was saying…

"Harvey Nichols, you embrace Christmas perfectly, you've been a Santa stand-in for years."

"True, but…" Harv began but Kandy looked steamed suddenly.

"You always know what the children want for Christmas…"

"It's not magic. I just know…" Harv's mind raced back. How did he know? And while he was at it, when and why did he start standing in for Santa anyway?

"No, it is *magic.* You see the inner child." King Kandy's tone softened. "You possess a very special gift that is a Santa Claus prerequisite. Why when fate knew Chris couldn't go on, why do you think fate sent Belle to Nantucket? To *you?"*

Harv narrowed his eyes thinking of all the events leading Belle into his life.

King Kandy cleared his throat. "I'm getting ahead of myself." He stopped speaking as they dashed along the snow.

Harv allowed the quiet for a time, but his mind swirled on

the subject of Belle and fate.

"Belle is like no one I've ever met." His eyes misted, looking off into middle space, wishing he could see her now, apologize, whatever it took.

"You'll save Christmas, then?" King Kandy asked, hopeful.

"If that's what it takes to get Belle to marry me—of course, I'll save Christmas!"

King Kandy pulled a gigantic floral hanky from his pocket and dabbed his brow. Bits of glitter clung where he wiped and soft chocolate oozed here and there.

"Isn't there a lot to learn in such a short time?" Harv asked on board now that he understood the mission.

"You'll do fine. But first you have to marry Belle." Kandy paused. "Patch things up with the lass first, then marry her, and then save Christmas!"

"I will. You can count on it." Then Harv softened. "Thank you for helping me understand. Would you be my best man?"

King Kandy was speechless.

"It would mean a lot." Harv wanted this man by his side. He hadn't met Nickolas or Nicole yet, but he already liked King Kandy.

"In the land of Nantucket?" he asked very small.

"Well, yes," Harv said waiting.

"I rarely leave Candy Land, except of course to go to Santa's Village…"

"You could arrange it, if you wanted?" Harv asked leading. After all, the man was magic personified.

Then he took a deep breath. "It would be lovely to go to your Land."

"Nickolas and Nicole will be there," Harv threw in for extra bait. "You could travel with them."

King Kandy looked off into the horizon deep in thought.

"Just say you'll think about it," Harv said and let him off the hook. There was time to decide the details.

When they arrived at Santa's Village, Harv was awed more than ever. The energy in the air literally sparkled and every shoppe in sight was a flutter of activity. Real-life elves were everywhere and the Toy Factory that dominated the street's end sported red-and-white twisted-stripe smoke rising from its chimney.

"There's a theater?" Harv gestured, amazed Santa's elves would have a movie house.

"Oh, yes, and it only shows Christmas movies!" King Kandy let out a deep laugh. "That's Nickolas's gym." He pointed to a building with a dozen chimneys on the roof, each a different diameter. As Harv noted them, Kandy volunteered, "Those are for practice, my boy! Practice!" Kandy laughed long and loud.

"Practice sliding down the chimney. I get it," Harv said with a nod, eyeing with interest as they passed Santa's Post Office and the Naughty and Nice Building.

"Right, and inside is his gym equipment to rehabilitate his knees."

Harv imagine himself practicing with those chimneys and cleared his mind, not quite putting himself in Santa's boots just yet.

The Dollhouse Factory piqued his interest most of all as dollhouses were his favorite toys to design and build. The Ribbon and the Gift Tag Shoppes looked like toys themselves only bigger. Everywhere they went elves waved and saluted. A few of them even bowed. At first Harv found it entertaining, and then charming, and then he was moved.

"They know who I am, don't they?" he asked quietly.

Kandy tipped his chin. "They've been expecting you, or should I say, hoping you would come."

"I didn't know what to expect but, well, I love it. It fills me with warmth … it's like I've always thought it would be." Harv found himself smiling from deep down.

"Think you could live here?" King Kandy tossed out.

Harv stopped and inhaled, turning to see Kandy's face. "Live here?"

"You wouldn't have to give up your old life. Just Christmas."

Harv perked up. "Oh, well…"

King Kandy chucked his shoulder. "I don't see why you couldn't maintain a dual citizenship; Santa's Village and the Land of Nantucket."

"True." Harv grinned; this had promise.

"And?" Kandy pressed, leaning in.

"It might be doable …" Harv released a breath he didn't realize he'd been holding. "But there's also Walter to think about. He's getting ready for the first grade." Harv took a scan around them. "Do you have internet?" Kandy nodded once. Harv hummed. He could manage it. Homeschooling when needed. It could work.

"Nicole has talked about a school for the elves for years. Maybe this could be her incentive!" he said with a laugh. "And Belle would be there when she was ready to retire."

"As Mrs. Claus," Harv let slip.

"She'll always be Mrs. Claus. It is hers all the way."

They were now past the reindeer barn and up to Santa's Chalet. King Kandy slowed his reindeer to a stop.

"Here we are," he said with finality.

"Are you coming in?" Harv asked suddenly anxious.

"After a bit. I will take my boys to the barn. Let them visit and cool down."

Harv said thank you and turned for the residence. After a deep inhale, he trotted up the front steps and onto the porch. When he rang the bell, "Santa Claus is coming to Town" played from the speaker.

"Coming," a singsong voice called out and then the click-click of heels on a wooden floor. The door opened to the loveliest older woman he had ever seen. Her silver hair was swept up with little dangly bits wisping around her cherubic face. Her cheeks were rosy, her big round eyes were sky blue, and they shot open in amazement. "Oh!"

Harv was afraid she was going to faint. "Mrs. Claus…"

She threw her arms around his neck. "I know who you are! Come in! Come in!" She released Harv and hollered out, "Belle, dear, can you come down to the foyer?"

Harv was tugged into the room by the elbow and he turned his gaze to the staircase. The sound of feminine footsteps on the wooden treads reached his ears along with the tiny click-clicking of possibly a dog with her. Harv moved into the great room, oblivious to his surroundings with his mind absorbed with seeing Belle and what he might say to make everything right. Belle was halfway down the massive staircase, Sprinkles right behind her when she looked up.

"Harv!" she breathed and jogged the rest of the way down, right into his open arms.

Harv swept her off her feet. "I should have believed you," he said in her ear, holding her close, her beautiful aroma filling his senses to the utmost. After a long while, they finally pulled apart enough to see each other's faces.

"It's a lot to believe," Belle commiserated, her eyes watery. "You're here now. You believe now." She hugged his neck again and spoke more words into his hair.

"Yes, I do, I do. And I was afraid, not of you, but of me," Harv admitted wanting to come clean all the way.

"I know. I understand. Really…"

"I've always been a part of Christmas. I always believed in it. I don't know when I lost my faith and I didn't even know I had until I met you. You are my world. You are what I need to remind me that I was made for Christmas and I was made for you…"

Harv said it all in a whoosh and then slowed down. He had

so much more to say, about how she saved him in more ways than one, how she changed him and made his life better. He and Belle spoke similar sentiments into each other's ears as they embraced yet again and it was a full minute before they parted to simply exhale in each other's gaze.

The seconds ticked, and with lopsided grin, Harv finally looked around, noticing his surroundings. "This place is incredible…"

They stood in a gigantic lodge-type room with plump sofas facing each other, a four-foot-square solid wood coffee table between them. Papers were scattered on the table, more on the floor. A red tray with what looked like a cup of cocoa, and a plate of cookies, sat next to the paperwork. His eyes shifted to a roaring fireplace—big enough for two Santas to come down together. Three huge white dogs snored in front of it, basking in its warmth. Two oversized red leather chairs were pulled up to the fire, again with a table between them, again scattered with papers. So many papers... An oak library table, big and heavy, dominated a wall of glass windows. The table had an ancient carved chair pulled up to it. Another lamp lit low, and more papers in piles, some tidy, some literally in heaps. On the floor next to it were three burlap sacks as huge as the table, open, loaded with what looked like letters. Some had drifted to the floor. Harv walked first to the windows, and the view, and then looked down at the letters. They were addressed, for the most part, to simply "Santa."

Belle looped her arm through his. "Maybe you passed the Post Office on the way through the village."

Harv nodded and she squeezed his elbow to her body.

"We're a bit behind. Usually Nickolas sits there…" She indicated one of the big red leather chairs by the fire. "…and reads them."

Harv gave himself a little shake. He was at Santa's Village, in Santa's Chalet, looking at Santa's chair where he read letters from children who believed in Santa Claus. They didn't need convincing. They hadn't been disillusioned. They simply opened their hearts and believed in the magic of Christmas. And Santa. Belle broke into his thoughts.

"I'm so happy you came! How is Walter?" she asked, her eyes filled with love for his son.

"Miss Tabatha and Magee are watching him." Harv again pulled her close and Sprinkles tried to angle between them. "Belle," Harv began, his voice low, "I know all of this sounds crazy and I know it's bigger than both of us, but so is love. I love you—I want to share my life with you …" Without hesitation, he dropped to one knee, looking up into her beautiful face. "Marry me, Belle. Together we can do anything. Together it will fall into place because we'll have each other."

Leaning low, Belle threw her arms around his neck, tears of joy escaping, and nodded. "Yes! Yes!"

King Kandy had slipped in, and he and Nicole watched from the foyer, both dabbing wayward tears. Sprinkles abandoned his efforts of separating Belle and Harv and ran over to them, yapping noises of happiness at their presence.

Belle and Harv looked over after another long embrace.

"Congratulations, my boy! Belle! This is a great day!" King Kandy bellowed. Nicole stepped up and engulfed Belle into a hug before opening an arm to pull Harv in, too. Doing his happy dance, Sprinkles filled the air with yips of glee.

"I asked King Kandy to be my best man," Harv said to Belle when Nicole set them loose. "Do you think Nickolas will give you away?"

Suddenly, Belle, Nicole, and King Kandy froze, all three saying at once, "Nickolas!"

twenty-six

"WHAT DO YOU MEAN, HE'S NOT HERE?" NICKOLAS bellowed. "That scoundrel! Running away! Not wanting my Belle! Leaving, disappearing!" His face became the ruddy red of a brick chimney.

Miss Tabatha was too stunned by his outburst to say anything. Ken and Magee cowered, shocked that Santa Claus had such an explosive temper.

Walter jumped up on one of Miss Tabatha's antique Windsor chairs and shouted, "Grandpa! Grandpa!" He looked him right in the eye. "Dad left for the North Pole to get Belle! To bring her back and marry her!"

"What is this, my boy?" Nickolas asked his brow raised.

"Dad went to get her!" Walter said slower, still standing on the chair.

Nikolas's scowl dissolved into a gigantic beam. He opened his arms to Walter who jumped off the chair and into them.

"Why didn't you say so?" He swung Walter around, and Miss Tabatha, Magee, and Ken exhaled with relief. "This is a horse of another color! We need to celebrate! Tabatha, my fine woman, bring on the celebration!" Just as the chatter began in earnest, Nikolas demanded, "When did he leave?"

"Yesterday," Walter said. "Is he there yet, Grandpa? Has he found her? Is it very far? Are there direct flights?"

Nickolas laughed until his big bowl full of jelly belly shook.

"Oh, no, my boy, there are no direct flights, none whatsoever. I've been traveling since early yesterday myself!"

"You possibly crossed paths," Ken suggested.

"Very possibly! I was on some of the smallest planes I've ever seen! Including the puddle jumper that brought me to the Isle of Nantucket!"

"That would have been Gavin, our resident pilot," Ken filled in finally getting with the program.

Not listening, Nickolas was back on Harv. "But if Harv is up there, I need to talk to Nicole! She's met him by now! She can tell me what she thinks!"

"My guess is Nicole has her hands full," Miss Tabatha said coming forward.

Nickolas agreed with a humble nod. "But she's there and I'm here. Hmmm."

"And they're together," Miss Tabatha finished.

By now they were sprawled around the living room furniture. Ken had started a fire, Magee had gone to the kitchen and returned with the sack of Chocolate Chunkers Nickolas had gotten at the bakery and a box of cutouts she found on the counter.

"Nickolas," Miss Tabatha began, "what matters is what *Belle* thinks. I've seen her cry for this young man. She loves him, he loves her. He's gone to fix things between them. You have to decide if he is good enough for you."

Nickolas caught Miss Tabatha's eye and lowered his head. "I'm an old man, set in my ways, and I apologize for my behavior. Nicole reminds me often to think before I speak. I'm sorry Tabatha, you're right."

Miss Tabatha gave a kind nod. "You are forgiven. Let's give them a little time. They'll call and tell us their plans."

"But what if…" Nickolas started to wind back up.

"Give them a chance."

After a new exhale, the twinkle returned to Nikolas's eyes. "You know what, Miss Tabatha, I knew the moment we met that I had met my match!"

"Nicole, how can we get back in time for the wedding? It is scheduled for this weekend." Harv sat at Belle's side in the greatroom. Nicole had him opening letters to Santa to get a feel for the task. He had toured the Toy Factory and most of the village. He even tried the chimney workout, and though he had no way of explaining it, he whooshed right down the trial chimneys. The town elves had cheered which only further sealed the deal.

They telephoned Miss Tabatha and Belle convinced Nickolas that Harv was not only perfect for *her,* but he was perfect for the entire world. She also spoke to Walter to reassure him she would be coming back, that there would be a wedding, and yes, she'd be his new mom. Walter's tears of joy were evident over the phone.

"I believe I have the answer," Nicole began, "Let's take a walk to the barns." Sprinkles followed, not wanting to miss a thing.

"This is one place I haven't seen," Harv offered as Nicole threw open the enormous barn doors. He stood, mesmerized.

"There is lots yet for you to see and discover!" Nicole said warmly. "We've only scratched the surface."

As the doors opened and light poured in, Harv stared in amazement. The barn was set up as a garage for sleighs. Nicole took his hand and pulled him in.

"This one we use to hop over to Candy Land." Nicole pointed to a lovely red and green sleigh with holly leaves and berries stenciled on its side. "And this one…" She gestured to a bigger version. "We use when he have to make deliveries."

"Deliveries?" Harv repeated.

"Everyday things," Nicole said with a kind smile. "Books for King Kandy or new robes from the tailor, maybe new wands for Lolli…"

"Oh-kayyy," Harv said stretching out the word and gawking at the upcoming examples.

"This was Nickolas's father's everyday sleigh. We use it sometimes for parades."

They continued on, passing countless sleighs for countless purposes. Practice ones for the reindeers, tiny ones for the dogs, but as they reached the back of the barn, things took on a golden aura.

"This…" Nicole rested a hand tenderly on an elegant red and green. "Is one we use when we need to fly."

"Fly?"

She nodded. "It is our get-around for when we need more than what the land sleighs will do."

"I see," Harv said still in awe.

"And this one …" They had moved to a magnificent sleigh, red and green again with gold trim, ropes of golden bells. It had a generous front seat with a gold bar that looked like a safety bar on an amusement park ride. The seat was red leather, tufted and shiny. There was a small backseat and then a large open area for cargo … or a sack full of toys.

"This is our beloved Christmas Eve sleigh." Nicole tenderly ran a hand along the leather seat.

"How does it fly?" Harv sounded ridiculous but he needed to know.

"It *just does,* my dear. No one has ever answered that question any better than that. Of course, the reindeer help quite a bit."

"Is it dangerous?" Harv asked next, his mind inevitably going to Belle's first husband.

"It can be," she said and turned aside with, "Especially if

one has been drinking."

She walked on. A red velvet drapery with gold fringe concealed a section of the barn. She pulled it back with the flick of her wrist. Even Belle was in awe.

"Nickolas has been working on this."

Harv's eye landed on a fabulous sleigh with a streamlined look, bigger, bolder, and grander. Painted gold with red and green trim, it had a full front seat with gold cord seatbelts and the same protective bar.

Belle rushed forward. "This is the one he was working on!"

"It's faster," Nicole offered. "Safer, bigger, and has safety features built right in."

The back seat was generous and also had seatbelts. The cargo area had a gold mesh cover that looked as though it could drape over, and secure, anything, and then loop in place. The sleigh runners were thicker and it sported gold-plated exhaust pipes.

Nicole noticed he noticed. "That is the backup rocket system. He saw it in a movie and thought—why not? It had been a stretch for Nickolas, but he was excited about it."

"Impressive!" Harv walked over and looked in the front. There were gears and controls, then he laughed. "Are those cup holders?"

Nicole smiled. "Nickolas always felt a hot mug of cocoa would be wonderful. There's also a repair kit, a glove box, and I had the elves put in a tiny make-up mirror." She gave a laugh. "Your speedometer, odometer, and sky-ometer." She pointed to the various dials. "And your GPS is here." Nicole grew serious. "If you are planning on getting married this weekend on Nantucket, I think we ought to take this on its maiden flight."

Harv looked at the sleigh and back to Nicole.

She gave a single slow nod holding his eye and Belle reached for his arm to hold close.

"Fly the sleigh?" Harv choked.

"Yes." Nicole turned drill sergeant and began instructions. "Christmas Eve is right around the corner." Harv was still shaking his head in tiny increments and Nicole *tsked*. "Harv, dear, you need to jump in if you're coming. We haven't time for subtle."

"Fly in the sleigh to Nantucket?"

Nicole moved to arrange a soft blanket on the sleigh's rear seat. "The reindeer do most of the work. You program the GPS to Nantucket and you're off. King Kandy and I will ride in the back. Nikolas is already there, so after the wedding, the three of us can fly home commercial."

"Umm."

Belle took his hand. "I know you can do it." She looked up at him, her eyes shining with faith in her soon husband.

Harv took a deep breath. "Okay! Let's do it! Can I practice?"

"You and King Kandy take a few spins around the neighborhood while Belle and I pack."

"When do you want to leave?" Harv swallowed his nervous fear, a bead of sweat trickling down his back.

"At dusk, we only fly at night."

"Won't people, uh, see us anyway?" Harv ran a hand through his unruly hair.

Nicole laughed, "Oddly enough, they rarely do." King Kandy entered the barn and Nicole pulled Belle for the exit. "Okay, boys, get to it!"

Once back inside the chalet, Nicole gave a deep exhale. "That didn't go too badly." She turned to Belle. "What are you wearing for your wedding?"

"Oh, no… I don't know," Belle said and drooped.

Unfazed, Nicole chirped, "Come along, my dear, we're going to the attic!" Grabbing Belle's hand, they headed up the grand staircase.

"What's in the attic?" Belle asked as they climbed. She'd never been to the chalet's attic and now her curiosity went on overdrive.

Nicole threw open a rounded door that creaked as she pushed. Belle peered in and was shocked at the immense space. Dust motes danced in the beams of light that poured in from the sky lights. Other corners looked locked in glum and shadows, but Nicole tripped a switch, and the space flooded with soft light.

Belle blinked taking it in. There were piles of forgotten furniture, some obscured with huge drop cloths, and much like Tabatha's attic, bunches and bunches of trunks. Artwork leaned against the walls, one huge painting in front of another. An endless sea of boxes, some neatly labeled, others higgly piggly.

"I know, I know," Nicole began. "Someday I'm going to organize all this." Then she grinned. "But not today."

She headed deeper into the farthest recesses as Belle trundled behind. They passed iron dress-forms, a dappled rocking horse, and enormous pieces of luggage. Under the eaves were a series of armoires and old wooden wardrobes. Nicole contemplated a moment and finally walked to a mahogany number. Carefully, she pulled open the massive mirrored door. Gold glitter seeped out and danced in the air as if alive. Nicole paid no heed and rifled through the hangers as Belle watched on.

When she found what she sought, Nicole pulled out a flowing ivory velvet gown with a white fur hem. She gave it a shake and more glitter dusted off in every direction.

Belle watched—spellbound. The dress had the classic sweetheart neckline, low and dipping, but outlined in white fur. The bodice tapered to a tiny waist and from there the skirt escaped into yards and yards of shimmering velvet fabric. The glitter moved with sentience and again she thought of Miss Tabatha.

"Miss Tabatha is my twin sister," Nicole offered, her eyes to the dress, swishing back and forth. She then rolled her gaze to Belle's. "Fate is wonderful, eh?"

Belle offered a nod, smiling at how wonderful her fortune had been. Of all the places in the world to land after a crash, and to have Mrs. Claus's twin sister living in the same town as Harvey, the next Santa… It boggled her mind and she gave a soft laugh.

"Being Mrs. Claus comes with a lot of magic," Nicole offered in a professor's tone. "Don't ever let it get old."

As Nicole swirled the skirt again and Belle pictured the movement if it were worn. The sleeves were long, tight, and tapered to fur-trimmed wrists.

"Hold this, my dear." Nicole thrust the dress into her arms and reached back into the wardrobe. She pulled out an equally impressive ivory velvet full-length cape also edged in white fur, but this time thicker, bolder. It had a mammoth hood that fell onto the back of the cape in folds. Nicole fluffed it out with her hands, her own eyes glistening. Then she turned to Belle.

"This was my wedding dress and cape. I think it will fit you and I'd be honored if you'd wear it."

Belle broke down, and as the glitter danced with her arms full of velvet, she let the tears come. Nicole took her by the elbow.

"Let's go down and you can try it on."

Together they closed the mysterious attic of forgotten things and headed down.

twenty-seven

"MISS TABATHA! YOU HAVE TO CALM DOWN!" MAGEE shrieked. Then stopped, hearing herself. She and Miss Tabatha both broke into peals of laughter.

"Oh, Magee!" Miss Tabatha set down a bowl of white roses. "I'm so nervous. You'd think I was getting married!"

"Me, too," Magee agreed. "Do you think the garland around the porch looks right?"

Miss Tabatha headed out by her side. "It's spectacular! All that hemlock feathering out, and the way you twined the white roses in!" Then she paused, fingering a soft branch along the porch railing. "We could be wedding planners…"

"You mean, if you didn't run the Tuck You Inn and I didn't run The Bake Shoppe?" She laughed. "And if we were much, much younger? Wedding planning is exhausting!"

"I know, I know," Miss Tabatha conceded and looked at the forgotten mansion next door literally buried in overgrowth, long empty. It tickled her mind now and again to do something with the place. So far, nothing poked her enough into action.

Magee followed her line of sight. "We'll get some of the high school boys to clean up that frontage. Folks could park there, too."

Tabatha nodded. "Fine idea." She rested her hands to her bosom and sighed. "I say again, the island needs a wedding planner, or in the least, a place always ready for an event. I know all this preparation is exciting, but I swear I can't wait to have my quiet inn back again. Why, I left my house slippers in the living room right by the fireplace and they're coming tonight!"

Magee rolled her eyes at Miss Tabatha's idea of mess.

They admired the massive front door festooned in garland, and started to head back in. But they heard a *tap tap tap* and looked around. Nothing. More *tap tap tap*. Finally, they looked up. There on the roof sat Nickolas and Walter, both wearing tool belts, both with their necks draped with Christmas lights.

"Okay, my boy, roll me out another length."

Walter unwound a measure of lights and Nickolas scooted backwards tapping with his hammer until they were in place.

"Save me! Tabatha, did you know they were up there?"

Miss Tabatha screamed, "What do you two crazy men think you're doing on my roof? What if you slip? No father of the bride! No ring bearer! No wedding! No Christmas! And what would I tell Belle and Harv?"

They kept tacking the lights in place ignoring her.

"And Nicole," she yelled. "What would I tell Nicole? Santa killed himself on my roof?"

"Ho-ho-ho, Tabatha, I'm on a roof! That's what I do! That's what I've always done! We're perfectly safe!" But as he said it and swung his arms his tack hammer got away from him and slid down the shingles until it crashed on the porch. Both Miss Tabatha and Magee shrieked.

"Use my hammer," Walter said handing over his ballpeen. "Honest, Miss Tabatha we're fine! Anyways, Grandpa says I need to get comfortable on a roof. I need to practice!"

"Someone help me!" Magee and Miss Tabatha both ran their hands through their hair worried sick.

"Besides, think how awesome it'll look tomorrow for the wedding! We're gonna test them tonight when it's dark!"

Nickolas nodded. "He's a natural! And I wouldn't let anything happen to him. Go back and finish the inside." Still they stood. Nickolas softened his voice. "Go on, we're fine."

They relented, but as they headed in, they heard him bellow. "You don't want to make us nervous, ho-ho-ho!"

Tabatha and Magee closed the big door. "I swear I need a drink!" Magee said looking wired.

"How about some cocoa with peppermint schnapps!"

"You're on!" Magee said and they headed to the kitchen.

Tuck You Inn shone from top to bottom. True to his word, the Episcopal priest made sure his nephew could perform the wedding. They originally thought of having the ceremony at the inn but then Magee and Miss Tabatha got sentimental, and with no one really to consult but Nickolas and Walter, changed it to the Old Episcopal Church.

The church ladies were festooning it and begged them not to worry. There would be more seating, and it seemed Nickolas had ingratiated himself to everyone in the village he met and invited them.

The reception would be at the inn. A tent for dancing had been erected on the back lawn overlooking the ocean. Another tent had been set on the side yard as a bar. Unknown to Miss Tabatha and Magee, Nickolas and Walter had already covered the tent roofs with lights; the inn was the last to go.

"Do you think Nicole will bring something for Nickolas to wear?" Magee fretted.

"She said not to worry."

"We were lucky to get that little tux for Walter."

"And you were smart to get one for Harv. Who knows if he's thought that far ahead."

Miss Tabatha sipped her laced cocoa. "Nicole said she had something for Belle.

"They're bringing a best man, and they asked me to be matron of honor, and you to be a bridesmaid."

Magee wiped a tear. "At our age …"

"Magee, hush. You're a fraction of my age. Anyhoo, who cares how it looks? We'll be right there cheering them on right up close."

"What time do you think their flight will get in?" Magee absently ate a cutout.

"I'm not sure, Nicole was sure vague on that point. I've scheduled the rehearsal dinner at Neptune's for 9:30 in case they're late."

"Do you think we have enough Santa cookies?" Magee looked at the foil wrapped trays.

"I do, and those cutouts shaped like wedding cakes really turned out. Not to mention the beautiful cake itself."

In the living room, on its own table, stood a magnificent creation of peppermint chocolate and white peppermint cake, and butter cream frosting. Cascading down the sides were intricate tiny white-chocolate boxes as Christmas packages.

"We still don't have a bride and groom for the top," Magee said wistful.

"Sure we do. Nikolas left this for you." Tabatha pushed a pearlized-cardboard box her way.

Magee lifted the lid and her smile lit up the room. "It's Harv and Bell in Santa's sleigh!" she exclaimed lifting the item to examine the details. "How in the world… it even looks like those two!"

Tabatha nodded and sipped, having already peeked. As Magee attested, the groom sported shaggy black hair under his plastic Santa hat and the bride long blonde tresses cascading to her mid-back, floofing over her fur-trimmed cape hood. The sleigh had been stenciled with delicate holly and ivy boughs and shimmered with gold fleck on red paint. All minutiae had been attended and Tabatha had no doubt the couple would display that treasure forever.

Magee marveled another long moment and tucked the item to her pile of necessaries. Miss Tabatha changed gears.

"I wish Belle had been here to consult on the flowers."

"We know she had poinsettias at her last wedding, so I think you were right to go with white roses."

"And ivy and mistletoe," Miss Tabatha added.

Their conversation was interrupted by Walter's screams. They ran outside and there, hovering and preparing to land, was the most magnificent thing anyone had ever seen. A spectacular gold sleigh trimmed in red and green, with eight reindeer.

Nickolas hobbled out to meet them and as he threw open his arms proclaimed, "Harvey Nichols! The next Santa Claus! Welcome home, son! Welcome home!"

King Kandy helped Belle and Nicole out of the sleigh, and the reindeer nickered and bobbed their heads, happy to see Nickolas again. but Nickolas had his arm around Harv's shoulders.

"You did it, my boy! You flew her!" Nikolas draped an arm about Harv's shoulders, beaming with pride. He wiped back a joyful tear with his huge red-and-white striped hanky.

"Thank goodness!" Harv said grinning, thrilled and relieved. "Had no choice if we were going to make it for our own wedding!"

Walter ran up to his dad who scooped him up in an embrace. "I knew you'd come back with Belle!" Happier than he'd ever been before, Walter then spied King Kandy in his purple robes and candy mosaic boots. "King Kandy! King Kandy!" He jumped from his father's arms to the king's.

Belle and Nicole unpacked the sleigh, handing things to the shellshocked Magee. Introductions went around again when Ken from Union Street Inn returned. Ken stood dumbfounded. Yes, he'd heard about Nikolas being Santa, but to see the sleigh?

Neighbors and townspeople began to gather and the rumor that Harv was going to be the next Santa Claus had spread in their whispers. Harv jumped upon the edge of the sleigh.

"You people of Nantucket are the only family Walter and I have had for many years. We love you and appreciate you all very much. Tonight, I'd like you to meet my *new* family. Nickolas and Nicole and their friend King Kandy."

The crowd went wild.

"What you have witnessed is a miracle," Harv continued when the cheers abated. "But it is no bigger than the miracle of love I feel for Belle. This is a miracle that, as a family, we need to protect, cherish, and nurture. I know you will all use discretion so we can keep this tradition going. You are all invited to our wedding tomorrow. Thank you each and every one of you for your love and support."

Nickolas came forward and his voice boomed out. "Harv is right. We all have a responsibility to remain discreet, not today and tomorrow, but always because I am declaring the Isle of Nantucket Santa's second home. I am deputizing you all as our helpers, and I am renaming your island as the Isle of Nantucket, Most Magical Land on Earth!"

Anew, the crowd went wild with cheers and tears both. It was a while before everyone gathered was able to meet and shake hands with the North Pole visitors.

Eventually the townspeople departed for home, the sleigh was stashed in the hardly-used storage barn on Tabatha's property, and the deer were made comfortable in the carriage house attached to the abandoned mansion next door. With a happy calm settling over the town, the wedding party left to dine.

Dinner at Neptune's was elegant yet as comfortable as a family reunion. Nickolas had finished sizing up Harv the minute he knew he could fly the sleigh, and Harv felt as if he'd always known Nickolas. Belle, Nicole, Miss Tabatha, and

Magee watched, fascinated by the two men bouncing from one subject to the next. Walter was still in awe and barely touched his lobster cocktail with fries.

In time, Nicole pulled her attention from the men to speak details with Tabatha and Magee. "Okay, let's talk about this wedding."

Tabatha leaned in. "St. Paul's Episcopal is over 150 years old with a lovely whitewashed stone exterior with Tiffany stained glass windows."

"How wonderful!" Nicole exclaimed.

"Wait until you see them," Miss Tabatha beamed, "They were made by the Tiffany Studios in 1904 and represent some of the best art glass ever produced. They're rare in an ecumenical setting because they depict landscapes and flowers with no figures. I can't wait for you to see them. But as far as the wedding itself goes, we will keep it traditional. We won't do the bride or groom's side in the seating since most of the town will turn out. Nickolas will walk Belle down the aisle and Harv asked King Kandy to be his best man."

"Yes. I brought tuxedos for all the men, but you said you had Walter covered." Nicole let out a breath.

"But what should we wear?" It had finally dawned on Magee there really was going to be a wedding.

Miss Tabatha stopped, she hadn't thought about it either.

"I brought my ivory suit," Nicole began.

"I have one," Magee beamed.

"So do I," Miss Tabatha joined in. "Good! We three will look elegant without detracting the attention from our Belle. She told me she's wearing your dress."

Nicole misted. "Oh, girls! Do you think we'll be able to get through this?"

Tabatha sniffled with her. "I have some lovely vintage lace handkerchiefs to help."

And as they tucked into their meal the chatter went on hold. When their brandies were brought out, Nickolas began toasting, and from there, the evening wore on as though they'd all always been together.

"Dad, I can't tie it!" Walter wailed struggling with a tiny bowtie.

"Where's the clip-on?" Harv asked still dressing himself.

"Isn't that cheating?" Walter raised a little eyebrow.

"Not at all, it's still a bowtie." Harv popped it on.

"Do you have the ring?" Walter asked as the ring bearer.

"Right here." Harv patted his pocket. "I'll hand it over to you at the church."

"Can I see it again?"

Before dinner last night, Walter, Nickolas, and Harv made a stop at Johnson's Jewelers. Brenda, the elegant proprietress, met them as they rolled in and in short order she understood the situation. The ring Brenda brought out was a single carat surrounded by tiny diamonds set at irregular spaces. When the three men looked at it, they all said the same thing.

"It looks like a snowflake!" Then, "Perfect!"

Brenda was delighted to not only meet what could potentially be three generations of Santa Clauses but to help find Belle and Harv a fabulous ring. They guessed on the size and Brenda assured them they could bring it back for sizing if need be.

Harv pulled it from his pocket and flipped open the small velvet box for Walter who peeked in.

"It *does* look like a snowflake, Dad, doesn't it?"

"It does."

"Do you think she'll like it?" Walter wanted everything to be perfect.

"I think she'll cry."

"Is that good?" Walter worried his bottom lip.

"Sure! There is such a thing as happy tears."

Reassured, they took one last look in the mirror and headed out. They soon slipped in the back door of St. Paul's to get into place.

Belle was in the bride's room nervous. She had on Nicole's magnificent velvet gown and cape with a bouquet of white roses and ivy sitting on the side table. Magee, Miss Tabatha, and Nicole fussed over everything, her hair, her face, her dress, her train. Miss Tabatha doled out the lace handkerchiefs and they all dabbed and reassured Belle she looked spectacular.

"It's time!" Magee said, then changed tempo. "I can't believe you got a tux made for King Kandy! And he agreed to wear it!" she teased Nicole.

"Don't forget Nickolas. Both of them like to wear what they wear. I specifically told Harv not to let me down and make sure they wear them." Then she got a little misty. "You know girls, not only is our Belle getting married, but I am officially turning over the Mrs. Claus title today. I looked forward to this day so much, but now that it's here?" She sniffled. "I am a sentimental old fool."

"I won't let you down," Belle promised.

"Time to go," Miss Tabatha said hating to interrupt.

"One last thing…" Nicole got out a silver and gold drawstring purse decorated with enormous gemstones. She opened the string, and to everyone's surprise, took out a handful of what looked like gold and silver glitter. She tossed it into the air over all of them and they caught on Belle's gown, adding a hint of sheen.

"Moonbeams and Magic," Nicole said, and Miss Tabatha

and Magee were pretty sure she meant it literally. "It's a tradition in case you have any doubts or fears about anything to come, this will remove them and make it all easier." Nicole closed the pouch with a tearful smile. "Okay, girls, we're ready! Nickolas should be at the back of the church to walk you down the aisle and Harv will be at the altar waiting to marry you." She gave Belle a last feather of a kiss and they all slipped out.

There was no organ music, just a baby grand piano. The crowd was silent, holding their breath. Walter led the procession carrying a red-and-white striped pillow with the ring box on it. He gave a quick wave to Billy as he made his way to his dad and his new life. Magee came down the aisle meeting her husband, a last-minute recruit, at the altar.

Miss Tabatha was next, fighting the tears. King Kandy held out a hand, looking dashing in his tux. Up close, she realized his cummerbund appeared to be constructed of cut rock candy. He winked, and she took a deep breath.

Nickolas linked arms with Belle and they began their walk. Cameras flashed, and Belle beamed. "You know, my girl, I think you found the perfect man."

Belle stopped mid-aisle and gave Nickolas a kiss on the cheek. Then they headed the rest of the way.

When Harv saw Belle, his heart caught in his throat. The ceremony was tender, and traditional, and far too short. After the pronouncement of man and wife, and the traditional kiss, Belle and Harv faced their guests beaming with joy. When the pianist switched to *Santa Claus is coming to Town,* the congregation went wild, and the true party began.

Jinx & Jefferson II

IT WAS CHRISTMAS EVE BACK IN WIND STAR. JINX AND Jefferson had been at their shoppe Fairchild's since early morning taking care of an endless stream of customers. Now it was late, and the last person had left. The Pekingese pooches were asleep in their baskets, and Jinx had taken off her shoes.

"I think that about does it," she said to Jefferson. "I'm closing out the Visa."

"Are you disappointed we didn't get to Nantucket this fall?" Jefferson asked with a frown.

"No, hon, not really," Jinx responded, sending him a kind half-shrug. "I'm sure nothing happened that we can't see next year."

With practice, she pulled bills from the aged cash register to slip into the zippered bank bag. For weeks, the counter had been sea of giftwrap and sales check books, items customers had swapped out, and a box of baked goods from the patisserie[v] down the street.

"The island isn't going anywhere, and you were *bang-on* about our hectic schedule. Shew!"

Finished with the money, Jinx nearly turned when her eye fell on a wrapped package not in their signature shoppe paper. Jefferson caught wind of her attention but gave a shrug. With the closest scissor, she carefully opened the seam to discover a copy of *Nantucket Magazine.*

"Oh, Jefferson," she said in tearful happiness.

Jefferson stepped close to see over her shoulder. "Honest, it isn't from me. Look, there's a card."

Curious now, Jinx opened the envelope to discover a vintage-style Christmas card. A second envelop in that one had more weight and she opened it to find open-ended plane tickets to Boston's Logan Airport, plus a gift certificate to the Union Street Inn.

"What in the world?" Jefferson began as Jinx read the card aloud.

"'"A travel voucher and subscription to *Nantucket Magazine* has been entered in your name.'" Jinx scrolled then to the handwritten note behind it. *"Hope you'll come to our fine Isle of Nantucket. Signed, Santa."*

E*N*D

Harv & Belle's story continues, so follow the author on Amazon or at www.LittleRoniPublishers.com to be alerted of every new release!

Coming Soon from Jacqueline Gillam Fairchild and Little Roni Publishers

Santa Claus has a summer house on Nantucket? How absurd! But ace reporter Max will leave his New York City loft for a ferry to the island in order to satisfy his young nieces' demands to find out if this is true.

When he meets the beautiful and mysterious Noel, a part-time dress designer newly arrived to the island herself, he begins to change his tune.

Is the entire island hiding Santa's secret, and if so, what would it take to crack the exclusive circle of insiders? Whatever the case, Max needs to remember the magic of Christmas before Noel walks out of his life forever.

The Nantucket Tuck You Inn Series, Book Two, Looking for Santa, coming soon from Little Roni Publishers.

Recipes

- Belle's Christmas Tree Cookies
- Snowballs
- Christmas Nut Horns
- Rudolph Reindeer Cookies
- Miss Tabatha's Tuck You Inn Magic Cocoa

Belle's Christmas Tree Cookies

3 cups flour
1 cup sugar
1 egg
1 cup butter-at room temperature
1 ½ teaspoons baking powder
½ teaspoon salt
2 teaspoons almond extract
Parchment paper

* Mix all dry ingredients together

* Mix sugar and butter until well blended and fluffy. Add egg and almond extract. Add dry ingredients.

* Take one sheet of parchment paper and place a handful of dough on it (about the size of a large orange). Set all of this on your cookie sheet. Cover with another sheet of parchment paper and roll out. If you need more dough to cover the sheet of parchment paper, add it now and reroll. Take this cookie sheet and place it in the refrigerator for about 15 minutes to firm the dough.

* Remove top sheet of parchment paper.

* With your Christmas tree cookie cutter, cut trees.

* With the tip of a knife peel away uncut dough and return to your bowl to be rolled.

* Continue on more cookie sheets until all dough is used up. If there are scraps, Walter likes Belle to bake them in little odd shapes for munching.

* Bake in a preheated 350-degree oven for about 10 minutes depending on how thick you made your cookies. In the Aga, use

the baking oven and bake 8-10 minutes. Do not let cookies become brown. Pull them when the edges start to turn deep tan. Make sure the centers are firm.

* Let cool preferably on a wire rack to help them cool faster and to prevent the cookies from still baking on their cookie sheet.

Frosting:

1 egg white at room temperature and 1 ¾ cup powdered sugar. Mix and use immediately. Note: Belle likes to make her frosting in small batches as needed. If you run out, make up another batch rather than make too much and letting it sit. M&M's for trim. There should be blue ones unless Walter has picked them out.

Carefully frost one cookie at a time and while the frosting is still very soft cover in M&M's. Save a yellow M&M for the star. Let sit until very dry. Cover your small bowl of frosting in between cookies. Note: You could tint the frosting green for your tree, but if you put enough M&M's on top you can leave it white. Makes about 2 dozen depending on the size of your cutter and the thickness you roll your cookies.

Snowballs

1 cup sugar
½ cup butter
2 eggs
2 cups flour
2 teaspoons baking powder
½ teaspoon salt
1 teaspoon coconut or almond extract
¾ cup milk (in a pinch you can make up powdered milk)
Frosting and coconut

- Mix butter and sugar and then add the eggs. Mix all dry ingredients. Mix extract with milk. Alternate adding dry ingredients with the milk mix until all incorporated.
- Using standard cupcake pans lined with papers (which you will peel off) or heavily sprayed with vegetable spray, fill 12 cupcake cups.
- Bake in a preheated 350-degree oven about 20 minutes until a knife tests clean. In the Aga use the baking oven, on the rack. Check after 15 minutes.
- Cool completely.
- Peel paper liners if used and discard.

Frosting:

½ cup butter, at room temperature
3 cups confectioners' sugar
3 tablespoons milk (can use powdered milk in a pinch)

½ teaspoon coconut or almond extract*

- Mix all together until fluffy.
- Frost cupcakes top to bottom and of course sides.
- Roll in coconut.
- Garnish with a glitz snowflake or star pin.

Note: Because of all the handling with the frosting, this is not a real delicate cake recipe. In a pinch you can use a cake mix but go for a yellow one, they tend to be a little tougher than a white one. You can make these one day and place in an airtight container in the refrigerator and serve up to 3 days later. Don't wait too long, and make sure they are well wrapped.

* Walter is so fond of these Snowballs that Belle has started purchasing her coconut in commercial quantities. To play it safe, buy two standard bags of sweetened coconut. They are best when rolled on very thick.

Christmas Nut Horns

2 sticks butter
2 cups flour
1 egg yoke
½ cup sour cream

- Mix all together and form into balls about the size of a small orange. 6 balls. Chill.

Filling:

2 cups ground or heavily chopped pecans and walnuts (though they are quite lovely with one type of nut).
1 teaspoon cinnamon
1 ½ cups white sugar
Mix all together
Powdered sugar for rolling
Parchment paper or silpats

- Take a ball of chilled dough. Place on parchment paper that has been covered in powdered sugar. Flatten the dough with your hand and then sprinkle this with more powdered sugar. Roll into a round circle about 7 inches. Sprinkle with a handful of the cinnamon filling. Pat filling into the dough. Cut into 12 pie shaped slices. Roll each slice up jelly roll style. Tuck the ends underneath. Bake in a preheated 350-degree oven until lightly brown and the sugar has crystallized. About 12-15 minutes. In the Aga, use the baking oven rack. To freeze, place between layers of parchment and put in an airtight container. Yield 36 cookies

Rudolph Reindeer Cookies

1 stick butter (room temperature)
1 cup sugar
1/2 cup light molasses
1 egg
2 cups flour
1 tsp. salt
1 tsp. soda
1 tsp. cinnamon
1 tsp. ginger (ground)
1 teaspoon maple flavoring.
Parchment Paper

- Mix sugar and butter. Mix in egg, maple flavoring and molasses. Mix all dry ingredients together and then add. Mix well. Chill dough before rolling out.

- Place a sheet of parchment paper on your cookie sheet. Take one glob of chilled dough. Cover with another sheet of parchment paper and roll out. Fill in with more dough as needed. Roll dough thin if you want a crisp shape or if you want it to bleed a bit, roll thicker. Walter likes these rolled thin enough to be crisp.

- Remove top sheet of parchment paper.

- With your reindeer cookie cutter, cut cookies. With the tip of a knife peel away all excess dough. Reroll dough until it is all gone. Put two reindeers (if large) on one cookie sheet.

- Bake in a preheated 350-degree oven for 8-10 minutes. Check to watch for burning. In the Aga, use the rack of the baking oven.

- Cool cookies on a rack.

- Trim: One bag mini pretzels in the classic shape (not sticks), red hots (one small bag goes very far as you will use one per reindeer nose). Gently press the pretzels on the reindeer's head and one red hot on the reindeer's nose before baking.

Note: This dough is wonderful for cutout high heels, but of course Belle would never make those since they're not Christmas.

Miss Tabatha's Tuck You Inn Magic Cocoa

Makes one Tabatha-sized Christmas Mug

¼ cup granulated white sugar
1 pinch of ground cinnamon
¼ unsweetened Hersey's cocoa powder
1 teaspoon vanilla extract
2 cups whole milk
1 extra-thick peppermint candy cane
5 Jumbo Marshmallows

- In a small saucepan, stir together the sugar, cinnamon, cocoa powder, vanilla extract, and ¼ of the milk as the cocoa warms, using medium heat. Stir continuously until smooth.
- Reduce heat to low and stir while slowly adding remaining milk.
- Heat to just shy of boiling and remove from heat.
- Pour into a giant mug (or two mugs), and garnish with the candy cane and marshmallows.
- Sip carefully and enjoy!

About the Author:

Jacqueline Gillam Fairchild writes about her experiences (and guests) from her tea room and retail shoppe. She owns and operates Her Majesty's English Tea Room and her British store Fairchild's. She often brings her beloved Pekingese Piewacket to work.

A former interior designer who studied pastry at Le Cordon Bleu, her business was a finalist for Gift and Decorating Accessories Magazine's Retailer of the Year award.

Her business won the coveted Icon Award from Americasmart Atlanta. Youtu.be/HK3_bUCqbWe.

Jacqueline is also a script writer and a cast member of the Grand Hotel Murder Mystery Troupe and American Immersion Theater.

Enjoy her daily blog at jgfairchild.wix.com/tea-room-life, and on Facebook at Her Majesty's English Tea Room.

Be sure to sign up for alerts as LRP is excited to publish more wonderful stories by Jacqueline in months to come.

www.LittleRoniPublishers.com

Publisher's Extras

The Origins of Candy Land

The game "Candy Land" was designed in 1948 by Eleanor Abbott, while she was recovering from polio in San Diego, California. The game was made for and tested by the children in the same wards on the hospital. The children suggested that Abbott submit the game to Milton Bradley Company. The game was bought by Milton Bradley and first published in 1949 as a temporary fill in for their then main product line, school supplies. Candy Land became Milton Bradley's best-selling game surpassing its previous top seller, Uncle Wiggily, and put the company in the same league as its main competitor, Parker Brothers.[1]

[1] Source, Wikipedia, https://en.wikipedia.org/wiki/Candy_Land#History

---

[i] "Jinx and Jefferson" show up in many of Jacqueline's books, linking her various series and installments regardless of whether or not they interact with the plot. We invite you to check all of Jacqueline's books found on her Amazon.com Author Page and join her ranks of rabid fans.

[ii] An Aga cooker is a stove that uses gentle, radiant circulating heat.

[iii] Silicone mats used for baking.

[iv] Dragée, a candy consisting of a center covered with a coating, such as a sugared almond or a chocolate.

[v] A shop where French pastries and cakes are sold.

Made in USA - Kendallville, IN
1195166_9781735933719
12.02.2020 1409